LOST WORLDS

Our fabled shores none ever reach,
No mariner has found our beach,
Scarce our mirages now are seen,
And neighborly waves of floating green,
Yet still your oldest charts contain
Some dotted outlines of our main. . . .

—Thoreau

LOST WORLDS

Lin Carter

DAW BOOKS, INC.

DONALD A. WOLLHEIM, PUBLISHER

1633 Broadway, New York, N.Y. 10019

I dedicate these legends of the
lost worlds to my favorite editors
—to August Derleth and Donald A.
Wollheim, Roy Torgeson and Ted White
—who are also among my best friends.

—Lin Carter

FIRST PRINTING, AUGUST 1980

1 2 3 4 5 6 7 8 9

DAW **BOOKS**
DAW TRADEMARK REGISTERED
U.S. PAT. OFF. MARCA
REGISTRADA. HECHO EN U.S.A.

PRINTED IN U.S.A.

Contents

ACKNOWLEDGMENTS & PERMISSIONS:

Riders Beyond the Sunrise first appeared in the book King Kull by Robert E. Howard and Lin Carter, Lancer Books, Inc., N.Y., 1967. Copyright © 1967 by Lancer Books, Inc. It appears here by arrangement with the estate of Robert E. Howard.

Thieves of Zangabal first appeared in the book *The Mighty Barbarians*, edited by Hans Stefan Santesson, Lancer Books, Inc., N.Y., 1969. Copyright © 1969 by Lancer Books, Inc.

The Seal of Zaon Sathla first appeared in the book *The Magic of Atlantis*, edited by Lin Carter, Lancer Books, Inc., N.Y., 1970. Copyright © 1970 by Lin Carter.

Keeper of the Emerald Flame first appeared in the book *The Mighty Swordsmen*, edited by Hans Stefan Santesson, Lancer Books, Inc., N.Y., 1970.

The Scroll of Morloc (with Clark Ashton Smith) first appeared in the magazine *Fantastic*, October, 1975. Copyright © 1975 by Ultimate Publishing Company, Inc. It appears here by arrangement with CASiana Literary Properties.

The Twelve Wizards of Ong first appeared in the book *Kingdoms of Sorcery*, edited by Lin Carter, Doubleday & Company, Inc., N.Y., 1976. Copyright © 1976 by Lin Carter.

The Stairs in the Crypt (with Clark Ashton Smith) first appeared in the magazine *Fantastic*, August, 1976. Copyright © 1976 by Ultimate Publishing Company, Inc. It appears here by arrangement with CASiana Literary Properties, Inc.

The Thing in the Pit appears here in print for the first time.

The Introduction:

LOST WORLDS OF TIME

Something young and alive and deep within me leaps and thrills when I read a phrase like, "Zamora, with its dark-haired women and towers of spider-haunted mystery" . . . or, "Ilek-Vad, that fabulous town of turrets atop the hollow cliffs of glass that overlook the twilight sea wherein the finned and bearded Gnorri build their singular labyrinths" . . . or, "the splendid city of Celephais, in the valley of Ooth-Nargai, beyond the Tanarian Hills". . . .

That something is within you, too, or you would never have plucked from the rack a book with a title like *Lost Worlds.*

For we are both human, you and I; and to be human is to possess a quality denied the beasts and the angels. Imagination! The sense of wonder; the thirst for marvels; the fascination for that which lies "over the hills and far away."

We are lovers of fantasy, you and I. I know that I am. I have been a fantasy buff all my life. Before I was old enough to read I was thrilled and delighted by two grand and glorious films, *The Wizard of Oz* and *Snow White and the Seven Dwarfs.* When I could, at last, master the secrets of the printed page, I turned to the Oz books, the Greek myths and Norse legends, Doctor Dolittle, Mary Poppins, the fairy tales of Grimm and Andersen, *Peter Pan,* Kenneth Grahame's marvelous *Wind in the Willows.* And so on . . . and on. Still later, films like Sir Alexander Korda's immortal *Thief of Baghdad* seized my imagination, as did the wonderful romances of Haggard and Merritt and the tales of Robert E. Howard and Clark Ashton Smith, and—

But this is turning into an autobiography!

7

I am trying to make some sort of statement about that quality of imagination which lures us into the world of fantastic literature, not tell the story of my inner life. Some of us are drawn into the incredible realms of science fiction—others to the weird, the macabre, the ghostly.

I have yielded for years to the attraction of those realms; yes, and yet others, too. But it is fantasy which delights me most. And, of all the worlds of fantasy literature, I seem most deeply fascinated by the lost lands of legend—by those far and mysterious realms and continents presumed by dreamers to have flourished in remote, prehistoric ages.

Primarily, I think, it is the unsolved *mystery* of those "evening isles fantastical" that teases my curiosity and captivates my imagination. *Did* the oceans drink down the shining cities of Atlantis? *Did* mighty Mu founder beneath the waves before history began? *Was* there ever a lost polar paradise of Hyperborea? Did the Seven Isles of Antillia ever exist, amid

The dragon-torn, the gong-tormented sea

or are they all but creations of pure fable?

It is the exquisite and tantalizing lure of these mysterious "lands that time forgot," the romance of these fabulous names, that attracts me. And, since we cannot look to science or history or archaeology for the age-lost annals of Atlantis or Ultima Thule or Lemuria, we must turn to the writers of fantastic fiction to satisfy our thirst for their marvels. Many a teller of tales has yielded to the same lure of these lost worlds of time that so captivates me—H. P. Lovecraft, Edgar Rice Burroughs, A. Merritt, Robert E. Howard, Clark Ashton Smith, Henry Kuttner, Avram Davidson, John Jakes, Poul Anderson, to name only a few recent or contemporary fantasts. Such as these have spun their splendid yarns out of the fabric of fable which clings about these ringing and fabulous names of lands that, perhaps, never really were.

For one reason or another, I find that over some fifteen years, I have written stories set in several of these romantic realms. In the beginning, it was never my deliberate intention to do so; like so many other things I have done, it just happened. But on the whole these stories please me, and I hope that they will please you, too.

Here is a whole bookful of them, anyway.

So come, let the world go by for a little while and, with me,

Push off, and sitting well in order, smite
The sounding furrows; for my purpose holds
To sail beyond the sunset, and the baths
Of all the western stars, until I die.
It may be that the gulfs will wash us down:
It may be we shall touch the Happy Isles,
And see the great Achilles, whom we knew. . . .

—Lin Carter

HYPERBOREA

Hyperborea was a remote and fabulous land in the Arctic "beyond the North Wind," discussed in the Greek myths and mentioned by such poets as Pindar. The Greeks assumed it to be a sort of polar Garden of Eden where everybody was happy, went around without any clothes on, and the ripe fruit plopped from every tree, so that nobody had to work for a living. Sounds rather like Bermuda to me.

In 1888, a flamboyant Russian-born spiritualist called Madame Blavatsky published *The Secret Doctrine*, a bewildering book which sets forth a rather gaudy cosmology that traces human evolution down through successive civilizations, beginning with "Polarea," then Hyperborea and finally Lemuria and Atlantis. Later writers in the Theosophical Society filled in the details of her rather sketchy chronology. In the 1930's the California poet, artist, sculptor, translator and short-story writer, Clark Ashton Smith, laid many of his finest fantasies in his own version of Hyperborea, which owes nothing to the Greeks, or to the Theosophists, for that matter.

Since 1973 I have been working with his unpublished notes and outlines for stories he never got around to finishing, complete with lists of coined-but-unused names of people and places. My "posthumous collaborations"—like those Derleth wrote "with" Lovecraft—are done in as close an approximation of Smith's lapidary style as I can manage, and they are also set in Hyperborea. Here are two of my favorites.

THE SCROLL OF MORLOC

with Clark Ashton Smith

The shaman Yhemog, dejected by the obdurate refusal of his fellow Voormis to elect him their high priest, contemplated his imminent withdrawal from the tribal burrows of his furry, primitive kind to sulk in solitude among the icy crags of the north, whose bourns were unvisited by his timorous, earth-dwelling brethren.

Seven times had he offered himself in candidacy for the coveted headdress of black *ogga* wood, crowned with fabulous *huusim* plumes, and now for the seventh time had the elders unaccountably denied him what he considered his just guerdon, earned thrice over by his pious and reverent austerities. Seething with disappointment, the rejected shaman swore they should have no eighth occasion to bypass the name of Yhemog by bestowing the uncouth hierarchical mitre upon another, and vowed they should erelong have reason to regret their selection of an inferior devotee of the Voormish god over one of his unique devoutness.

During this period many of the clans of the subhuman Voormis had fled into warrens tunneled beneath the surface of a jungle-girt and mountainous peninsula of early Hyperborea which had yet to be named Mhu Thulan. Their semibestial forebears had originally been raised in thralldom to a race of sentient serpent people whose primordial continent had been reft asunder by volcanic convulsions and which had submerged beneath the oceans an eon or two earlier. Fleeing from the slave pens of their erstwhile masters, now happily believed almost extinct, the ancestors of the present Voormis had wrested all of this territory from certain degenerate, cannibalistic subhumans of repellent appearance, whose few sur-

11

vivors had been driven northward to dwell in exile amid the
bleak glaciers of Polarion.

Of late, their numbers inexplicably in decline, their warlike
prowess unaccountably dwindling and the vengeful descend-
ants of their ancient foes growing ever more populous and
restive in the north, many of the Voormish tribes had sought
refuge in these underground dwellings. By now the furry
creatures were accustomed to the comforting gloominess and
the familiar, pervasive stench of their warrens and seldom did
they venture into the upper world, which had grown strange
and frightening to them with its giddy spaciousness of sky, lit
by the intolerable brilliance of hostile suns.

In contemplating self-imposed exile from his kind, the dis-
gruntled shaman was not unaware of the dangers. This particular region of the peninsula would someday be known as
Phenquor, the northernmost province of Mhu Thulan. During
this early Cenozoic period the first true humans were just beginning to seep into Hyperborea from southerly tropical
jungles whose climate had grown too fervent for them, and
all of Phenquor was a primal wilderness, uninhabited save for
the cavern-dwelling Voormis. Not without peril, therefore,
would the shaman Yhemog traverse the prehistoric jungles
and reeking fens of the young continent, for such were the
haunts of the ravening catoblepas and the agate-breasted
wyvern, to cite only the least formidable denizens.

But Yhemog had mastered the rudiments of the antehuman
thaumaturgies and had gained some proficiency in the arts of
shamanry and conjuration. By these means he thought himself quite likely to elude the more ferocious of the carnivora
to achieve the relative safety of the Phenquorian mountains.

By dwelling subterraneously, it should perhaps be noted
here, the Voormis were but imitating the grotesque divinity
they worshipped with rites we might deem excessively sanguinary and revolting. As it was an article of the Voormish
faith that this deity, whom they knew as Tsathoggua, dwelt in
lightless caverns far beneath the earth, their adoption of a
troglodytic existence was primarily symbolic. The eponymous
ancestor of their race, Voorm the arch-ancient, had early in
their history asserted that their assumption of a wholly subterranean habitat would place them in special propinquity to
their god, who himself preferred to wallow in the gulf of
N'kai beneath a mountain to the south considered sacred by
the Voormis. This dogma the venerable Voorm had pro-

nounced shortly before retiring into chasms near N'kai to spend his declining eons near the object of his worship.

The tribal elders considered the opinions of this patriarch infallible, especially in purely theological matters, for it was believed that he had been fathered by none other than Tsathoggua himself during a transient liaison with a minor feminine divinity named Shathak. With this ultimate patriarchal teaching the tribal elders now, somewhat belatedly, concurred; to obey the last precept of their spiritual leader was after all, a reasonable precaution considering the profound and disheartening conditions into which the race had so recently, and so abruptly, declined.

In reaching his eventual decision to shun the dank and fetid burrows of his tribe in favor of a radical change of residence to the vertiginous peaks along the northern borders of Phenquor, overlooking the frigid wastes of Polarion, the shaman Yhemog discovered himself ineluctably sliding into heresy. Unable to reconcile his private inclinations with the pontifical revelations handed down by the eponymous patriarch, he was soon implicitly questioning the validity of the teachings, a tendency which resulted in his eventual denial of their infallibility. Now rejecting as essentially worthless the very patriarchal dogmas he had earlier reverenced, he lapsed from the most odious condition of heresy into the blasphemous nadir of atheism.

This disappointment soured into bitter resentment and resentment festered into vicious envy and envy itself, like a venomous canker, gnawed at the roots of his faith, until the last pitiful shreds of his former beliefs had utterly been eaten away. And naught now was left in the heart of Yhemog save for a hollow emptiness, which became filled only with the bile of self-devouring rancor and a fierce, derisive contempt for everything he had once held precious and holy. This contempt cried out for expression, for a savage gesture of ultimate affront calculated to plunge his elder brethren into horrified consternation. Yhemog hungered to brandish his new-found atheism like a stinking rag beneath the pious snouts of the tribal fathers.

At length he determined upon a course of action suited to his ends. He schemed to steal into the deepest and holiest shrine of Tsathoggua and to purloin an antique scroll which contained certain rituals and liturgies held in religious abhorrence by the members of his faith. The document was among the spoils of war carried off by his victorious forefathers from

the abominable race which had formerly dominated these
regions at the time of the advent of the Voormish savages
into Mhu Thulan. The papyrus reputedly preserved the
darkest secrets of the occult wisdom of the detested Gnophkehs, which name denoted the repulsively hirsute cannibals
whom Yhemog's ancestors had driven into exile in the arctic
barrens. This scroll contained, in fact, the most arcane and
potent ceremonials whereby the Gnophkehs had worshipped
their atrocious divinity, who was no less than an avatar of the
cosmic obscenity Rhan-Tegoth, and was attributed to Morloc
himself, the Grand Shaman.

Now the Voormis had, from their remotest origins, considered themselves the chosen minions of Tsathoggua, their
sole deity. And Tsathoggua was an earth elemental ranged in
unrelenting enmity against Rhan-Tegoth and all his kind, who
were commonly accounted elementals of the air and were
contemned by those of the Old Ones who, like Tsathoggua,
abominated the airy emptinesses above the world and wallowed in dark subterranean lairs. A similar degree of mutual
animosity existed between those races which were the servants of Tsathoggua, among whom the Voormis were promi-
nent, and those who served the avatars of cosmic and
uncleanly Rhan-Tegoth, such as those noxious protoanthro-
pophagi, the Gnophkehs. The loss of the Scroll of Morloc
would, therefore, hurl the Voormis into the very nadir of
confusion, and contemplation of their horror at the loss
caused Yhemog to tremble with delicious anticipation.

The Scroll had for millennia reposed in a tabernacle of
mammoth ivory situated beneath the very feet of the idol of
Tsathoggua in the holy-of-holies, its lowly position symbolic
of the Voormis risen triumphant over their subjugated enemies. In order for the Scroll of Morloc to be thieved away by
Yhemog, ere he quit forever the noisome, squalid burrows of
his centuries of youth, he must first enter the most sacred
precincts of the innermost shrine itself.

For a shaman of his insignificance, but recently graduated
from his novitiate a century or two before, to trespass upon
the forbidden sanctuary was a transgression of the utmost
severity. By his very presence he would profane and contami-
nate the sacerdotal chamber, and this act of desecration he
must perforce do under the cold, unwavering scrutiny of
dread, Tsathoggua himself, for therein had stood enshrined
for innumerable ages the ancient and immemorial eidolon of
the god, an object of universal veneration.

The very thought of thus violating the sacred shrine to perform a despicable act of burglary in the awesome presence of the deity he had once vigorously worshipped was sobering, even disquieting. But unfortunately for the inward serenity of Yhemog, the fervor with which he embraced his new-found atheism transcended that of his former pious devotions. His iconoclasm had hardened his heart so that he despised his own earlier temerities, and now disbelieved in all ultra-natural entities far more than he had ever believed in them before. The venerable eidolon was but a piece of worked stone and naught more, he thought contemptuously, and the arch-rebel, Yhemog, fears no thing of stone!

Thus it befell that the traitorous and atheistical Yhemog slunk one night into the nethermost of the shrines sacred to Tsathoggua, having prudently charmed to sleep the scimitar-wielding eunuchs guarding the sanctuary. Past their obese, stertorously breathing forms, sprawled on the pave before the spangled curtain which concealed the innermost adytum from the chance profanation of impious eyes, he crept on furtive, three-toed, naked feet. Beyond the glittering tissue was discovered a chamber singularly bare of ornamentation, in dramatic contrast to the ostentation of the outer precincts. It contained naught but the idol itself, throned at the farther end, which presented the likeness of an obscenely corpulent, toad-like entity. Familiar as he was with the crude images hacked from porous lava by the clumsy paws of his people, the shaman was unprepared for the astonishing skill whereby the nameless sculptor had wrought the eidolon from the obdurate and frangible obsidian. He marveled at the consummate craft whereby the chisel of the forgotten artisan had clothed the bloated, squatting form of the god with a suggestion of sleek furriness and had blended together in its features the salient characteristics of toad, bat and sloth in an amalgam subtly disturbing and distinctly unpleasing. The ponderous divinity was depicted with half-closed, sleepy eyes which seemed almost to glitter with malice, and it had a grinning and lipless gash of mouth which Yhemog fancied smiled with cruel and gloating mockery.

His new contempt for all such supernatural entities dimmed before a rising trepidation. For a moment he hesitated, half-fearing that the hideous and yet exquisitely lifelike eidolon might stir suddenly to dread wakefulness upon the next instant and reveal itself to be a living thing. But the moment passed without any such vivification, and his derision and denial of the transmundane rose within him, trebled in its blind conviction. Now was the moment of ultimate profanation upon him; now he would renounce his former devotions by abstracting from beneath the very feet of the sacred image its chiefest treasure, the papyrus which preserved the arcane secrets of the elder Gnophkehs. Summoning the inner fortitude his atheistical doctrines afforded, thrusting aside the last lingering remnants of his superstitious awe of the divinity the idol represented, Yhemog knelt and hastily pried open the ivory casket and took out the primordial scroll.

Whereafter there occurred absolutely nothing in the way of preternatural phenomena or transmundane acts of vengeance. The black and glistening statue remained immobile; it neither blinked nor stirred nor smote him with the levin-bolt or the precipitous attack of leprosy he had almost expected. The relief which welled within his furry breast was intoxicating; he almost swooned with exultant joy. But in the next moment dire melancholy drowned his heady mood; for he realized now for the first time the fullest extent of the vicious hoax the practitioners of his cult had perpetrated upon him. So to delude an innocent young Voormis cub, so that the noblest aspiration it might conceivably dream to attain was the *ogga*-wood mitre of the hierophant, was an action of such odium as to excite within him a lust to desecrate this sacred place.

Ere spurning forever the moist and gloomy tunnels to seek a new and solitary life among the steaming quagmires and cycadean jungles of the upper earth he would commit a desecration so irremediable as to defile, pollute and befoul for all eons to come this innermost citadel of a false and cruelly perpetuated religion. And in his very clutches he held at that moment the perfect instrument of revenge. For how better to desanctify the temple of Tsathoggua than to recite before his most venerable eidolon, within his sacred and forbidden shrine, the abominable rituals the hated enemies of his minions used in the celebration of their atrocious divinity, his rival?

With paws that shook with the loathing, Yhemog unfolded the antique papyrus and, straining his weak, small eyes, sought to peruse the writings it contained. The hieroglyphics were indited according to an antiquated system, but at length he deduced their meaning. The dark lore of the Gnophkehs was centered upon placating and appeasing their grisly divinity, but erelong the shaman found a ritual of invocational worship which he judged would be exceptionally insulting to the false Tsathoggua and his self-deluding servants. It commenced with the discordant phrase *Wza-y'ei! Wza-y'ei! Y'kaa haa bho-ii*, and terminated in a series of ululations for which the vocal apparatus of the Voormis was inadequately designed. As he commenced reading the liturgical formula aloud, however, he discovered that the further he progressed the easier the pronunciation became. He also was surprised to find, as he grew near the terminus, that the vocables he had earlier considered jarring and awkward became curiously musical to his ears.

Those ears, he suddenly noticed, had unaccountably grown larger and now were not unlike the huge, flapping organs of the ridiculously misshapen Gnophkehs. His eyes as well had undergone transformation and now bulged protuberantly like those of the revolting inhabitants of the polar regions. Having completed the final ululation he let fall the Scroll of Morloc and examined himself in growing consternation. Gone was his sleek and comely pelt, and in its place he was now covered with a repulsive growth of coarse and matted hairs. His snout, moreover, had in the most unseemly manner extended itself beyond the limits considered handsome by Voormish standards, and was now a naked, proboscidean growth of distinctly Gnophkehian proportions. He cried out in unbelieving horror for he realized with a cold and awful panic that *to worship as a Gnophkeh* must, under certain circumstances, be defined in terms absolutely literal. And when his hideous lamentations succeeded in rousing from their charmed drowsiness the elephantine eunuchs beyond the sequined veil, and they came lumbering in haste to discover a detested and thieving Gnophkeh squirming on its obscene and hairy belly, gabbling incomprehensible prayers before the smiling, the enigmatic, and the lazily malicious eyes of Tsathoggua, they dispatched him with great thoroughness and righteous indignation, and in a certain manner most acceptable to the god, but one so lingering and anatomically ingenious that the more squeamish of my readers should be grateful that I restrain my pen from its description.

THE STAIRS IN THE CRYPT

with Clark Ashton Smith

It is told of the necromancer Avalzaunt that he succumbed at length to the inexorable termination of his earthly existence in the Year of the Crimson-Spider during the empery of King Phariol of Commoriom. Upon the occasion of his demise, his disciples, in accordance with the local custom, caused his body to be preserved in a bath of bituminous natron and interred the remains of their master in a mausoleum prepared according to his dictates in the burying grounds adjacent to the abbey of Camorba, in the province of Uthnor, in the eastern part of Hyperborea.

The obsequies made over the catafalque whereupon reposed the mummy of the necromancer were oddly cursory in nature, and the encomium delivered at the interment by the eldest of the apprentices of Avalzaunt, one Mygon, was performed in a niggardly and grudging manner, singularly lacking in that spirit of somber dolence one should have expected from bereaved disciples mourning their deceased mentor. The truth of the matter was that none of the former students of Avalzaunt had any particular cause to bemoan his demise, for their master had been an exigent and rigorous taskmaster and his cold obduracy had done little to earn him any affection from his students in the science of necromancy.

Upon their completion of the requisite solemnities, the acolytes of the necromancer departed for their ancestral abodes in the city of Zanzonga which stood nearby, while others eloigned themselves to more distant Cerngoth and Leqquan. As for the negligent Mygon, he repaired to the remote and isolated tower of primordial basalt which rose from a headland overlooking the boreal waters of the eastern main, from which they had all come for the funeral rites. This

18

tower had formerly been the residence of the deceased necromancer but was now, by lawful bequest, devolved upon Mygon as the seniormost of the apprentices.

If the pupils of Avalzaunt assumed that they had taken their last farewells of their master, however, they were to prove seriously mistaken. For, after some years of repose within the sepulchre, vigor seeped back again into the brittle limbs of the mummified enchanter and sentience gleamed anew in his jellied and sunken eyes. At first the partially revived lich lay in a numb and mindless stupor, with no conception of its present charnel abode. It knew, in fine, neither what nor where it was, nor aught of the peculiar circumstances of its unprecedented resurrection.

On this question the philosophers remain divided. One school holds that it was the unseemly brevity of the burial rites which prevented the release of the spirit of Avalzaunt from its clay, thus initiating the unnatural revitalization of the cadaver. Others postulate that it was the necromantic powers of Avalzaunt himself which were the sole cause of his return to life. After all, they argue, and with some cogence, one who is steeped in the power to effect the resurrection of another should certainly retain, even in death, a residue of that power sufficient to perform a revivification upon himself. These, however, are queries for a philosophical debate for which the present chronicler lacks both the leisure and the learning to pursue to an unequivocal conclusion.

Suffice it to say that, in the fullness of time, the lich had recovered its faculties to such a degree as to become cognizant of its interment. The unnatural vigor which animated the corpse enabled it to thrust aside the heavy lid of the black marble sarcophagus and the mummy sat up and stared about iself. The withered wreaths of yew and cypress, the decaying draperies of funereal black and purple, the sepulchral décor of the stone chamber wherein it now found itself, and the unmistakable nature of the tomb furnishings, all served to confirm the reanimated cadaver in its initial impressions.

It is difficult for us, the living, to guess at the thoughts which seethed through the dried and mold-encrusted brain of the lich as it pondered its demise and resurrection. We may hazard it, however, that the spirit of Avalzaunt quailed with none of the morbid trepidations an ordinary mortal would experience upon awakening within such repellent environs. Not from shallow impulse or trivial whim had Avalzaunt in his youth embarked upon a study of the craft of necromancy, but from a fervid and devout fascination with the mysteries of death. In the swollen pallor of a corpse in the advanced stages of decomposition had he ever found a beauty superior to the radiance of health, and in the mephitic vapors of the tomb a perfume headier than the scent of summer gardens.

Oft had he hung in rapturous excitation upon the words which fell, slowly, one by one, from the worm-fretted lips of deliquescent cadavers, or gaunt and umber mummies, or crumbling liches acrawl with squirming maggots and teetering on the verge of decay. From such, rendered temporarily animate by his necromantic art, it had been his wont to extort the abominable yet thrilling secrets of the tomb. And now, he, himself, was become just such a revitalized corpse! The irony of the situation did not elude the subtlety of Avalzaunt.

"Once I yearned to know the terrors of the grave, the kiss of maggots on my tongue, the clammy caress of a rotting shroud against my tepid flesh," soliloquized the cadaver in a croaking whisper from a dry and shrunken throat crusted with the salts of the bitter natron. "I thirsted for the knowledge that glimmers in the pits of mummied eyes, and burned for that wisdom known only to the writhing and insatiable worm. Tirelessly I perused forbidden tomes by the feeble luminance of guttering tapers of corpse-tallow to master the secrets of mortality, so that should ever the nethermost pits disgorge their crawling vermin I might aspire to dominion over the legions of the living dead—among the which I, now, myself, am to be henceforward numbered!"

Thus that mordant humor in its present circumstances was readily perceived by the revitalized corpse.

Among the various implements of arcane manufacture which the pupils of Avalzaunt had buried in the crypt beside the mortal remains of their unlamented master there was a burnished speculum of black steel wherein the cadaver of Avalzaunt beheld its own likeness. It was skull-like, that sere and fulvous visage which peered back from the ebon depths of the magic mirror. Avalzaunt had seen such shrunken and decayed lineaments upon prehistoric mummies rifled from the crumbling fanes of civilizations anterior to his own. Seldom, however, had he gazed upon so delightfully decomposed and withered a visage as this bony horror which was his own face.

The lich next turned its scrutiny on what remained of its lean and leathery body and tested brittle limbs draped in the rags of a rotting shroud, finding these imbued with an ada-

mantine and a tireless vigor, albeit they were attenuated to a
degree which may only be described as skeletal. Whatever
the source of the supranormal energy which now animated
the corpse of the necromancer, it lent the creature a vigor it
had never previously enjoyed in life, not even in the long-ago
decades of its juvenescence.

As for the crypt itself, it was sealed from without by pious
oeremonials which rendered the portals thereunto inviolable
by the mummy in its present mode of existence. Such precau-
tions were customary in the land of Uthnor, which was the
abode of many warlocks and enchanters during the era
whereof I write; for it was feared that wizards seldom lie
easy in their graves and that, betimes, they are wont to rise
up from their deathly somnolence and stalk abroad to wreak
vengeance upon those who wronged them when they lived.
Hence was it only prudent for the timid burghers of Zanzonga, the principal city of this region of Hyperborea, to in-
sist that the tombs of sorcerers be sealed with the Pnakotic
pentagram, against which such as the risen Avalzaunt may
not trespass without the severest discomfiture.

Thus it was that the mummy of the necromancer was pent
within the crypt, helpless to emerge into the outer world. And
there for a time it continued to sojourn; but was in no wise
discommoded by its enforced confinement, for the bizarre architecture of the crypt was of its own devising, and the building thereof Avalzaunt had himself supervised. The crypt was
spacious and, withal, not lacking in such few and dismal
amenities as the reposing chambers of the dead may customarily afford. Moreover, the living corpse bethought itself
of that secret portal every tomb is known to have, behind
which there doubtless was a hidden stair that went down to
black, abysmal deeps beneath the earth where malign and potent entities reside. The Old Ones they are called, and among
these inimical dwellers in the tenebrous depths there was a
certain Nyogtha, a dire divinity whom Avalzaunt had often
celebrated with obscene rites.

This Nyogtha had for his minions the grisly race of
Ghouls, those lank and canine-muzzled prowlers among the
tombs: and from the favor of Nyogtha the necromancer had
in other days won ascendancy over the loping hordes. And so
the mummy of Avalzaunt waited patiently within the crypt,
knowing that in time all tombs are violated by these predators from the Pit, who had been the faithful servants of

Avalzaunt when he had lived, and who might still consent to
serve him after death.

Erelong the cadaver heard the shuffle of leathery feet as-
cending the secret stairs from the gloomy abyss, and the
fumbling of rotting paws against the hidden portal; and the
stale and vitiated air within the vault was, of a sudden, permeated with a disquieting effluvia as of long-sealed graves
but newly opened. By these tokens the lich was made aware
of the Ghoul pack that pawed and whined and snuffled hun-
grily at the door. And when the portal yawned to admit the
gaunt, shuffling herd, the lich rose up before it, lifting thin
arms like withered sticks and clawed hands like the stark
talons of monstrous birds. The putrid witchfires of a ghastly
phosphorescence flared up at the command of the necromancer, and the Ghoul herd, affrighted, squealed and grov-
eled before him. At length, having cowed them sufficiently,
Avalzaunt elicited from the leader of the pack, a hound-
muzzled thing with dull eyes the hue of rancid pus, a fearful
and prodigious oath of thralldom.

It was not long before Avalzaunt had need of this loping
herd of grave robbers. For the necromancer in time became
aware of an inner lack which greatly tormented it and which
remained unassuaged by the supernatural vigor which animated its form. In time this nebulous need resolved itself
into a gnawing lack of sustenance, but it was for no mundane
nutriment, that acrid and raging thirst which burned within
the entrails of the lich. Cool water or honey-hearted wine
would not sate that unholy thirst: for it was *human blood*
Avalzaunt craved, but why or wherefore, the mummy did not
know.

Perchance it was simply that the desiccated tissues of the
lich were soaked through with the bituminous salts of the natron wherein it had been immersed, and that it was this acid
saltiness which woke so fierce and burning a thirst. Or mayhap it was even as antique legends told, that the restless
legions of the undead require the imbibement of fresh gore to
sustain their unnatural existence. Whatever the cause, the undead necromancer yearned for the foaming crimson fluid
which flows so prodigally through the veins of the living as he
had never thirsted for even the rarest of wines from terrene
vineyards when he had lived. And so Avalzaunt evoked the
lean and hungry Ghouls before his bier. They offered him
electrum chalices brimming with black and gelid gore drained
from the tissues of corpses; but the cold, thick, coagulated

blood did naught to slake the mummy's thirst. It longed for fresh blood, crimson and hot and foam-beaded, and it vowed that erelong it would drink deep thereof, again and again and yet again.

Thereafter the shambling herd roamed by night far afield in dire obedience to the mummy's will. And so it came to pass that the former disciples of the necromancer had cause to regret the negligent and over-hasty burial of their mentor. For it was upon the acolytes of the dead necromancer that the Ghoul horde preyed. And the first of their victims was that unregenerate and niggardly Mygon who still dwelt in the sea-affronting tower which once had been the demesne of the necromancer. When, with the diurnal light, his servants came to rouse him from his slumbers, they found a blanched and oddly shrunken corpse amid the disorder of the bedclothes, which were torn and trampled and besmirched with black mire and grave-mold. Naught of the nature of the nocturnal visitants could Mygon's horror-stricken servants discern from the fixed staring of his glazed and sightless eyes; but from the drained veins of the corpse, and its preternatural pallor, they guessed that he had fallen victim to some prowling vampire in the night.

Again and again thereafter the Ghoul herd went forth by the secret stairs within the crypt of Avalzaunt, down to those deeps far beneath the crust of the earth where they and their brethren had anciently tunneled out a warren of fetid passageways connecting tomb and burial ground and the vaults beneath castle, temple, tower and town. After nine such grisly atrocities had befallen, some vague intimation of the truth dawned upon the ecclesiarchs of Zanzonga, for it became increasingly obvious that only the former apprentices of the dead necromancer, Avalzaunt, suffered from the depredations of the unknown vampire creatures. In time the priests of Zanzonga ventured forth to scrutinize the crypt of the deceased enchanter, but found it still sealed, its door of heavy lead intact, and the Pnakotic pentagram affixed thereto undisturbed and unbroken. The night-prowling monsters who drained their hapless victims dry of blood, whoever or whatever they might prove to be, had naught to do with Avalzaunt, surely; for the necromancer, they said, slept still within his sealed crypt. This pronunciamento given forth, they returned to the temple of Ymboth, in Zanzonga, satisfied with themselves for the swift and thorough fulfillment of their mission. Not one of them so much as suspected the existence of the stairs in the crypt, whereby Avalzaunt and his Ghouls emerged in the gloaming to hunt down the unwary and abominably to feast.

And from this vile nocturnal feasting the mummy lost its gauntness, and it waxed sleek and plump and swollen, for that it now gorged heavily each night on rich, bubbling gore; and, as is well known to those of the unsqueamish who ponder such morbidities, the undead neither digest nor eliminate the foul sustenance whereon they feed.

Erelong the now bloated and corpulent lich had exhausted the list of its former apprentices, for not one remained unvisited by the shamblers from the Pit. Then it was that the insatiable Avalzaunt thought of the monks of Camorba whose abbey lay close by, nigh unto the very burial ground wherein it was supposed he slept. These monks were of an order which worshipped Shimba, god of the shepherds, and this drowsy, rustic little godling demanded but little of his celebrants; wherefore they were an idle, fat, complacent lot much given to the fleshly pleasures. 'Twas said they feasted on the princeliest of viands, drank naught but the richest of vintages and dined hugely on the juiciest and most succulent haunches of rare, dripping meat; by reason thereof they were rosy and rotund and brimming with hot blood. At the very thought of the fat, bubbling fluid that went rivering through their soft, lusty flesh, the undead necromancer grew faint and famished, and he vowed that very night to lead his loping tomb hounds against the abbey of Camorba.

Night fell, thick with turgid vapors. A gibbous moon floated above the vernal hills of Uthnor. Thirlain, abbot of Camorba, was closeted with the abbey accounts, seated behind a desk lavishly inlaid with carven plaques of mastodonic ivory, as the moon ascended toward the zenith. Rumor had not exaggerated his corpulence, for, of all the monks of Camorba, the abbot was the most round and rosy; hence it was from the fat jugular that pulsed in his soft throat that the necromancer had sworn to slake his thirst.

In one plump hand Thirlain held a sheaf of documents appertaining to the accounts of the abbey, the which were scribed upon crisp papyrus made from calamites; the pudgy fingers of the other hand toyed idly with a silver paperknife which had been a gift from the high priest of Shimba in Zanzonga, and which was sanctified with the blessings of that patriarch.

Thus it was that, when the long curtained windows behind the desk burst asunder before the whining pack of hungry Ghouls, and the hideously bloated figure of the mad-eyed cadaver which led the tomb hounds came lurching toward the abbot where he sat, Thirlain, shrieking with fear, impulsively thurst that small blunt silver knife into the distended paunch of the corpse as it flung itself upon him. What occurred after that ordinarily ineffectual blow is still a matter of theological debate among the ecclesiarchs of Zanzonga, who no longer sleep so smugly in their beds.

For the bloated and swollen paunch of the walking corpse burst open like an immense rotten fruit, spewing forth such stupendous quantities of black and putrid blood that the silken robes of the abbot were drenched in an instant. In sooth, so voluminous was the deluge of gore that the thick carpets were saturated with stinking fluids, which sprayed and squirted in all directions as the stricken cadaver staggered about in its throes. The vile liquid splashed hither and yon in such floods that even the damask wall coverings were saturated, and, in no time at all, the entire chamber was awash with putrescent gore to such an extent that the very floor was become a lake of foulness. The liquescent vileness poured out into the hallways and the corridors beyond when at length the other monks, roused by the shriekings of their horror stricken abbot, rose from cot and pallet and came bursting in to behold the ghastly abbatial chamber and Thirlain himself crouched pale and gibbering atop his ivory desk, pointing one palsied hand at the leathery rind of desiccated flesh that was all that remained of Avalzaunt the necromancer, once the vile fluids his mummy retained had burst forth and drained him dry.

This horrendous episode was hushed up and only distorted rumors ever leaked beyond the abbey walls. But the burghers of Zanzonga marveled for a season over the swift and inexplicable resignation from his cozy sinecure of the pleasure-loving Thirlain, who departed that very dawn on a barefoot pilgrimage to the remotest of holy shrines far-famed for its wonder-working relics, which was situated amid the most hostile and inaccessible of wildernesses. Thereafter the chastened abbot entered a dour monastic order of stern flagellants, famed for their strict adherence to a grim code of the utmost severity, whereby the austerities of the newly zealous Thirlain, together with his over-rigorous chastisements of the flesh, made him an object of amazement among even the most obdurate of his brethren. No longer plump and soft and self-indulgent, he grew lean and sallow from a bleak diet of moldy crusts and stale water, and died not long thereafter in the odor of sanctity and was promptly declared venerable and beautific by the Grand Patriarch of Commoriom, and his relics now command excessive prices from the dealers in such ecclesiastical memorabilia. As for the remains of the Necromancer, they were burnt on the hearth of the abbey at Camorba and were reduced to a pinch of bitter ash which was hastily scattered to the winds. And it is said of the spirit of the unfortunate Avalzaunt that at last it found rest in whatever far and fabulous bourn is the final haven of perturbed and restless spirits.

MU

Mu was invented in the 1920's by a British-born eccentric and oddball named James Churchward (or "Colonel" James Churchward, as he liked to call himself), and it is more or less identical with the Lemuria of the Theosophists; that is, it was a lost continent in the Pacific just like Lemuria. Churchward wrote of it in a series of marvelously wacky works of pseudo-non-fiction with titles like *Cosmic Forces of Mu* and *Sacred Symbols of Mu,* and so on. They are a lot of fun to read if you don't try to take them seriously.

In 1933, *Weird Tales* published a charming story by Hazel Heald called "Out of the Eons," which was laid in Mu. It was actually one of H. P. Lovecraft's ghostwriting jobs and Miss Heald had little to do with it.

I always enjoyed that story, with its fancy, high-falutin' prose; so I paid it the compliment of imitation in the yarn which follows next. (At least, I *hope* it's a compliment!)

This story has never been published before.

THE THING IN THE PIT

The following narrative from the shocking and chaotic Zanthu Tablets is an excerpt from a fragmentary and conjectural translation which their discoverer, Harold Hadley Copeland the archaeologist, made some years before his death in an insane asylum in San Francisco in 1926.

I

The innumerable iniquities of Yaa-Thobboth, hierophant of Ghatanothoa the Monster on the Mount, I, Zanthu, wizard and last priest of Ythogtha the Abomination in the Abyss, had endured with uncomplaining fortitude, but this ultimate affront I could not let pass in silence.

For uncountable millennia the fortunes of my cult had been on the wane, even as, during the same ages, the rise to victory of those who worshipped the Monstrosity that dwelt ever atop the heights of Yaddith-Gho had been an unbroken succession of triumphs. It was now many millennia since that Year of the Red Moon* when the over-bold T'yog, high priest of the worship of Shub-Niggurath, sought to break asunder the power of Ghatanothoa forever, and came to so unthinkable an end that even that dread chronicle, the *Ghorl Nigräl*, dares not whisper a single hint of his fate. Seizing upon the moment, the infamous Imash-Mo, who was high priest of Ghatanothoa in his day, proclaimed to all the Nine Kingdoms that his loathsome and noxious divinity was thus

---

* Von Junzt, in his *Unaussprechlichen Kulten* (XXI, 307) estimates this date as B.C. 173,148.—*Translator.*

28

proven supreme over all the thousand gods of primordial and everlasting Mu. And, alas, Imash-Mo had long since gained ascendancy over the weak and easily swayed Thabou, king of the province of K'naa, wherein rose the demon-possessed mountain of Yaddith-Gho; and King Thabou hastened to ratify the supremacy of Ghatanothoa even over the might of Cthulhu, the Lord of R'lyeh, himself.

Lustrum by lustrum, cycle by cycle, the wealth, power and following of the cult of Ythogtha declined thereafter, even as did all of the other of the thousand cults of primal Mu. In vain did my priestly predecessors warn that the vengeance of the affronted gods would someday smite the Nine Kingdoms of Mu, and mayhap trample all of the mighty continent beneath the seething waves of ocean, as ancient prophecies reiterated was to be our eventual doom. But naught could avert or even retard the remorseless decline of the worship of Ythogtha.

II

When I, in my turn, assumed the scarlet pontificals and the brazen rod of my office in the Year of the Whispering Shadow*, I swore by the Gray Ritual of Khif, by the Vooric Sign, by the Weedy Monolith, and by the might and glory of terrible Ythogtha, that my god should achieve his triumph and his revenge during my pontificate.

Alas, I had reckoned without the cunning and the ambition of Yaa-Thobboth! For no sooner had the brazen rod been set into my grasp and the Thirty-One Secret Rituals of Yhe been given over to my keeping than the villainous high priest of Ghatanothoa let pass the ultimate affront against the dignity of my office and the splendor of my god.

For this Yaa-Thobboth had at length prevailed upon the palsied and enfeebled Shommog, monarch over K'naa, and a writ was proclaimed banning any other form of worship of the Great Old Ones than that approved by the followers of Ghatanothoa. The copper gates of the temple of Shub-Niggurath were sealed; the greenly lit adyta of Cthulhu were

---

* Evidence in the *Ponape Scripture* (particularly the astronomical data in Versicle 9759) suggests this date may be equivalent to roughly B.C. 161,844; von Junzt does not include any reference to this period, as his commentary breaks off several milennia earlier.—*Translator*.

deserted; and, temple by temple, across the breadth of the
Nine Kingdoms, the supreme power of Ghatanothoa the
Monster on the Mount was proclaimed.

Now King Shommog was regnant over the province of
K'naa while I and my few acolytes dwelt in the land of
G'thuu to the north, beyond the River of Worms and the
Carven Basalt Cliffs and the Catacombs of Thul. But great
had the authority of K'naa grown in the eleven thousand
years since the reign of King Thabou and the hierophancy of
Imash-Mo, and in these moon-dim, latter days, the power of
my land of G'thuu was shrunken and seldom did mine own
monarch, the degenerate Nuggog-ying, dare oppose the will
or whim of the King of K'naa. Thus it seemed inevitable that
the last vestige of reverence for the Abomination in the
Abyss should gutter and die, and in the very pontificate of
one who had sworn to restore Him to the heights of His
former tremendous might.

III

In despair, I withdrew to the crumbling ruins of my palace
which stood of old upon the very brink of that profound and
shadowy chasm, the Abyss of Yhe, wherein the victorious
Elder Gods had hurled the great Ythogtha and had sealed
him therein forever under the potency of the Elder Sign and
wherein to this day unbreakable bonds of psychic force im-
prison him, even as foul Ghatanothoa is prisoned in that immemorial and cyclopean citadel atop Mount Yaddith-Gho,
and Great Cthulhu slumbers in his Sunken City on the
ocean-whelmed and eon-lost Black Island, and terrible Zoth-
Ommog lies chained amid the Deep beyond the Isle of the
Sacred Stone Cities.*

* The cryptic *Ponape Scripture* says that Ghatanothoa, Ythogtha,
and Zoth-Ommog, are, "the Sons of the mighty Cthulhu, Lord of
the Watery Abyss and dread and awful Potentate of drowned
R'lyeh." While neither the *Scripture* nor any other text of Elder
Lore known to me records the planet wherefrom Cthulhu descended to this world, the *Scripture* says of the origin of his three
sons: "the Spawn of Cthulhu came down from remote and ultra-
telluric Xoth, the dim green double sun that glitters like a demonic
eye in the blacknesses beyond Abbith, to whelm and reign over
the steaming fens and bubbling slime pits of the dawn eons of
this Earth, and it was in primordial and shadowy Mu that They
were great." Von Junzt (XXI, 29-a) cannot identify Xoth save to

Even in the uttermost nadir of my despair, it were unwise for me to neglect the awful duties of my sacerdotal office and thus I turned from a dreary contemplation of this most dire of all the thousand iniquities of the infamous Yaa-Thob-both to that scrutiny of the Thirty-One Rituals demanded of my office. This precious document, of which the Earth affords no single other copy*, and which dates from the most extreme antiquity, was indited by the hand of Niggoum-Zhog, the First Prophet, himself, in the dim eons before the Old Ones had yet dreamed of creating man. The Secret Rituals themselves were inscribed in fiery and metallic inks upon leaves of parchment fashioned from *pthagon* membrane and bound betwixt twin carven and gem-studded plates of rare, precious *lagh* metal brought from dark Yuggoth where it rolls upon the Rim in the most remote of terrestrial eons by the shadowy Elder Ones. My seething brain a chaos of incoherent images, I perused one by one the Thirty-One Secret Rituals of Yhe, and in the last, most potent and terrific of them all, I found the answer to my dilemma.

For that Thirty-First Ritual contained the formula which is called "The Key That Openeth The Door To Yhe," and which the primal and elder Prophet warns is not to be spoken aloud save in the final extremity of ultimate Doom.

Therein, in my madness and desperation, I found the answer for which I sought—*aii, n'ghaa xuthoggon R'lyeh! Iä*

---

say that it lies in the same star cluster as Zaoth, Abbith and Ymar. The above reference to the "Isle of the Sacred Stone Cities" and the Deep that lies off its shores, together with geographical data hinted at earlier in the *Zanthu Tablets*, enables me to identify tentatively the place whereat Zoth-Ommog the Dweller in the Deeps lies imprisoned as a submarine chasm off Ponape. —*Translator*.

* The hierophant Zanthu is in error here, for the surviving fragments of the Susran myth cycle list a copy of *The Yhe Rituals* from *Elder Mu* as among the necromantic tomes in the library of the great magician Malygris, according to the inventory recorded by the sorcerer Nygron, and an incredibly ancient copy of the *Rituals* was in the possession of the Saracen wizard Yakthoob, Alhazred's mentor, according to the Irem chapter of the *Necronomicon* (Narrative II). A copy, perhaps the same Yakthoobic redaction, is rumored to have been found in a sealed tomb in Egypt about 1903.—*Translator*.

Ythogtha! A million generations yet unborn shall curse my name!

IV

And thus was I resolved to open the Door to Yhe, by which term is meant to render null the strictures of the Elder Sign and to release the Primal One, the Abomination in the Abyss, from the chains of psychic force which have imprisoned him in the depths of the great Chasm for innumerable eons.

To set free Ythogtha from his Abyss would be at a single stroke to render him the most awesomely powerful of all the thousand gods of antique Mu, and thus to elevate myself, as His hierophant and prophet, to the supreme and most potent priest in all of the Nine Kingdoms.

The ambitions of Yaa-Thobboth would thus be ground into dust; the too easily dominated King Shommog would in a breath be divested of all authority, to the elevation of mine own monarch, Nuggog-ying; the wealth and might of the province of K'naa would drain away like shallow mud before the sucking tides, and mine own realm of G'thuu would achieve ultimate prominence over the kingdoms of Mu. What man dares condemn me if, in the last extremity of my need, I set my hand against the decree of the Elder Gods themselves!

Thus I went down the Hidden Stair to the secret crypt, burrowed deep into the bowels of the planet beneath the age-crumbling foundations of my palace, and there I caused my mute Rmoahal slaves to open the trapdoor, one single massy slab of hewn and polished onyx, revealing a black depth from which blew ever a chill and noxious wind.

And, steeling my soul, I called upon the power of the Xothic Key, and summoned slithering from his noisome burrows the Father of Worms himself, even undying and putrescent Ubb, leader and progenitor of the dreaded Yuggya—the Burrowers Beneath—the prehuman servitors of my god, who squirm and slither in the slime about his feet.

Like a great, glistening mass of putrid white jelly was Father Ubb, and his squat and quivering trunk supported naught but a swollen head wherein drooled a pink-rimmed, obscene orifice lined with triple rows of adamantine fangs. Now the Yuggya serve my lord Ythogtha and his brother, Zoth-Ommog, even as the Deep Ones serve Cthulhu and the Tcho-Tchos their lords, Zhar and Lloigor; and as the Flame-

Creatures strive ever to free Cthugha and the Serpentmen of Valusia sought to unchain their lord, Yig, so do the Yuggya tirelessly gnaw at the bonds that hold Ythogtha and Zoth-Ommog.

Emerging at length pale and shaken from my converse with Father Ubb, whose unholy stench is that of Abboth Itself, I gained the upper air with relief. But I had won the aid of the Burrowers Beneath to my great endeavor, and together we swore to open the Door to Yhe, though we incur the wrath of the Elder Gods upon remote and rubicund Glyu-Vho!*

I chose the Day of the Writhing of the Aurora as most efficacious for my endeavor; and thence to the brink of the mighty Abyss of Yhe went I forth, with my few frightened acolytes in my train, and in the Hour of the Singing of the Green Vapor I stood upon the cliffs overlooking the gloom-veiled depths of the chasm and made the Scarlet Sacrifice while behind me arose the wailing chorus of mine acolytes in the uncouth and alien rhythms of the Yuggya Chants.

I performed the Red Ablution; I brandished the Xothic Key; I traced upon the trembling air in characters of supernal fire the Hieroglyphs of Yrr; I performed the Quaar Exorcism; I called upon the Dholes in eon-forgotten Aklo; I employed the lore of the Forbidden Litany; I summoned the Xlath Entities from beyond the extraspatial region of Asymmetrical Etheric Polarity.

I adored the Black Flame in a manner which maketh my soul to shrink and shudder within me to this hour; I called upon all of the gods of archaic Mu—upon the Great Ones (saving only the noxious and tyrannical Ghatanothoa), and upon the Lesser Ones, upon Yig the Serpent-Father, and shadowy Nug, and Yeb of the Whispering Mists, upon Iod the Shining Hunter, and Vorvadoss of Bel-Yarnak, the Troubler of the Sands—and upon Him Who Is To Come, and upon Father Dagon and Mother Hydra, who rule the Deep Ones who are his servants in the green sea.

And I uttered in a great voice The Name Which Is Not Ever To Be Uttered Aloud. . . .

* In an often-quoted passage of the *Necronomicon*, Alhazred identifies this name, which is primal Naacal, as that of the star known to the Arabic astronomers of his day as *Ibt al Janzah*, which is to say, Betelgeuze.—*Translator.*

Above me the stars trembled and burned pale as waxen tapers in a draught . . . all save for the scarlet eye of Glyu-
Vho, which blazed more brightly than before.

Beneath my heel the Earth shook with tremors; and from
the dimly lit west, where titanic mountains march the breadth
of Mu, deep subterranean thunders mumbled and cold black
craters burst into flame, filling angry heaven with seething
smoke.

Mine acolytes huddled before me, white faces hidden in
shaking hands. And there was a great silence upon the Earth
for seven breaths of time.

V

And then my heart leapt up within me for Lo! I had released the first of the seven bonds that had, from the immemorial depths of forgotten time, held prisoner the
Abomination in the Abyss.

And *he* lifted himself above the brink of the vast chasm of
Yhe and gazed down upon his arch-hierophant.

Very terrible was Ythogtha to the sight of men, and more
huge than my mind could scarce accept.

Like a black glistening moon he rose above the brink, a
gigantic hemisphere of quaking slime, vaster than any mountain. Faceless and neckless was he, save that from his front a
terrific beak thrust forth. Cruel and terrible was this curved
beak of blackest adamant, and it measured many thousands
of paces in its length.

And then, half a league farther along the brink of the
chasm, a second black, glistening, beaked head rose into
sight—and another!—and then yet a third colossal beaked
head rose above the lip of the Abyss!

*And then it was true terror smote me to the heart, for I
saw and knew my Lord in his awfulness* . . . and we trembling mortals were dwarfed by him, like motes before the
ponderous *yakith*-lizard were we . . . and, suddenly, horribly,
I knew what I had done.

The acolyte huddled at my feet knew in the same instant,
and squealed and wallowed in terror, wriggling from before
the altar of the Abomination . . . to flee, staggering and
stumbling, white to the lips, with wide, mad, staring eyes that
burned with pale fire like sick moons . . . and I, too, quailed
to the depths of my being and turned on trembling limbs,
hurling from me with sudden horror the loathsome volume of

the Rituals, which fell into the Abyss from which ultimate
and mind-blasting Nightmare had but part way emerged . . .
and I ran—*ran*—while the Earth shook and great crevices
opened to split the land asunder . . . ran, while mountain after mountain erupted in flame and thunder, and the sea
boiled madly, and a great terrible shaft of unearthly light
burned down the star-gulfs from distant Glyu-Vho . . . ran,
even as down that star-beam descended, from the remote
luminary that flamed like a wrathful and revenging eye
athwart the volcano-shaken west, terrible great Things like
Towers of Flame . . . which I knew to be either the Elder
Gods or their servants . . . while sky-tall and burning towers
swept the Abyss with their lightnings—and I fled through the
gates of Yu-Haddoth, where dwelleth my king, but which lay
now in smoking ruin, shaken by the great tremors of the
Earth—and I scourged the panic-stricken multitudes before
me—*who knew not the true nature of the monstrous Thing
I had almost freed*—drove them shrieking into the vidya
vahans, the ancient sky chariots of doom-fraught Mu . . .
while the ground shook and the towers fell and mountain
after mountain erupted . . . and we fled through the storm-
torn skies and across the wind-lashed waves . . . fled all that
unending night of flame and doom and chaos, while behind
our sky-borne keels immemorial Mu crumbled under the
mighty waves that beat in from the angry sea, and broke
apart, shaken to its unstable core by the convulsions of
outraged nature, lashed by starry fires of the Elder Gods . . .
on we flew at length into a distant land near the Hidden
Gates of elder Shamballah itself . . . but mere distance can
not erase from my terror-frozen brain the ultimate glimpse
of nether-most hell that shook my soul when I saw . . . and
knew . . . that vast and beaked and mountainous head of the
Thing in the Pit . . . *that awful and eon-accursed Thing whose
prodigious FINGERTIPS I had seen.*

LEMURIA

Lemuria was really invented by the geologists, not the occultists, and they postulated its former existence to explain how the same species and fossils could be found on opposite sides of the ocean. It was originally in the Indian Ocean, by the way, before Madame Blavatsky and her gang moved it to the less crowded Pacific.

Hardly any fantasy writers have bothered much with Lemuria, which explains why I set my first novel there. Atlantis was the province of Kuttner, Smith, Gaskell and de Camp, but Lemuria was fair game. That first novel was about Thongor the Mighty, barbarian warrior of time's dawn, cast very much in the mold of Conan. The book proved so popular that it is still in print and has fathered a half-dozen sequels and several short stories.

Following next are the first two short stories, laid earlier in Thongor's career than are the novels. They were both written at the request of Hans Stefan Santesson, who wanted them for his sword and sorcery anthologies.

Since both of Hans's anthologies have been out of print for ten years or so, it's about time they were reprinted.

THIEVES OF ZANGABAL

I

In the Hall of Seven Gods

The priest Kaman Thuu was old and skeletal, his lean body wrapped in a robe of crimson velvet whereon the symbols of the Seven Gods of Zangabal were worked with stiff gold thread. Jeweled rings flashed and glittered on his clawed fingers and his eyes burned keen in his shaven, skull-like head.

"We are agreed then," he purred. "For twenty pieces of gold you will rob the house of Athmar Phong the magician and fetch back to me the mirror of black glass you will find in his workshop. And this task you will fulfill this very night."

"Aye," the bronzed young giant grunted sourly, "but I like not the task."

"I have already explained that you have naught to fear at the hands of Athmar Phong," the priest reminded him silkenly. "This is the first day of Zamar, the first month of spring. On this night the magicians of the Gray Brotherhood to which Athmar Phong is sworn, meet on a mountain plateau far to the north of here for their vile and sorcerous sabbat. Thus will the magician be absent tonight, and thus you may thieve the mirror for us in utter safety. . . ."

"So you claim," the youth growled, "and so it may well be. But it is never wise to meddle in the affairs of wizards, and their houses go seldom unguarded. What if this Ptarthan sorcerer has left behind a demon to watch over his treasures?"

A cold amusement flickered in the clever eyes of the gaunt priest. He ran his gaze over the broad shoulders, the long and powerfully muscled bare arms, and the heavy-thewed chest of the young barbarian who sat before him in the veiled antechamber of the temple. And he let his gaze linger on the

37

massive hilt of the great two-handed Valkarthan broadsword
that hung at the lean waist of the young thief in its long scabbard of dragon leather.

"Surely you are not . . . *afraid?*" he suggested slyly.

The young barbarian flushed angrily. His strange gold eyes,
that burned with sullen, wrathful fires under scowling black
brows in his tanned face under the thick, unshorn mane of
black hair blazed with sudden temper. Then they cleared, and
the youth threw back his head and laughed.

"Gorm!" he rumbled. "You sit here secure in your silken
nest, a pure and holy priest of the Gods of Zangabal who
would never sully his sanctified fingertips with blood or
crime—and pay another man to take risks and dare the perils
you would shudder to face—and then taunt him with a hint
of cowardice!" The burly young barbarian laughed again, and
spat on the marble flags and the fine Pelorm carpet. "Wizards
and priests! You are alike, the both of you—and I would
have dealings with neither, if I had my way!"

The gaunt skull-face of Kaman Thuu tightened and his
voice grew harsh and contemptuous. "Would you rather
starve like a whining beggar in the back alleys of Zangabal,
barbarian? Because that you will do if you refuse the task I
have set you. Remember, the Thieves' Guild is powerful in
our city: to make your living as a thief here you must join
the guild, or fight both your brother thieves and the city
guard each time you attempt a robbery. And to enter the
guild, you must pay a heavy fee in gold. For weeks, by your
own account, you have fought over scraps like a half-starved
animal, stealing from the bazaar, lifting a fat purse, scrabbling like an *unza* for a bare subsistence. I alone have offered
you gold for a task: reject my offer, and you perish miserably
either of a starved belly or at the hand of the guild—"

The young barbarian—his name was Thongor—waved
away this cloud of words with a grunt of surly acknowledg-
ment.

"I know all this, priest. And I also know why you come to
me, an outlander, with your offer—because the self-respecting
thieves of Zangabal have already rejected you. By Gorm the
Father of Stars—even the cunning thieves of Zangabal dare
not steal from this Ptarthan mage! But I must do it, or starve:
so save your breath. But I still ask: what if this Athmar
Phong has left a demon to guard his house while he is absent? I have fought beasts and men ere now, but no warrior
can pit naked steel against hell-spawn and live!"

The priest smirked, narrowed thoughtful eyes.

"There is some truth in what you say, barbarian. Athmar Phong *is* reputed to hold a familiar spirit or elemental bound to his service. That is why we of the Temple are willing to entrust to your hands a rare amulet which is one of our treasures—"

He dipped one bony, bejeweled hand into his crimson robes and brought forth a small object of curious workmanship which he set gently on the tabletop between them, moving to one side the empty wine bottle and the remains of the meal of broiled *bouphar* steak which had somewhat appeased his guest's ravenous appetite.

The thing was as long as a man's middle finger and made of colorless crystal. It glittered in the orange light of the candelabra. Thongor picked it up gingerly, turning it so it caught the light. He scrutinized the amulet but could make nothing of it. The surface of the lucent crystal was engraved with a pattern of tiny hieroglyphics in some unknown language. He grunted sourly. A simple barbarian, bred in the savage wilderness of the frozen north, far from perfumed cities and silk-clad men, he had a healthy warrior's contempt for all this foul, sly witchery. Still, there was an odd glitter to the thing: and his fingers tingled with faint currents of some uncanny force locked within the very structure of the crystal. . . .

"What does this gewgaw do?" he rumbled mistrustfully.

"This amulet is called the Shield of Cathloda," the priest told him in a severe tone. "It is a rare protective amulet which diverts and absorbs the attack of magical forces, and it was made a thousand years ago in Zaar the Black City far to the east. It will rechannel or cancel anything up to ninth-order forces. Fear not, even if Athmar Phong has left magical traps or a guardian Famílulus of some kind, you will walk safely and unharmed. . . ."

Thongor studied the crystal cylinder for a few moments. Then he stood up, slipping the amulet into his pocket-pouch and drawing an immense hooded black cloak about his brawny shoulders.

"Very well, priest," he growled. "I will chance it for your gold . . . although something tells me it is a bargain I will yet live to regret—if I live!"

II

Black Catacombs

The priest thereupon led him forth from the veiled antechamber and into the central nave of the colossal temple. At this hour of night there were no worshippers in the vast domed hall, which was murmurous with whispering echoes and filled with vague depths of gloom.

At the far end of the hall, which was lined with titanic pillars of gray stone that loomed up into the darkness of the vault above like stone sequoia, stood towering idols hewn from seven kinds of stone: the Seven Gods they worshipped here in Zangabal on the Gulf. Thongor eyed them grimly, unimpressed. The winged colossi, bearing mystic attributes and symbols in their many arms, tridents, stylized thunderbolts, crowns, swords and less-recognizable accouterments, glared down at him, their stone faces shining in the dim gleam of coiling blue flames which glided heavenwards from a vast bronze bowl on the alabaster altar. The superstitions of the barbarian were bred deep in him, stamped deep in blood, brain and bone: but he knew them not, these alien godlings of the tropic, jungle-clad southlands: he swore only in the name of Father Gorm, the grim divinity of the dark northern wastes of ice and snow.

The priest led him around to the rear of the seven-fold dais whereon were upreared the stone colossi. And there he touched a hidden catch. A panel of thick marble sank from view, soundless and sudden as a feat of magic, revealing the yawning mouth of a black cavern. Thongor growled, napehairs bristling at the thought of entering the ominous secret portal.

"This hidden route will carry you to the house of Athmar Phong," the priest said smoothly. "You will follow the yellow symbols only: they are shaped like the Yan Hu glyph—you know the characters of our southland language, do you not?"

"Aye," he nodded curtly.

"Then follow only the yellow Yan Hu, and it will lead you to the pits under the magician's house. Let me caution you not to stray from the path thus delineated, for other characters mark other routes, such as, for example, the Shan Yom glyph, marked in red, which leads to the waterfront. You will come up beneath the house and will thus avoid the many magical traps or defenses the Ptarthan wizard has doubtless set over his walls, his doors and his windows."

Despite the priest's soothing words, the brawny young warrior still hesitated at the threshold of the black tunnel's mouth.

"What are these cursed caverns—how came they here?" he demanded. "Since I bear your crystal toy, why should I not take my chances with the front gates and walk the streets under the open skies like a man? I am no skulking *unza* to slink through your stinking sewers!"

The priest answered smoothly: "These cavernous passageways are very old; indeed, their origins are lost in the dim mists of the ancient past. But the chronicles of our Temple tell that at the end of The Thousand Year War with the fall of Nemedis in the east, the Children of Nemedis came thither to found the Nine Cities of the west. It was Yaklar of the House of Ruz was Lord of the founding of Zangabal, and it is written that the hidden ways were here even ere the walls of the city were first raised. More than this we know not, but by means of this secret the Temple is mighty in Zangabal, and even the Sark in his palace is beyond the reach of our eyes and ears, for the tunnels extend even under the royal precinct. But come, barbarian, you must linger no more: night passes swift-winged, and you must accomplish the theft of the Black Mirror ere dawn or be surprised in the midst of the task by the returning of Athmar Phong. . . ."

The gaunt priest stood by the open portal until the grim-faced young warrior had vanished in the darkness of the tunnels; then he released the secret spring and closed the hidden door again,

He stood for a moment, fingering his lean jaw with bony fingers. With luck, the mirror would be in his possession before the first hour of morning, and with it—*power!* Power to bend even the strong will of Athmar Phong to do his bidding. Power to command the secret of the mirror, by which he thought he saw a clear path from this place to a higher . . . to the throne of Zangabal itself! He smiled a slow, evil smile at the thought.

And as for the barbarian—well, why should he squander even a portion of the gold his wiles had wrung from temple worshippers? The youth could be disposed of without loss:

luckily, he was not even a member of the Thieves' Guild, which was a stroke of good fortune, as the guild took a disquieting degree of interest in the disappearance of their members. But no one would even miss the outlander.

His hand went to the small glass phial concealed in a secret pocket of his robes. There was enough powder of that deadly narcotic called Rose-of-Dreams within the small phial to destroy a dozen such as Thongor of Valkarth.

Thongor strode through the darkness, his strange gold eyes questing about distrustfully and one hand at the hilt of his mighty broadsword. The cavernous passage was black as the depths of his savage Northlander hell, and it reeked of dead things long unburied.

Dangling stalactites hung from the arched roof overhead, glistening wetly in the faint light. The very presence of the hanging spears of stone denoted the awesome age of these secret passages beneath Zangabal, for Thongor understood that such were slowly built up over eons of sluggish calcareous drippings. He would almost have assumed the passages to be the work of nature from such evidence, but the walls and floors of the tunnels clearly showed the handiwork of the builder. For although obscured by centuries of neglect and decay, the ancient marks of stone-working tools were still visible along his path. He wondered grimly what unknown people of Earth's remotest dawn had built these subterranean ways, and for what mysterious purpose? Oft had he heard whispered myths of the pre-human Dragon Kings of lost Hyperborea, buried countless ages ago under the fathomless snows of the polar north. Legend told that the mystery race of lost Hyperborea, sprung from the gliding serpent and not the jungle ape, as were the races of men, had ruled all of old Lemuria before the creation of Phondath the Firstborn, the Father of All Men. Could it have been the shadowy Hyperboreans who cut these passages through the depths of the world?

Shrugging, he put such questions aside. It was futile to puzzle over such mysteries, since he had no answer to the riddle. He strode forward, his black leather boots crushing the mold and pooled slime which bestrew the stony floor.

And then he came to the branching of the tunnel. One offshoot led away to his left, but it was marked with the Shan Yom symbol painted on the wall in strange pigments that glowed with cold crimson fires. The other passage, to his right, was emblazoned with the phosphorescent yellow glyph of Yan Hu. He took the right-hand way.

Cold water dripped from the roof above, slow drops splashing in black pools, beslimed and foul. Small sounds came to his ears as he strode forward: the squeak and scurry, the rattle of tiny claws rasping over wet stone: the tunnels were aswarm with *unza*, the hideous scavenger-rodents of Lemuria. He could see the gem-like wink and glitter of small red eyes from the black mouths of side tunnels as he moved forward. He ignored the scrabbling rats, but his hand tightened on the hilt of his broadsword: the *unza* are eaters of flesh, and where they slither thick may also be found larger creatures.

Once a black serpent slid in front of him and he recoiled, choking back a curse. But the viper glided on, ignoring him even as it ignored the rats.

And once the foaming torrent of a subterranean river cut across his path. He crossed it by means of a narrow, arched bridge of stone. Icy spray splattered him from the black waters as they rushed by beneath his heels, and his feet slipped on the treacherous slimy mold which encrusted the stone arch, but he plodded forward grimly.

He sullenly cursed the ironies of fate that had cast him up on this shore. Nine years had passed since he had found his way down across the mighty mountainous spine of the Lemurian continent, the Mountains of Mommur, from the frigid wastes of his native Valkarth. As a boy of fifteen he had been the lone survivor of his clan, the Black Hawk people of Valkarth who perished in a mighty battle with their sworn enemies, the Snow Bear tribe. The boy, Thongor, armed with the mighty broadsword of Thumithar his sire, had cut his way through the cities of the south. He had been an assassin, a wandering adventurer, a bandit—the last profession ending on the slave galleys of Shembis from which he had escaped, leading a slave mutiny and stealing the very galley whereon he had toiled.

Thence he had sailed south to Tarakus, the pirate city which lay at the foot of the Gulf of Patanga, where it mingled with the wind-lashed waters of Yashengzeb Chun the Southern Sea. The youth, Thongor, had brawled and battled his way to power in the red roaring Kingdom of Corsairs. As one of the proud Captains of Tarakus he had swaggered through the narrow spray-swept streets of the little seaport, draped in costly brocade, emeralds and rubies blazing about his corded throat, and the wealth of a dozen merchant ships piled in the basement of his stone house. But, alas, his vile Valkarthan temper had been his doom, and he had slain the Pirate King in a duel still legended among the wild rogues of the Corsair Kingdom; he had fled with half the Tarakan navy at his heels, bearing off only the rags on his back and the mighty broadsword of his kingly sire. Thus, during the year past, he had fought his way through the jungled southland to the docks of Zangabal, hoping to enter the Sark's service as a mercenary swordsman. But, that failing, he had fallen back on his old profession of thievery, and thus had come to the present perilous impasse—serving a black-hearted priest by robbing a dangerous and potent magician!

Suddenly a black wall swung up before his face, and Thongor jerked his attention away from his wandering memories . . . his underground journey was over, and the house of Athmar Phong lay before him.

III

The Magical Workshop

Thongor ran his hands lightly, questing, over the wall of black stone that confronted him. The marked path ended here, that much was certain; behind this wall, then, must lie the pits below the house of the Ptarthan mage. But how to pass the wall?

Growling a curse on that smirking priest who had not fore-warned him of this barrier, he fumbled about in the dark and at last—more by happy accident than by careful plan—his fingers found the hidden spring and depressed it. The smooth wall sank soundlessly into the earth and the warrior stepped forward into a gloom-drenched room cut from smooth, heavy stone.

He did not, as yet, seek to close the opening thus made. You can never be certain how swiftly you may wish to leave the house of a wizard, and a smart thief never closes a door behind him if he can help it.

The basement was piled with crates and bales of barrels. Thongor did not waste time looking them over; he prowled through the darkness of the room, every sense at the alert, the great broadsword naked in his hand.

Soon he encountered a stone stair against the farther wall, and followed it up to the next floor on silent feet. Pushing through a heavy hanging of purple cloth, he found himself in a room so weirdly furnished that at first all he could do was blink and stare and blink again, standing in the doorway.

The walls were of smooth stone faced with gray plaster and lined with shelves of dark wood. Along these were stacked and piled a jumble of curious things. Bottles and jars and flasks filled with colored liquids and nameless powders, bundles of dry, withered leaves and grotesquely shaped roots, little cloth bags tied with drawstrings and filled, perhaps, with strange drugs and deadly powders.

And books—more of these than Thongor had ever seen before. Huge, ponderous tomes made of crinkly sheets of rough parchment crudely bound in heavy leather or carven wood or painted ivory panels.

This, he knew, must be the magical workshop of Athmar Phong. A massive desk of oily black wood, carved all over with grinning devil masks, stood to one end of the room, its top littered with hieroglyphic charts and curious instruments of brass and crystal. A man's skull of browned bone stood as a paperweight on one corner of the desk, and rubies were set in the sockets of the skull for eyes. They glinted with malign small lights, following his movement as he crossed the room.

A monstrous stuffed dragon hawk, a winged flying demon, hung from wires suspended from the rafters.

In a globe filled with milky fluid, a human brain floated.

Thongor noticed that this room was well lit, although he could not discover the source of the illumination. Gazing about, he could see no windows, nor were there any lamps or candles or torches to be seen; nevertheless the chamber was bathed in a harsh, sterile light that leeched most of the color out of things. A prickle of unease crawled down his spine, and, as he could not see the Black Mirror the priest had sent him here to fetch, he hastily quitted the silent room and pushed through a velvet-hung doorway into an adjoining chamber.

Whereas the first room had been cold and grim and workmanlike, with its harsh gray illumination and bare stone floors, this second chamber was a nest of silken luxury. The air reeked with heavy perfumes from a fat silver incense lamp on a low tabouret of blond wood inlaid with small panels of delicate ivory, exquisitely sculptured with shockingly detailed pornographic tableaux. A long, low divan lay along the farther wall—and there, languorously coiled amid a nest of bright-colored cushions, a young girl of breathtaking loveliness watched him from dark almond eyes.

The shock of discovering the room was inhabited by another stunned Thongor for an instant—but no longer. The hair-trigger reflexes of a barbarian warrior took over. The keen point of the great broadsword came up and hovered a half-inch from the base of the girl's throat.

"One sound—one word—!" Thongor growled.

The girl smiled slightly and continued to regard him from under thick, sooty lashes. Thongor looked her over curiously. She could have been eighteen, but no older, for her sleek golden body was as slim and graceful as a young panther. A thin gown of green silk was drawn partly across her white body, leaving bare one arm and one long slender leg, and a silver disc gleamed upon the tip of each breast. Her long thick hair was fire-red with gold gleams shot through the silken tresses. Thongor had never seen a red-headed girl before, but he knew that some of the slave women in the harems of the Southland kings used color dyes, which may have explained the dazzling shade of her tresses, which were plaited into one thick braid with strands of glowing pearls.

Her face was filled with fresh young beauty. Dark, tiptilted eyes under thick black lashes, a full-lipped warmly crimson mouth; and soft delicate skin of flawless pallor.

"Thank the gods you have come!" the girl breathed in a low, quiet voice, deep and husky. She writhed a little on the silken divan, and her thin covering slipped away a trifle, revealing the naked curve of her thigh and a slim hip. Slowly, so as not to trigger him into action, the girl lifted into view her slim bare arms; they were bound at the wrist with manacles made of small gold chains.

"Who are you, lass? The wizard's concubine?" he demanded roughly, still holding the great sword at her throat.

"The wizard's slave . . ." she sighed. Then, before he could speak, she continued in a rush of words: "Athmar Phong stole me from my people when I was eleven; for seven hideous years I have been his helpless slave, the subject of evry vile whim and loathsome fancy that came into his black, putrid heart!" the girl panted. Her young pointed breasts rose and fell, straining the green silk of her covering tautly with every breath.

"For seven years I have dreamed and prayed that someone would come to free me from this hideous bondage . . . and at last *you* have come to break my chains and set me free!"

Heedless of his lifted sword, the girl slid from the couch and knelt before Thongor, the heart-shaped oval of her face lifted to him, tears trembling on her sooty lashes.

"Free me . . . free me, warrior . . . and I will gladly be *your* slave!" she whispered.

Thongor was young, and he had been without a woman since leaving Tarakus a year before, so it is not surprising that the blood rose hotly within him. Growling a calming word or two, he sheathed his sword and bent to snap the slender golden chains that bound the girl's wrists. Then he lifted her from her knees in his strong arms. She curled languorously against him, her slim arms sliding around his waist, her naked legs smooth and soft against his bare thighs. The pulse thundered in his temples as he felt the warmth of her breasts pressing against his bare chest through the scant silk covering that was all she wore. She lifted a trembling mouth to his lips . . . another instant and he might well have forgotten the dangers of this place, and the perilous mission that had brought him . . . another instant and he might have lost himself in the warm softness of her. . . .

But even as her panting kiss seared his mouth, even as his brawny arms encircled her hips, one sly hand slipped into his pocket-pouch—and the girl sprang halfway across the room and turned to laugh mocking at him—clenching the Shield of Cathloda between her fingers!

IV

A Voice in the Dark

For a moment, he stood frozen with shock, his senses still tingling with her warmth and softness. She stood across the room, her lips parted—and laughed.

But not the delicate laughter of a young girl! Peal after ringing peal of harsh metallic mirth roared from her soft, warm lips—and even as he stared uncomprehendingly, dazed with the swiftness of the change—hellish fires blazed up in her almond eyes. They flamed like pits of burning sulphur. And now that she laughed, her lips were drawn back revealing hideous yellow tusks, like those behind the black, bristling jaws of the savage Lemurian jungle boar.

She began to . . . *change*.

Her limbs blurred, then grew transparent as smoke, then remolded themselves. A ghastly parrot beak thrust from the warm oval of the girl's face. Blazing orbs of yellow fire seethed with hellish mockery beneath her arched brows. Her hands became scaly bird claws, armed with ferocious talons.

"Fool of a mortal," the bird-demon croaked in a clashing iron voice, "I knew of your presence within the house of my master from the first moment you set foot herein . . . and I chose a form that would lull your suspicions—"

Thongor struck!

The girl-thing had fooled him for instants—but now the fighting instincts of a Northlands warrior turned him into a battling engine of destruction! One hand flashed out—scooped up the round silver incense lamp and hurled it straight as an arrow into the demon's half-transformed face. The thud of heavy silver against flesh was audible the length of the room. The monster, its body still a weird blend of exquisite human female and grisly bird-thing, staggered back from the impact.

The silver lamp broke open, and glowing pink coals splattered the half-changed body of the demon guardian! In an instant, the disarranged piece of green silk the devil still wore went up in a flash of flame. Blazing coals dashed down between the white soft breasts of the girl-like torso, raising terrible weals and blisters. The parrot beak gaped open, screeching with agony and fury.

Thongor had not paused, as would a civilized child of the southern cities, to use reason: instinct alone told him that if the demon still wore flesh—that flesh could feel pain!

He followed the flying brazier with the small tabouret on which it had stood. This he hurled like a powerful catapult straight at the ghastly scaled claw that clutched the protective talisman. The blunt edge of the wooden tabouret caught the slim girl's wrist which had only partly changed into demon's claw. The bone snapped with the sound of a dry branch cracking. The claw sagged limply as the demon howled—and the amulet fell!

Thongor dove across the room. His flying body crashed against the tender girl legs of the monster and sent it reeling back against the farther wall, while he scooped out one hand to catch the talisman. Luckily the fragile crystal thing had fallen on thick, soft carpets—had the floor been of bare stone, his only hope of escaping alive would have smashed to a thousand tiny shards.

Swift as he was, the demon was swifter. Even as he went crashing back against the wall, it—changed. The body crumbled into a coiling length of smoky stuff—and one arm snaked out, inhumanly long, to snatch the fallen amulet almost out of Thongor's fingers.

The young warrior came to his feet in a rush, steel singing as he tore his sword from its scabbard.

The demon melted before him, reassembling itself across the room. Only the hand which grasped the all-important amulet had remained solid on this plane as the demon moved: Thongor took a swipe at it, but missed.

Now he lunged for the monster, swinging up the mighty broadsword, deep chest thundering forth his primitive challenge. The great sword swung glittering up and came hissing down—to clang against the scaled, reptilian body of the demon, by now fully transformed to its usual appearance on the earth plane.

It was like swinging at a wall of solid steel! The shock traveled up Thongor's arms to the shoulders, numbing and paralyzing even his mighty thews. The demon's breast was solid as iron. It was astonishing that the blade of the sword did not shiver to fragments from the impact. But they had wrought well, those wonder smiths of age-old Nemedis from which the ancient sword had come: potent spells and power-

ful runes had filled the great steel sword with terrific power.
The blade held, although nicked: but the ringing shock
numbed Thongor to the shoulder and the sword fell from his
nerveless fingers to clang like a stricken bell against the stone
floor that lay beneath the carpets.

His arms temporarily helpless, Thongor lashed out with a
booted foot. Howling with harsh mockery, the great yellow
beak of the demon was open: Thongor's booted foot crashed
into its mouth, crushing the beak to gory ruin! Green hell-
blood spurted from the crushed face of the devil, and again it
went reeling back against the wall.

Thongor began to understand the limitations of the thing.
It had complete control over its body, could doubtless transform itself to the likeness of any creature in earth, hell or
heaven—but it was slow of thought. Anticipating a blow
from the great Valkarthan broadsword, it had increased the
density of the matter whereof its breast was composed until it
reached the hardness of solid metal—but had not thought to
extend the same protection to the rest of its body!

Thus, if the young barbarian could keep it off balance, he
might yet defeat the creature, or at least wrest the talisman
from its clutches. He dove after the monster as it fell squall-
ing to the floor, its face a bubbling gory wreck.

He landed squarely upon it, both heavy booted feet crashing down upon its groin.

It was naked now, the green silk covering burnt away by
the scattering coals, and sexless as a stone to the eye, at
least—but still vulnerable to such a brutal blow. He heard it
voice a shrill shriek of bestial agony. Alien organs crunched
and popped under his weight, and more of the green gore
splattered from pulped flesh.

But it availed him little. For a second only it squalled and
flopped in pain—then it hardened its body to the density of
steel all over. He could feel it happening even as he grappled
with the wriggling thing.

They were both on their feet in a moment, battling lustily.
Thongor swung balled fists into the thing's gut and groin, but
only tore the skin from his knuckles and numbed his hands
again. He shouldered it with terrific force, hoping to break
free, and for a moment he took the monster-thing by surprise
and shoved it off balance. He heard bird-clawed feet rip
through the soft carpeting and squeak against naked stone as
it fought to regain its feet.

Then two great hands like twin iron vises closed about his throat and—*squeezed.*

Blood roared in Thongor's ears like pounding surf. A red haze thickened before his eyes, obscuring his vision. Dimly he could see the demon's beaked face—now repaired and whole—snarling into his own. But the crushing pressure on his throat sent needles of unbearable torment lancing through and through his brain like thrusts of pure blinding flame.

He fought desperately with every atom of strength in all his mighty form. Lashing out with strong legs, he sought to crush the clawed feet of his foe or entangle his legs and knock him off balance—but to no avail. The demon increased the density of its body, and thus its weight, till it stood as unmovable as a pyramid of solid stone. Thongor rammed his burly shoulders into its chest, thudded balled fists into midsection and groin—but again, to no avail.

He could not breathe. The howling brute was crushing the very life out of him. Strength drained from his knees; he sagged toward the floor, still battling like a titan. His vision had darkened now, so that he could hardly see. He knew his face must be black from congested glood, a snarling tiger mask of grim ferocity. The blood roared in his ears like a thousand seas plunging over the edges of the world to shatter like a thunderclap against the foundations of eternity.

He fought on, as consciousness ebbed and darkness closed around him like black rising waters.

He passed into utter blackness, still fighting.

V

Ald Turmis

Thongor came awake like some great jungle cat. His savage heritage had honed his reflexes to exquisite keenness. He did not come awake through slow, foggy, transitional stages, as softer city-bred men awaken, but all at once—from total unconsciousness to full, tingling alertness like a jungle predator whose slumbers are disturbed by the faint, distant snapping of a twig.

A dim remote light beat about him.

Cold, rough, wet stone was against his naked back and his

numb wrists were stretched against the wall of rock, clamped helpless with thick bands of icy metal.

He was in a large, empty chamber cut from naked stone. This his hearing told him instantly: he could hear the faint echoes of water dripping down through the foundations of the building above. From the darkness, the moisture, the foul stench, he reasoned that he must be in some dungeon cell beneath the house of the Ptarthan wizard. His cloak was gone, his sword and other weapons and accouterments— even the pocket-pouch at his wrist, where a few lonely coins were stored against hunger.

But these things mattered little. He was surprised to find himself still alive!

And alive he was, or all the myths were wrong—for surely no disembodied spirit could feel such pain as went throbbing and pulsing from every nerve in his body. He took a deep breath and felt the red waves of pain beating against the very citadel of his mind. His body felt as if every inch of it had been beaten with leather clubs. But he still lived.

"I wasn't sure whether you were alive or not," drawled a young man's lazy voice very close to him. Thongor felt the icy drench of shock go through him, and twisted his head about—ignoring the soreness of bruised muscles—to find he had a cell mate.

His companion was a slim, dark young man, Thongor's age or perhaps a year or two younger, who wore the simple black leather harness of a lone fighting man unattached to the service of any house or lord. The young warrior wore a scruffy beard of perhaps two weeks's growth, and was somewhat soiled from the filthy dungeon.

Thongor took him in in one swift, measuring glance. The young man was well-bred, with intelligent dark eyes and a not-unpleasant smile, if a trifle dispirited and sardonic, and he had about him the trim, supple, hard-muscled look of a good fighting man.

Thongor relaxed, grunting.

"I live," he said simply. "Why are you not bound, as am I?" he asked immediately, for his companion was secured only by a single chain about one booted leg which was fastened to a ring set in the wall.

The young man grinned faintly. "Because Athmar Phong's pet devil had no trouble in knocking me witless—in contrast to the battle *you* put up. I gather he doesn't consider me of any particular danger. Unlike you—he must judge you a worthy opponent, even for a demon. I could hear the fight all the way down here; it must have been a magnificent brawl!"

"It was," Thongor grunted, "but I lost it. Who are you, and why are you here?"

The dark youth raised a quizzical brow. "For that matter—I might ask the same of you, my friend!"

The barbarian grinned. "Be it so: I am Thongor, a warrior out of Valkarth in the Northlands. I sought to steal a magic mirror from this Ptarthan sorcerer, but it seems I have a few things to learn about the profession of thievery. And you?"

His companion smiled wryly. "I am named Ald Turmis, and my city, Thurdis, lies across the gulf from here. *Belarba*," he said, and Thongor returned the familiar Lemurian word of greeting. The Thurdan regarded him closely.

"Our sanitary facilities are somewhat limited, but I used most of what water we have to clean you up a bit," he said. "There is still a little, if you thirst."

"I thirst, but also, I hunger," Thongor admitted. "I don't suppose there is any—wine?"

Ald Turmis laughed. "For a man who has just escaped alive from a battle with a demon, there should be wine aplenty! But there is a jug of ale, and some meat."

Since the barbarian was bound in such a way that he could not use his hands, Ald Turmis had to help him eat and drink. Thongor downed the strong, sour ale in great gulps, and felt his head clear and new life spread through his battered body. The meat was cold and dry and tough, but it was meat; he ate until his hunger was appeased, then he lay back with a grunt of contentment. With a full belly, a man could face the future on its own terms.

Ald Turmis had been looking thoughtful. At last, when the barbarian had eaten, he spoke up.

"I don't suppose," he began carefully, "that it was a certain Zangabali priest named Kaman Thuu who hired you to rob this house. . . ."

Thongor blinked. "How did you know?"

Ald Turmis shrugged. "I, too, am down on my luck, Valkarthan. I have been traveling about the cities of the gulf, seeking a place to sell my sword. I should have stayed home in Thurdis, it seems, for the new Sark of that city, Phal Thurid by name, has ambitions of conquest and empire and is hiring an enormous mercenary army. But, at any rate, I have thus far failed to find a sinecure, and turned to thievery. This same Kaman Thuu offered me gold to steal a certain mirror from the house of Athmar Phong. That was half a moon ago, and I have been languishing in this cell ever since."

"Gorm's Blood!" Thongor rumbled. "That sneaking pig of a priest! He didn't tell me there had been others!"

Ald Turmis smiled narrowly. "If he had, you might not have followed his wishes."

"There is truth in that," the barbarian growled. "Why does he seek so diligently for this cursed mirror? 'Tis not a wench's vanity, that's sure: he is as ugly as a skull."

"Oh, but it is a very famous mirror—the Mirror of Zaffar, 'tis called. He was a mighty wizard of Patanga in ancient days, and this magic glass holds therein imprisoned a great Demon Prince, who must obey him who holds the Zaffar's Mirror. All the secrets of time and space, all the wisdom of past ages, all the cryptic lore of age-lost and legended Hyperborea are his, who possesses the mighty mirror. Doubtless our priestly friend seeks power, as was ever the way of priests . . ."

Thongor's gold eyes burned amber and fiery as the eyes of lions.

"Well, if I ever get free of these chains, I will smash his cursed mirror over his shaven pate, for not giving me warning I was walking into a trap," he growled.

VI

Naked Steel

For a time they slept, the two of them, their talk done. Food and drink and rest did much to restore Thongor's animal vigor. When he awoke again, rested and refreshed, he tugged at his bonds restlessly.

"Enough of snoring our time away," he rumbled, nudging Ald Turmis to wakefulness with one foot. "This Ptarthan mage will return hither with dawn. It must be near that now, an hour or so hence, perhaps. If we are ever to free ourselves we must do it soon, for once the wizard has us in his grasp we are doomed men. Naked steel cannot battle against blasts of magic."

"We are already doomed men," Ald Turmis yawned. "For

bare hands cannot battle naked steel, and I have long since
given up trying to break my chains."

"But I have not yet tried," Thongor said quietly, and there
was something in the level quality of his voice that made Ald
Turmis feel a thrill of hope.

"You have the body of a gladiator, Thongor, and the thews
of a god, but surely you cannot burst our chains?"

There was a note of question in his voice, but Thongor
merely grunted and turned to examine his bonds. His arms
were spread against the stone wall at his back, and his wrists
were held flat by bands of iron riveted to the stone. The position was cleverly thought out: thus bound, he could only employ a portion of his strength to free himself, and could use
little if any leverage. Still, a man can try.

He took deep breaths, his massive chest swelling with
power. Great ropes of sinewy muscle writhed across his
naked shoulders and down his mighty arms. He set his back
firmly against the stone, and strove against the bonds. Although his face blackened with effort and the thews of his
torso hardened like solid rock, the bonds gave not. He
relaxed, breathing deeply, then he threw every ounce of
his surging strength against the bonds once more. Ald Turmis
watched with growing fascination. The primal, brute strength
of this half-naked barbarian was something beyond his experience.

City-bred men are for the most part shielded against the
raw world of nature—for that is the purpose of cities. Raised
behind walls, guarded by armies, they but rarely are forced to
pit their naked strength against the savage wild.

But Thongor was born on the wintry steppes of the most
terrible wilderness on all the continent. The child of hunters,
born to bare rock and numb snow and howling winds, in a
cruel land surrounded with merciless enemies, men, beasts
and the hostile forces of nature, he was driven to fight for
survival almost from the very hour of his birth. At an age
when most boy children can scarcely walk, Thongor had
battled with his brothers against hungry wolves knee-deep in
frozen snow, with only a piece of rock for a weapon. Hunting the great white bear of the north, he had lived for days
alone on the mighty glaciers with no nourishment but the hot
blood of his kill to sustain him. The struggle for survival in
the savage wilderness is brutal and fierce: the weak die
swiftly; only the mightiest of men survive. Thongor had survived the cold, the harsh winds, the ferocious competition,

and the cruel years of his boyhood had driven the hard
strength of barbarian manhood deep within him.

The iron band—*broke!*

Like twin shadows, Thongor and Ald Turmis prowled
through the darkness of the secret passage within the walls of
the wizard's house on silent feet. They went armed with
lengths of chain, since both the great Valkarthan broadsword
and the Thurdan's slim rapier had been wrested from them
when they were captured. But a length of iron chain is better
than no weapon at all, and in this dark house of magic and
mystery a man felt better with a weapon in his hands.

Privately, Ald Turmis thought they were fools not to flee
when they had the chance. But Thongor could be grimly
stubborn: he sought his great sword, and would not leave
without it.

It had been comparatively easy, with one shackle broken
and one arm freed, to break free of the other. Then, with his
bare fingers, the mighty Valkarthan had pried open a link of
the chain that bound Ald Turmis to the ring set in the wall.
Arming themselves with lengths of the very chains that had
bound them, the two young warriors stole silently from their
cell and into the depths of the cellars of the house. Their first
thought had naturally been of escape, for the concealed door
to the network of underground tunnels still lay open. But
soon they had discovered the tunnels extended directly into a
secret passage within the house itself, as well as into the base-
ments. Thus the Valkarthan had refused to flee like a thief in
the night and insisted they use this rare opportunity to re-
cover their weapons, at least. Ald Turmis had argued, but to
no avail. To the civilized Thurdan, his sword was little more
than a tool, and easily replaced. But to the grim barbarian,
the mighty broadsword was like a part of his body: he had
lived with it by his side too long to abandon it now through
fear.

The wizard's house had many rooms and many floors.
Cleverly concealed eye-holes, hidden among the wall decora-
tions, permitted them to spy on the contents of these chambers.

The first room they inspected in this manner was a labora-
tory given over to alchemy. A great stone fireplace covered
most of one wall and upon its hearth a magic fire of yellow
and purple flames crackled, heating the simmering contents
of strange glass spheres. A profusion of chemical equipment

cluttered long low tables of porcelain and steel. Glass and ceramic containers of bewildering design bore colored fluids of unguessable nature. And strange instruments of the alchemic science loomed in the wavering, colored light of the mystic fire: crucibles and athanors, curcubits and aludels, and all manner of peculiar devices beyond their knowledge even to name.

The second room was given over to an even more terrible purpose. Herein stood huge vats of milky crystal, filled with thick, soupy fluids. Naked bodies lay within, immersed in the cloudy depths of these vats. They could not tell if these were the bodies of human beings or of animals: all they could see was the gleam of pallid flesh. But Thongor guessed the loathsome purpose of the equipment, and his hackles rose along his nape.

"Breeding vats!" he growled. "Look against the farther wall!"

And indeed it seemed that the Ptarthan wizard was engaged in the ultimate blasphemy itself, the attempt to duplicate the miracle of life. For steel-barred cages ran the length of the farther wall, and therein resided the grisly results of the wizard's experiments, or those of them which had gone awry. After one fascinated look, Ald Turmis spat a heartfelt curse and turned his eyes away from the hideous, deformed hybrids that wriggled, slithered and mewled behind the steel bars. There was one creature whose pink, glistening body was almost covered with eyes . . . eyes that wept with unutterable sadness, almost as if the thing had brain and wit enough to realize its own loathsomeness.

Another was a horrible blending of naked young girl and monster plant. Her bare body glistened wetly, pallid and unhealthy, although beautifully and perfectly formed. But her wrists and ankles ended in hairy thick roots, and her bald head was faceless—a thick profusion of pink, fleshy flower petals.

"By the Nineteen Gods," Ald Turmis cursed, "why does he let the pitiful things live—they should be put out of their misery with clean steal, and burnt!"

"Come," Thongor growled, "there are other rooms." They went on and came to a chamber whose walls were hung with silk that rippled black and crimson like leaping flames. From the vast, complex pentacle traced with glowing chalks against a floor of black marble, the nature of this third chamber was easy to guess. They needed not the stench of brimstone that

permeated the air to know that this room was given over to
the wizard's conjurations. Here he performed those forbidden
rituals whereby one might summon up demons from below or
spirits from beyond. The very air tingled with unholy magic.
They passed on.

Many other rooms were thus inspected, and these were
given over to wizardly arts almost beyond conjecture.

There was one that was completely lined with mirrors.
Walls, ceiling and floor were one vast glittering sheet of reflecting glass. Mirrored wall reflected mirrored wall and thus
on into infinity. The purpose of this mysterious chamber was
beyond the comprehension of the two swordsmen, but something about the room was unsettling. It was as if space itself
was twisted and distorted among those endlessly reflecting
self-mirroring walls. They caught a weird glimpse of an
endless nothingness that lay beyond the strictures of space
. . . yawning gulfs of glittering emptiness stretched away.

From this terrible glimpse into the Abyss, they tore their
gaze with difficulty. The shadowy vastness of dim light held
their attention almost with a fascination almost hypnotic.

In this room of mirrors, a man could become forever lost
in rapt contemplation of endless infinity, his mind wandering
trapped and helpless between glittering planes of nothingness. . . .

They came at last to the central hall of the wizard's house,
and Thongor stifled a grunt of satisfaction. A stone dais of
many steps supported a sparkling crystal throne, and there on
the topmost step lay their two swords.

"Come!" he grunted, fingers questing for the spring that
would release the secret door. The hall was untenanted; the
guardian demon nowhere in sight. The door slid open noise-
lessly and they stepped forth into the hall.

And the demon laughed!

VII

Swords Against Sorcery

The hall was broad and high. Stone columns worked with
weird runes and glyphs rose to support a cupola of scarlet
crystal overhead. A floor of polished stone tile rang under-

foot. Tall stands of glittering brass held up enormous branching candles of perfumed wax which cast a wavering gold light over the dark emptiness of the wizard's Seat of Power. Hangings wrought of curious fabrics, depicting nightmarish visions drawn from Ultimate Chaos, hung between the columns: in the flickering light, distorted demoniac figures leered and grimaced from these tapestries.

But Thongor spared but a swift, all-encompassing glance on the decor. He spun to confront the devil-guardian whose mocking laughter pealed through the vaulted hall in a thunder of echoes.

"There!" Ald Turmis yelled hoarsely.

Thongor turned, iron chains swinging in his hands. The demon had fooled them by rendering itself invisible to sight. Now it melted into being atop the dais whereon towered the sparkling crystal throne of its master.

Seven feet tall it stood, straddling their swords, which were laid at the foot of the throne like an offering. The heart of Thongor grew cold at the appearance of it. Now it had taken on its normal form for this plane—a scaled and reptilian thing with a bird's beak and hooked claws. A jagged scarlet crest adorned its blunt, triangular skull, and a serpent's tail lashed the stone steps. Burning eyes blazed sulphurously down at them with cruel triumph.

"Foolish mortals, not to flee when you had the chance!" it roared. "For now you perish! I had hoped to spare you for my master's pleasure, but now—*die!*"

Thongor crouched, the chain swinging loosely, ready for whatever might occur. Ald Turmis backed across the hall toward one of the towering candelabra as the demon launched itself at Thongor.

It sprang like a dragon-cat of the jungle, claws bared and glittering. But in the very middle of its incredible leap, it *changed*. A sheet of flame enveloped the hurtling form—it shrunk into a ball.

The globe of flame hurled directly toward Thongor.

At the last possible moment, the barbarian leaped aside with a lithe tigerish bound. The globe of fire flashed through the space where he had stood.

And, as he leaped aside, Thongor swung the heavy iron chain with all the strength in his mighty arms and shoulders. The heavy iron links whistled through the air and caught the flaming sphere a terrific blow.

Thongor had learned something of the demon's nature.

While its powers were great, the limitations that were imposed upon it by nature on this plane gave him a certain degree of hope. True, it could change to seemingly any form—but then it was bound by the natural limitations of that form.

For example, as a flying globe of flame the thing was virtually substanceless, light and flimsy. It could not have simultaneously the lightness of flying fire and the iron-hard density of its bird-devil form.

Hence the smashing blow of the heavy iron chain burst the burning globe into a shower of flying fragments. Bits of flame splattered over the floor. Of course, the demon could reform—but that would take a few seconds of time.

Thongor seized that momentary advantage. In three lithe bounds he had cleared the steps of the dais, snatched up his mighty sword and tossed the slim rapier to Ald Turmis.

Rivulets of flame snaked over the floor and merged into a burning globe again. But now Thongor was doubly armed: the great broadsword was clenched in his right hand and the heavy length of iron chain dangled from his left. He was ready to pit himself against the demon—as ready as he would ever be. If it came at him in its fire form again, he would again smash it to flying sparks.

But the seething sphere of flames darkened—blurred. It became a monstrous shadowy form, which congealed and hardened. Bird-like wings branched from hunched shoulders, but they were wings of—steel! The neck elongated and the beak thrust forth. The demon shaped itself into the likeness of a fantastic bird of metal. The feathers that clad its form and its mighty wings were hard, cold metal, like dagger blades! The long beak thrust forth like a spear point. The metal bird-thing rose into the air and sailed at Thongor where he stood atop the dais. Wings of glistening steel beat clangorously, heavily, but they supported the clumsy monster aloft. And Thongor's blade and chain would prove feeble weapons against the steel-clad flying monster—

Then, unexpectedly, Ald Turmis struck. The demon, whose intelligence was limited, had almost forgotten his presence. Concentrating on his primary foe—the giant barbarian—he had neglected to attend to the young Thurdan swordsman who stood in the shadows.

The youth turned and seized up the brass candle stand. Seven feet in the air it loomed, and it was heavy as a man—but desperation lent Ald Turmis new strength, and with a mighty heave he tugged it up and hurled it square against the steel bird as it lurched in flight.

The crashing weight of the massive brass stand brought the steel bird down. It clanged thunderously against the marble pave, and the steel-sheathed wings *cracked!* The long serpentine neck broke and the spear-beaked head went rolling and clattering across the tiles.

"Well thrown!" Thongor boomed.

Ald Turmis flashed a grin and sprang from his place by the wall to snatch up the severed head. Perhaps he had some wild hope of preventing the demon from reforming thereby. If so, the hellish powers of the monster were too swift for him.

The cold metal of the head melted into smoke in his hands. A cloud of green vapor leaked through his clutching fingers and floated across the floor. The broken bird of steel now collapsed into a swirling mass of emerald smoke into which the head portion mixed and mingled.

A bodiless streamer of dense green vapor, the demon rose. It floated through the air borne by the gusts of the wind.

Straight for the place where Thongor stood astride the high dais it drifted . . . to settle about his throat!

VIII

The Shield of Cathloda

As the smoke-serpent floated toward him, Thongor struck. His great broadsword swung through the vaporous body of the thing, but harmed it not. The banner of vapor was momentarily broken by the passage of his sword blade but it melted together almost instantly.

It swirled about him and for a moment he was hidden in the green smoke. Then two vaporish tendrils uncoiled from the mass and lashed about the throat of the young warrior. As the clammy fingers of vapor touched his flesh they congealed—hardened—took on weight and density.

Slithering tentacles of tough leathery flesh tightened in a stranglehold, cutting off his air.

Thongor's weapons clanged against the steps of the dais as he snatched at the tightening tentacles of the smoke-thing. His iron fingers tugged to loosen the crushing coils. Green vapor seethed about him. Starved for air, his lungs strained, his mighty chest heaved.

The sinuous tentacles sank into his flesh with incredible strength. He fought on, as more and more portions of the green cloud solidified about his struggling form. One tendril curled about his narrow waist, constricting, squeezing with a crushing grip. Another lashed about one booted foot—seized a firm hold—then snaked out and coiled around his other leg—tightened, and tightened, toppling him off balance and sending him crashing against the top of the dais.

Ald Turmis came yelling across the room, brandishing his slim rapier, to aid him in his thrashing struggle against the kraken-form. But before the gallant young Thurdan could spring to the aid of his embattled comrade—chance, or fate, intervened.

Thrashing about, striving for a firm hand-hold on one of the green tentacles that were slowly crushing the life from his body, Thongor's hand slid along the surface of the topmost step of the dais—and closed about the glassy rondure of a slim ovoid.

The demon exploded!

One moment Thongor lay tightly enmeshed in a tangle of emerald coils—and the next instant the tendrils disintegrated into green vapor! The whirling vapor was flung from the proximity of his body by some tremendous power.

It was as if, out of nowhere, an invisible wall had sprung into being about the half-strangled warrior, and, thrusting in all directions outward from his body, shattered the very substance of the tentacled demon—sundering it atom from atom.

At the moment of the explosion, there came as well a thunderous tormented cry, an agonized howl that shook the hall and sent the flames of the tall candelabra flickering.

Ald Turmis had but reached the base of the nine-tiered dais when the buffeting wind of this inexplicable explosion knocked him to his knees. Open-mouthed with astonishment, he stared about. Scudding wisps of green vapor were flying in every direction from about the barbarian, who lay prone and gasping at the foot of the crystalline Chair of Thaumaturgy.

Even as he watched, Ald Turmis became aware that the demon was unable to reform into a single wholeness again, for the shredded smoke was melting into emptiness even as it floated about the hall. Wisp after coiling wisp dissolved slowly. And, as the last echoes of that demoniac bellow faded, the last wisps of vapor disintegrated.

And the demon was—gone.

Atop the dais, Thongor stumbled to his feet, gulping huge breaths of air into his starved lungs. He, too, peered about uncomprehendingly. Then, recalling the cold smooth cylinder his fumbling hand had grasped, he looked down at what he held. And burst into croaking laughter. "It seems I owe that foul toad of a priest, Kaman Thuu, a debt of thanks after all," he grunted hoarsely. And he held up his hand for Ald Turmis's inspection.

There in his palm lay—the Shield of Cathloda!

IX

The Return of the Sorcerer

Thongor rejoined his comrade at the base of the dais. Despite the ferocity of the tentacled assault by constricting, steely limbs, Thongor's massive body was unharmed. A few bruises, a few more aching muscles, a smear or two of blood where rasping ropes of sinewy tendril had torn away a few square inches of his tough hide—but nothing more serious than that.

"It was the talisman," he explained to Ald Turmis, "the protective amulet the old Zangabali priest lent me ere first I entered into this cursed and devil-haunted house! 'Tis proof against every conjuring—it nullifies every spell—drives thither every magical or demonic thing that comes near! Now that I think on it, the demon was helpless to harm me when I first encountered it. With devilish cunning, the hell-fiend assumed the form of a beguiling wench. And once it had distracted my attention, it stole the talisman,—'the Shield of Cathloda,' old Kaman Thuu called it—from my pocket-pouch."

"But—I don't understand!" Ald Turmis said, in a puzzled voice. "Why should—"

"If I had not borne the shield on my person, the demon could have simply fallen on me the instant I entered the wizard's house and torn me apart—or tried to. But as I was protected by the amulet, it was unable to do me hurt . . . at least until it had seduced me with its girl form and distracted my attention from the amulet!"

"I begin to see," the Thurdan said slowly. "So it fetched

the Shield of Cathloda here and set it beside our swords at the foot of the throne, in offering to its master when he should return from the sabbat."

"Aye," Thongor grunted. "And in my thrashing about, I chanced to grasp the amulet—which automatically invoked its protective powers. The thing is small and glassy—I did not even notice it when I grabbed up our swords."

"So when you seized upon the amulet, it tore the demon asunder. But why—how?"

Thongor shrugged impatiently. "How should I know? I know naught of sorcery and such-like. Perchance it formed an invisible barrier about me, repelling the devil-thing. But it happened so swiftly that the demon was blasted apart . . . and, since the amulet destroys the magical power of whatever ensorcelled thing it touches, the demon itself was demolished. For it must have been held present on the earth plane by a powerful spell of black wizardry: 'tis abnormal for hell-spawn to gain entry into this plane of being; their natural home is far from here."

"So," mused Ald Turmis, "when the touch of the amulet canceled the spell which gave the demon freedom of movement on this plane, it disintegrated, returning to whatever pit of hell was its natural place. And lucky for us it happened as it did, for the vile thing had well-nigh strangled the life out of you—and would have made short work of me soon after!"

"Aye!" Thongor grunted, touching his bruised and swollen throat with tender fingers, wincing with pain. "Thank Gorm I blundered on the crystal thing when I did. But, now, Ald Turmis, let us leave this accursed place, and swiftly. We have our swords—and here lie our cloaks and warrior harness—let us shake the dust of this place off our heels and repair to the nearest inn. 'Twill take a jug or two of strong red wine to wash the stink of magic from me, and I can taste it already!"

But Ald Turmis, looking past him to the top of the dais, made no answer. Instead he went pale and clutched Thongor's arm mutely.

Thongor grunted questioningly and turned to see what had alarmed his comrade. And he saw—

Even as the ruddy glow of dawn lit the crystal dome above them and bathed the shadowy hall with tremulous radiance—whirling darkness grew about the empty throne atop the tier of stone steps.

Was it the hell-spawned guardian returning to this plane?

Or was it—his master?

X

The Living Statues

Like a churning cloud of dust motes in a skirl of wind, particles of darkness seethed about the crystal throne.

Gradually the whirling motes drew closer together, forming a dark pillar. Seven feet tall the blurred shadow-shape loomed, and the vapor grew slowly solid.

The tall lean figure of a man melted out of the dense blackness, wrapped from head to heel in a long black cloak whose collar lifted to peaks like horns beside his head.

"Gods of hell!" Ald Turmis swore—*"The sorcerer returns!"*

And it was so. Even as they watched, the gaunt form became solid flesh. Still garbed from throat to toe in the stiff black cloak, whose strange fabric glittered with tiny star-like points of light, the lean man stood. He seated himself in his Chair of Power and let long naked hands go out to clutch the arms of the chair. These arms ended with great knobs carved from the sparkling crystal whereof the throne chair was hewn, and each facet of these knobs bore inset a potent magic talisman. Enthroned in his high place, touching with his naked hands the sigils which commanded unseen sources of power, the wizard was enshrined, invulnerable—a Pole of Power—the connecting node between the Universe of Matter and the unseen half-world of tremendous forces which lay behind the structure of the cosmos.

Robed in power, beyond the reach of mortals, Athmar Phong gazed down at them calmly.

He was a veritable giant of a man. Had his towering height been less, he would have seemed a grossly fat man; as it was, his abnormal tallness made him less obese. But massive flesh lay on his giant bones. His weight must have been twice that of an ordinary man like Ald Turmis.

His face was a gross caricature of cold, cynical command. Hairless, he gazed down at them like some colossal buddha, his face a passionless mask of heavy flesh. Cold slitted eyes looked down at them with placid contempt. There was callous cruelty in the set of his thick lips, brutal virility in the arrogant curve of his nose, remorseless and superhuman intelligence in the huge bulging brows of his naked pate.

"Thieves in my house," he said calmly, "and clever ones at that. For, whether you know it or not, mortals, the guardian of my treasures was a demon of the Seventh Circle. I am amazed that mere men of brawn such as you had the cunning and the wit to destroy so mighty an entity of the Transmundane."

His voice was like his face: heavy, slow, soft and cold. The words glided from almost motionless lips.

"Whoever sent you here must have armed you with a potent Name of Power. Let me warn you, then, think not to employ such a Name against Athmar Phong. Enthroned, I sit at a nexus of the unseen forces, shielded from such powers as you might bear against me by currents of the Ineffable. The Name would rebound against yourself, leaving me unshaken. But let me see. . . ."

The heavy eyelids lifted, baring orbs of utter blackness. No whites were visible about those blazing pupils: nor did they look like the eyes of a fully human creature.

Thongor stiffened, his senses stirring with an eerie chill. The cold gaze of Athmar Phong thrust at him like needles of steel. His own gaze was locked and held in the grip of a superior will. He felt a weird sensation within his skull—as if cold tendrils of thought were prying through the secret places of his mind.

An instant only, and the tendrils were withdrawn.

Ominous satisfaction curved the lips of Athmar Phong in a slight, subtle smile.

"So it was my old friend Kaman Thuu sent you here, dog of a barbarian. I shall repay him trebly for this deed! Yonder youth also, as I recall, came thither at his urgings; him we took captive half a moon ago, and I thought him well secured in certain cellar chambers set aside for uninvited guests. I see the lad hath cunning enough to force an exit—or did you aid him with those great brawny arms, eh?"

Beside Thongor, Ald Turmis snarled an oath and his knuckles whitened on the hilt of his rapier. The Ptarthan wizard smiled cynically.

"I read your thoughts as well . . . rash, impetuous youth, 'tis best I immobilize the two of you before you cause hurt to yourselves—"

Before either Thongor or Ald Turmis could think or move

or speak, the wizard's hand tightened on one of the talismans set within the hand-grip of his throne.

A shaft of scintillating azure light speared from the crystal throne. The two young swordsmen stood bathed in the cold blue light, and the wizard smiled as Ald Turmis cried out sharply and Thongor growled an astonished oath.

"I—cannot—move!" the Thurdan said in an anguished voice.

His face gleamed wetly white, and as Thongor looked he saw an unnatural pallor sweep over the lean strong body of his comrade, who was naked but for a ragged clout.

"Numb . . . cold," Ald Turmis groaned. His voice sounded hoarse, as if the muscles of his throat were half paralyzed. The wizard chuckled above them, a gloating sound that roused a warning growl from Thongor's deep chest. He, too, felt a momentary chill pass over his body as he stood in the shaft of blue light. But then his fingers tightened over the cold ovoid of the Shield of Cathloda which he still clutched in his right hand, and the brief sensation of numbness vanished instantly.

The blue ray dimmed and died. The wizard withdrew his fingers from the circular sigil.

"The Immobilizing Ray," he said softly. "Your flesh will slowly grow harder and more dense until you twain will turn to stone. Lovely statues to adorn my hall . . . yet statues that live and think, for your souls will be held captive within your petrified flesh for all eternity. Fit punishment indeed, for the tools of that treacherous priestling, Kaman Thuu."

The giant wizard shifted in his throne. He stretched out one hand toward empty air.

"Poor mortals!" he said mockingly. "You searched my halls in vain, for that which you sought but could not find was here beside my Throne all this while, though shielded from the gaze of uninvited guests. Behold—the Mirror of Zaffar!"

One great naked hand whisked aside a blur of bright cloth from a silver pedestal. Atop the glistening stand an oval disc of thick black glass caught the dim radiance of dawn with sullen, shifting fires. Thongor stared.

The mirror had been covered with a strange cloth whose stiff bright fabric was oddly difficult to see. The eye would not quite focus on it: something about its blurred brilliance made sight slide off it. So the mirror had been beside the throne all the while!

Beside him, Ald Turmis moaned in anguish. The weird pallor was more visible now. An ashen whiteness . . . the surface of his bare body looked rough and dry, almost . . . like stone.

And Thongor grimly knew that if he did not act, and soon, the young swordsman of Thurdis who had befriended him in the pits below would turn to enduring stone—a living statue, imprisoning the tortured soul of Ald Turmis for all time to come!

XI

The Breaking of Spells

The slow, heavy voice of Athmar Phong was speaking again, like the dull tolling of a leaden bell under thick water. Waves of words beat against Thongor's ear.

"Behold, o fortunate mortals, that which few eyes have ever looked upon—the supreme magical treasure of all the ages! Zaffar the Great, the mighty Thaumaturge of Patanga, wrought this mirror, and seven generations of time—as mortal men measure—went into its making! Seven thousand potent spells of power are sealed into the substance of this black mirror. Zaffar fashioned it from perdurable adamant, the strongest substance known to sorcery. Now it is fragile as glass . . . and bound helpless and raging therein lieth forever imprisoned the very self and substance of Aqquoonkagua, one of the Nine Thousand Princes of the Infernal Pit! Aye, a mighty and eternal Prince of Hell, older than the very Universe of Stars itself—a fragment of Elder Chaos and Old Night—caught and held within the Magic Mirror of Zaffar the Great! *Behold*—"

The Black Mirror was about the size of the *cherm,* the small, lightweight buckler the Lemurian warriors wore strapped to their left forearms. It was black as the heart of darkness itself, a disc of shimmering crystal thick as the breadth of two fingers.

As Athmar Phong touched it with his naked hands, it stirred with strange life. Thongor felt the hackles rise upon the back of his neck. *Within the shimmering darkness a crimson shadow—moved!*

For a moment Thongor glimpsed a great triangular head—it shouldered into view, peering through the mirror as through a black window. He saw one great glaring eye—a pit of blazing hellfire—and a wide, fanged maw open, working, screaming with silent fury. Then the captive Prince of the Pit slunk back into the darkness of its shadowy home and was lost to view.

"Gorm!" the barbarian grunted, feeling sweat trickle down his sides and bedew his brow. Strange and terrible were the ways of wizards with their uncanny arts. The mighty crimson demon was somehow reduced to two dimensions only, to him the flat surface of the mirror was an entire world, wherefrom he could never break free unless released by an outside agency. The concept was nightmarish. For an instant he almost pitied the scarlet horror locked in the surface of the ebon glass for unguessable eons.

A groan of mute suffering from the young swordsman at his side awoke Thongor from these dark thoughts. Ald Turmis, too, was imprisoned—and his prison was his own living flesh, slowly, inch by inch, petrifying into solid stone. A doom more terrible even than that of the enslaved Demon Prince. . . .

It was time for Thongor to act.

He had not moved since the Ptarthan wizard had sent the strange azure beam sweeping over him and his companion.

Secure in his high place, throned in the midst of his magical forces at the nexus of two universes, Athmar Phong little dreamed that the young barbarian was not rendered helpless by the immobilizing ray. But now Thongor swung into action.

He reached out and laid his hand upon the shoulder of Ald Turmis—the hand that held the all-potent Shield of Cathloda. The flesh of his comrade was dry and cold to his touch; the skin felt strangely *granulated*. But the nullifying powers of the protective amulet were enormous. Strong enough to whelm the spell of the blue ray, aye, and far stronger, as would soon be seen!

Ald Turmis cried out as the amulet touched his hardening flesh. A tingle of weird force swept through his body like lightning. Through every cell and organ, every gland and muscle and tissue of his body it swept, and the spell of Athmar Phong ebbed and was canceled before it. The young swordsman, suddenly freed from the effects of the spell, staggered and fell to one knee, gasping with relief.

On the sparkling crystal throne, Athmar Phong froze with

utter astonishment. Thongor threw back his unshorn mane and roared with laughter.

"Now, wizard—if swords cannot battle against sorcery, we will see what happens when I pit magic against—magic!" he thundered.

And before the wizard could move or think, Thongor whipped back his mighty arm—and hurled the all-potent amulet straight at the Black Mirror of Zaffar!

It flew glittering through the dawn-lit air. Straight as an arrow to its mark it sped, and when it touched the invisible forces that wove a viewless shield about the wizard's Throne of Power, great spells were broken. Canceled energies flashed through the spectrum of visible light. A terrific flash of eye-searing radiance lit the hall like some supernal sun.

Tears pouring from his blinded eyes, Athmar Phong screamed terribly, high and shrill like an animal in pain. He lurched to his feet, pawing at his seared eyes.

Hurled with the strength of Thongor's mighty arm, the Shield of Cathloda flew through the flashing energy fields—and crashed full into the Black Mirror.

The mirror came apart in a dark flash of released forces—it shattered to grains of black dust!

For a single flashing instant, as age-old spells were broken, tremendous energy was released. A seething ball of black flames surged about the crystal throne. The silver pedestal, at the very node and nexus of the canceled binding forces, flashed with intolerable heat. It glowed crimson, then canary, then blinding white. It slumped, crumbling slowly, like the shaft of a wax candle suddenly thrust into the roaring heart of a furnace. Glowing rivulets of molten metal slithered sluggishly over the topmost tier of the dais like serpents of liquid flame.

One blazing rivulet crawled between the staggering legs of the blinded, howling wizard. His glistening black cloak went up in a puff of fire. Suddenly sheathed from throat to heel in a sheet of flame, the wizard screeched and fell writhing to the steps. He rolled down them and crashed against the stone pave of the hall, crushing out the flames beneath his heavy weight. Panting, his flesh blistered and blackened, he staggered to his knees, sobbing with agony and naked fury.

But neither Thongor nor Ald Turmis could spare a glance for the unthroned sorcerer. Their gaze was riveted with horrible fascination at that which stood above the dais.

For the Shield of Cathloda had severed the seven thousand

spells which had bound the Demon Prince within the depths
of the encanted glass.

Now Aqquoonkagua was free!

XII

Flames of Hell

Up out of the whirling cloud of black flame grew a titanic
shape of terror.

Crimson it was, and covered with crawling fire; bestial of
shape, hulking and monstrous. Great sloping shoulders like
some mighty ape's, from which long arms swung, arms that
ended in huge three-clawed paws, that also smoldered and
smoked as if molded out of red-hot iron.

Up and up it went until it loomed forty feet above the
stone pavement. Flames slithered across its shaggy skin: the
fiery red light that beat up from it was dazzling. The room
swirled with smoke. Blistering heat like the breath of an open
furnace went baking across the hall in waves. Soot blackened
the walls and hung thick in the air.

Roaring, raging, the crimson thing stood free after long
weary centuries.

It had no neck. A heavy-jawed, ape-like head swung between the burly shoulders. Huge eyes blazed with fires of
madness under beetling brows. The fanged maw gaped and
slavered.

One great paw closed into a fist and came smashing down
on the soot-blackened, overturned throne. It burst to fragments, and was ground to dust under the weight of the blow.
The other paw reached down for Athmar Phong.

Naked, the wizard's heavy body sprawled panting at the
foot of the dais. Blind and horribly burnt, the Ptarthan sorcerer somehow knew or guessed what was about to happen.
Like a fat slug writhing under the gardener's hoe, he squalled
and wriggled on the hot pave as the flaming hand came down
upon him. Waves of heat beat from the grasping paw, crisp-
ing flesh and withering cloth to ash. The demon's hand was
huge as the wizard's body, and the three mighty claws were
big as smoldering logs. The searing heat of the demon's flesh

smote him first, and he kicked and screamed. Then the hand
came down upon him and snatched him up.

Thongor had seen much of battle and death and suffering,
but never had he heard such a cry from mortal lips as that
which now went ringing through the hall: a hoarse,
screeching bellow of ultimate agony and unutterable
despair—the sort of cry that rips the lining of the human
throat.

The naked wizard flopped and wriggled on the flaming
palm of the demon's hand. Then the claw closed over him
slowly—tightened—and the screams were cut off. The sicken-
ing stench of broiling human flesh filled the great hall. Ald
Turmis gagged and spat; Thongor's own gorge rose.

Bearing the smoking corpse of Athmar Phong in one great
paw the roaring, raging demon burst up through the dome of
dawn-lit crystal and was gone—back to whatever ultracosmic
hell it was the blasphemous rituals of the thaumaturge, Zaffar, had conjured it from, ages ago.

The broken dome collapsed, strewing the soot-smeared
pave with wreckage. Mighty stone pillars, shoved askew by
the demon's skyward passage, toppled slowly, shaking the
wizard's house to its foundations. Black cracks zigzagged
through the fabric of the walls. The house was coming down
upon their heads.

Thongor grabbed Ald Turmis's shoulder, shouting through
the roar of wreckage. They ran across the buckling stone
flags for the secret panel which still stood open. Thongor
snatched up their cloaks and harnesses as they sprinted for
freedom.

The terrific heat of the demon's crimson body had flamed
the tapestries and hangings in the hall. Overturned benches
and fallen beams blazed like oil-soaked torches. The ruined
hall was transformed into a thundering inferno within instants.

The two warriors plunged into the black door and vanished. Down the secret passageways they went. Room after
room, as they passed, were bursting into flame. It was weird
to see solid marble burn, and metal, and crystal too. The fires
that blazed within the demon's body were the fires of some
ultracosmic inferno—hotter than any flames of man's
knowledge. The terrible hellfires burned through stone walls
and floors, consuming everything in their path.

And thus it was that doom came down upon the house of Athmar Phong and he was nevermore seen by the eyes of men.

XIII

A New Day Dawns

The morning breeze blew fresh and clean from the great Gulf of Patanga, and the tang of wet salt was upon it. They drew in deep lungfulls of cold fresh air with hearty zest after the stench of the burning house and the reeking slime of the subterranean passage.

It was good to be alive, and free, watching the sun come up over the shoulder of the world. All things looked pure and clean and new in the clear strong light, and the horrors of the night were over. Thongor drank deep of cold red wine and stretched out his weary legs with a grunt of satisfaction.

They had found the secret door in the pits, the door that led to the branching ways of the subterranean network of tunnels beneath the city, and for a time they had followed the yellow Yan Hu characters that marked the way back to the Temple of Seven Gods. But Thongor had not survived this long in the Land of Peril—as the *Scarlet Edda* named all these realms of the devil-haunted Southlands—without evolving a strong and canny sense of survival. Why return empty-handed to the scheming priest? He would pay nothing for a task undone—and Kaman Thuu would not be very happy to learn the Black Mirror was now destroyed for all time. Instead, the barbarian recalled what the priest had said about Shan Yom glyphs wherewith side tunnels were blazoned in scarlet pigment. Hence he and Ald Turmis had taken this route, and come out in an empty alleyway beside the seafront where tall ships rode at anchor, waiting on the morning tide.

The two youths were filthy, hungry and exhausted from the trials of the night. But it would have been unlike Thongor to have come forth empty-handed from the wizard's house; so he had lingered for a moment in one of the lower chambers to snatch up a gemmed ornament or two wherewith he and Ald Turmis had purchased themselves a hearty breakfast in the quay-side tavern called The Sailor's Haven.

Across the rooftops of the city a pillar of oily black smoke stood against the morning skies. Blue and scarlet flames flickered through it strangely. The house at Athmar Phong was burnt to ashes and all his terrible sorceries were dust, aye, and the loathsome mewling hybrids of his blasphemous experiments in life-making had gone to rest at last.

"Whither now?" Thongor asked his companion. Ald Turmis emptied the last drop of wine from their third bottle and sat back with a sigh of repletion.

"The gods know, friend," he said. "But one thing at least is certain: 'twould be unhealthy for the two of us to remain here in Zangabal for long. Kaman Thuu has long arms and many cunning fingers. And he will not like this night's black business, you may set a wager on that!"

"I know," Thongor said lazily. "I have a mind to see the gates of Zangabal close shut behind my back and to strike out for another city. What about this Thurdis, the Dragon City across the gulf, whereof you spoke earlier?"

"Well, why not?" said Ald Turmis. "Phal Thurid, Sark of Thurdis, arms himself for conquest and I have heard he enlists a host of warriors. Surely, there is a place there for your mighty broadsword and my rapier. Shall we try our fortunes in the ranks of the mercenaries? There is a merchant galley flies the Dragon of Thurdis at the ninth quay. They sail with the early morning tide for home, and if you have any gold left after purchasing this magnificent feast whereof I can eat not a single bite more, perchance we can buy passage thither to Thurdis. Shall we go together for a while, Thongor, and see what Fate has in store for us?"

Thongor stretched lazily, like a great cat. His black cloak was slung about his bare bronze shoulders, and a gold coin or two still nested in the pocket-pouch of his warrior's harness. He arched to shake the dust of Zangabal from his heels, and to feel the gulf-wind blow fresh and clean in his face, and to explore the winding ways of a new city for a time.

"Well, why not?" he growled, and thus it was decided.

And thus were the feet of Thongor set upon the path that would lead him in the fullness of time to a destiny stranger and more glorious than that of other men.

But that is another story. . . .

KEEPER OF THE EMERALD FLAME

I

The Sign of the Skull

The Daotar Dorgand Tul shifted gingerly in the hard saddle, scratched irritably at the bite of a stinging insect, and wished for the thousandth time that he had entered the priesthood rather than obeying his father's desire by purchasing a commission in the legions of Arzang Pome, the Lord of Shembis.

He was a fat, soft-faced little man, with quick, clever eyes, a petulant mouth and a waspish temper. For all his silver-gilded cuirass, jeweled honors and the martial-looking longsword that hung at one plump thigh, he seemed distinctly out of place at the head of a punitive company of warriors. And, indeed, with every league his troop penetrated into the dense jungles his dissatisfaction with the military life grew more profound.

The bad-tempered little Daotar was hot and weary, and his buttocks and thighs ached from long hours on kroter-back. He sat slouched in the saddle, dreaming of a soft couch, cooling breezes from the gulf, nubile slave girls at his beck and call and tall frosted goblets of spiced wine. He wondered if he would ever feel comfortable again.

For seven days and nights now he and his troop of warriors had plunged ever deeper into the jungles of southern Kovia, until by now he was heartily sick of the whole business. The massive crimson boles of soaring lotifer trees rose all about him; snaky vines dangling from low branches overhead caught the plumes of his helm; stinging gnats whirled in buzzing clouds about him as he guided his plodding kroter through thick bushes of tiralons, the strange green roses of ancient Lemuria. Behind him, half a hundred footsore warriors toiled along, their mail smeared with sap and black with

75

mud, and they longed for the comforts of civilization no less than he.

For the ten-thousandth time he cursed this Northlander savage and his gang of bandits, whose elusive track they followed. The bold young Valkarthan raider had been harrying the caravan routes for the past six months, and his depredations cut deeply into the revenues of Arzang Pome, who delighted more in the clink of fat gold coins than in the caresses of all his women and his perfumed boys. At length, stung beyond endurance by the daring of the bold young bandit chieftain, the Sark of Shembis had sent a troop of warriors on his trail . . . and it was the sad fate of Dorgand Tul to be the commander of that troop.

The day was wearing on apace. Ere long the gold disc of Aedir the Sun god would expire in crimson splendor on the western horizon and the thick jungle night would cloak all of Kovia in darkness. It was the night that Dorgand Tul feared most, for then the monstrous predators were aprowl—the slinking vandars, the great black lions of the Lemurian jungles, the savage Beastmen, and—most dread of all—the colossal jungle dragons whose enormous size and ferocity rendered them virtually unkillable.

Dorgand Tul shivered at the thought. The days were exhausting and muddy and vile with the steaming jungle reek—but the nights were made hideous by the coughing roar of hunting reptiles and the glare of hungry eyes through the blackness, mirroring the flicker of the watch-fires. Already he had lost two spearmen of his troop to the jungle brutes, and, were it nor for the fact that his own tent was set each night in the very center of the camp, the plump little Daotar would have trembled to the depths of his soul for his own precious hide.

Just then his kroter shied, almost toppling him from the saddle. He seized the saddle horn in one fat fist, straightening the plumed helm, which had slipped down over his eyes, with the other hand and snarling a blasphemous curse as he saw the cause of the disturbance.

The bushes ahead parted and the muddy, haggard figure of one of his advance scouts appeared, making a sketchy salute.

"Well, what is it, Yazlar? Don't tell me you have lost their trail again?" he demanded shrilly. The old scout shook his head.

"No, Daotar. It continues straight ahead. I estimate they are now only about four hours ahead of us."

"Well, what then?"

The scout turned, gesturing for Dorgand Tul to follow, and vanished in the underbrush. The fat little officer thumped the kroter's ribs with his booted heel and guided the weary beast through the bushes, whimpering a curse as thorn-edged leaves stung his hand. The kroter shouldered through the glossy-leaved bushes, and Dorgand Tul found himself in a little clearing.

The glade was small, hedged about with densely packed trees. Reining the beast to a standstill, the officer glanced about, and then his eyes caught an ominous and grisly emblem and he froze, while a small thrill of apprehension ran over him.

A tall pole of gaunt black wood thrust up from the muddy earth at the edge of the clearing. Atop the pole was affixed a grinning naked human skull.

A cryptic hieroglyph was etched in crimson paint on the brow of the death's-head. The eyes of Dorgand Tul were caught and held by that coiling crimson symbol.

"The sign of Omn," whispered the old scout.

The fat little Daotar paled, swallowed, but could not tear his eyes from the blot of bloody color blazoned on the grinning skull. It held his gaze with a horrid fascination, like the cold enigma in the eyes of a snake.

"Did the bandits . . . pass it?" he asked at last, in a weak voice.

The old scout nodded, his lank gray locks swinging. "They did," he said somberly.

A flame of malignant delight blazed up in the eyes of Dorgand Tul. New energy surged within his weary, flaccid form. He snatched up the reins and wheeled the kroter about and plunged through the bushes by which he had entered the clearing.

The first bedraggled warriors of his troop were just catching up to him as he retraced his path. A scarred, hard-faced sergeant came forward to receive orders at the Daotar's impatient gesture.

"Turn the men about, my man. We shall camp for the night in that large clearing we passed through an hour or so ago. And then back to the city!" the Daotar crowed delightedly.

Then, at the look of blank incomprehension in the sergeant's eyes, he laughed with vicious humor.

"The barbarian in his flight has led his bandits past the

Sign of the Skull . . . and ere night falls across the world, he will be in the power of Shan Chan Thuu!" he smirked. The sergeant's eyes widened in black horrified amazement.

His lips parted and he whispered to himself a dread phrase at which his men shuddered . . . and which even cooled the malignant joy in the heart of Dorgand Tul, and made the fat officer fumble at his throat, where a protective amulet of blue paste dangled on a silver chain.

"The Keeper of the Emerald Flame! . . ."

". . . Only the Nineteen Gods can save Thongor of Valkarth now," the grizzled scout said under his breath.

II

Something in the Dark

Thongor of Valkarth was baffled.

He crouched in the crotch of a great tree, his keen gaze studying the jungle behind his track, and deep in his heart he felt a nameless qualm . . . a distinct yet shadowy unease.

Something was wrong . . . yet he knew not what!

Lithely he swung down from his perch, dropped to a lower branch and clambered down a dangling vine, to drop lightly to the thick grasses of the clearing as might a jungle cat.

His warriors, who had been resting while he sought the upper levels, rose now to their feet, turning questioning eyes upon their young chieftain as he appeared.

For a moment he stood silent, brows knotted in puzzlement. As the men of his band watched him, waiting for his words, there was not one man among them who did not gaze at him with admiration.

He was superb, the half-naked young barbarian, his bronze body threwed like some savage god. Black and heavy as a vandar's mane, his unshorn hair fell across his broad naked shoulders, framing a stern, impassive face, strong-jawed and manly for all his youth.

Beneath scowling black brows, his strange gold eyes blazed with sullen, wrathful, lion-like fires. Few men could meet the gaze of those somber, burning eyes, for behind them smoldered the fighting fury of a barbarian, whose savage heart had never learned the cooler temper of civilized men.

His powerful torso was clad in the plain black leather of a Lemurian warrior. A great cloak was flung back over his shoulders and a massive girdle bound his taut, rock-hard midsection. The leather strap of a baldric was slung across his chest from shoulder to hip, and therefore hung scabbarded a mighty Valkarthan broadsword. A crimson loincloth and black leather boots completed his war-harness.

"What is it, Thongor?" one of his lieutenants demanded, as the long silence of their young leader began to puzzle the men.

The barbarian shook his head.

"Strange, Chelim! The Shembian troops are—*going back!*"

Chelim, a tall, massive Zangabali with shaven pate and gold hoops in his ears, scratched his heavy, stubbled jaw thoughtfully.

"Maybe it's a trick?" he suggested. "Maybe they split up, one group returning, the other sneaking around, hoping to catch us off guard, once we were convinced they were all turning back."

Thongor grunted. "Not a chance. I counted heads as they went through that big clearing near the lightning-blasted tree. Every man-jack of the troop is bound in full retreat."

A scrawny, rat-like little man with one eye sniggered.

"Chief? Maybe seven days o' jungle muck and vandars in th' night convinced 'em this be no place for Arzang Pome's warriors, eh? A lot o' craven-hearted dogs, those Shembians, anyway?"

Thongor grinned. "Well, maybe you're right, Fulvio. At any rate, we'll take no chances on being surprised. We'll push on—even past nightfall—until we find a place that can be stoutly defended. On your feet, men. Mount up, and let's get out of here."

Night fell, shadow-winged, across the edges of the world. Stars glittered like jewels in the dark sky, and soon the great golden moon of elder Lemuria emerged from her palace of clouds to bathe the black jungles of Kovia in her silken, shimmering light.

Thongor and his bandits made camp in the hills, where sheer walls of rugged stone enclosed their position on three sides. The hill slopes were covered with loose fragmented shale. Thongor believed that it would be impossible for any force to creep up on their position without dislodging under-

foot a rattling miniature avalanche of broken rock, whose
noise would give warning of the advance of the foe.

They watered their kroters in the small stream that trickled
by the foot of the hills, built a fire to keep the beasts away
and made a rude supper, gnawing on cold joints of meat and
dry cheese, washed down with thin sour ale in waxed skin
bags.

Then, setting his sentries, Thongor curled up on a bed of
dry leaves under the shelter of an overhang of rock, wrapped
his great cloak around him against the night chills, set
Sarkozan, his great Northlander broadsword, near to his hand
and fell asleep almost instantly. Even his giant frame was
weary from the long trek through the jungles, and from boyhood he had learned the knack of falling asleep at will. His
boyhood, spent on the wintry plains of the wild north beyond
the Mountains of Mommur, had taught him the survival skills
known only to a barbaric people such as his own Black Hawk
tribe. To survive in a rugged, frozen land, where the forces of
hostile nature are leagued with savage enemies and monstrous
predators against human life, one learns early—or one does
not live long. Thongor learned—and lived.

It was now four years since all of his tribe had fallen in
battle against an enemy tribe. He alone had survived that
day-long holocaust of blood and iron—a boy of fifteen, alone
and friendless in a harsh world of savagery and death; strong,
brave, trained virtually from the cradle in the use of
weapons, but still—only a boy of fifteen.

Down across the wintry steppes had he come, and across
the rugged Mountains of Mommur. He was a hardy, bronzed
youth of seventeen when he reached at last the lush jungle
lands and splendid, glittering cities of the Dakshina, as the
Southlands of Lemuria were known. And for the two years
since that time, he had eked out a precarious living as thief
and wandering adventurer, and now, most recently, as a bandit chieftain in the wilderness of Chush and Kovia. He had
joined the caravan raiders eight months ago, and fought his
way up the ranks to the leadership of the band, slaying the
former chief, Red Jorn, in a bare-handed battle to the death.

Some might think it odd that a youth of nineteen, scarce
more than a boy, should lead a band of experienced warriors,
most of whom were half again, or twice, his age. Odd, perhaps, but not illogical. For Thongor, from the first hour he
had entered the ranks of Jorn's Raiders, had proved himself
bold, fearless and indomitable. As for his men, seasoned

veterans all, their very lives depended on the quality of the leadership of the band, and if the young barbarian, not yet twenty, could prove his superior gifts, they were willing to swallow the fact that he was younger than the least of them.

The secret of his swift domination of the bandit company may be summed up in a single phrase: at nineteen, Thongor had faced more perils, fought more foes, seen more of death, war and adventure, than any man of them.

It was his savage intuitions that roused him now—

The scrape of leather sandals on rough stone! The click and rattle of a dislodged pebble!

The boy snapped in an instant to full, tingling alertness. Yet, in the transition from sleep to wakefulness, not a muscle moved in all his mighty frame. To the eye of any watcher, he was still slumbering in heavy sleep.

Again, the faint sound. And now his keen senses told him it came from directly above his rude couch. Someone was descending the face of the steep hill. *Someone was crouched just above the rock under which he lay.*

He rose lithely to his feet, drawing a long dagger from his girdle. The broadsword he let lay—it would make too much sound to draw the blade, and he would need his hands free.

As silent as a jungle cat, the barbarian padded to the brink of the overhanging ledge.

Emerging from under the low rock, Thongor rose slowly to his full height, flattening himself against the side of the wall of stone.

Dimly, in the moon-silvered gloom, he could make out a crouching figure, black against the sky. It seemed to be surveying the bandit camp. One hand clutched a long spear, and it was the heft of this spear that had dislodged the pebble.

Like a striking snake, Thongor seized the unknown watcher. . . .

III

Jungle Girl

He dragged the fiercely struggling figure down to the ground and sought to pinion its lithe arms. But it was as if he had seized a spitting, wriggling armful of clawed fury. It writhed and snarled in his grip like a maddened wildcat. Sharp nails drew lines of scarlet across his bronze hide and drew stinging furrows in chest, cheek and shoulder.

Suddenly Thongor gasped with astonishment, released his captive, and sprang back. For in their struggle, his arms had gone around the chest of his opponent from behind, and his hands had touched—not the flat, muscular hide of a male warrior—but the warm, pointed breasts of a young girl!

Illana the Moon Lady had receded behind a cloud moments before; now she displayed the glory of her unveiled visage, and by the sudden wash of silver light Thongor could clearly see his foe.

It was a half-naked young girl, of his own age or a year or two younger, who crouched, stone-bladed dagger clenched in one small capable fist, challenging him to continue the combat.

Her slender body was bare save for a strip of fur worn low about her hips, and twisted about her slim loins. This and leather sandals and a bauble worn about her throat on a thong constituted her only garments.

Very lovely was she in the silver moonlight, her hair long, black, a shining cascade that poured over sleek shoulders and down her slender back to the firm rondure of her little rear. Her legs were long, adolescent, graceful. Her breasts were shallow but firmly rounded, warm, pointed. They rose and fell as she panted, and their surging rhythm drove his hot young blood to interesting speculations.

"Come, girl," he growled. "Forgive my rough handling—I knew not what you were in the darkness. Come, let us be friends—I make no war on women!"

She crouched, wordless, moonsilver glinting on the flinty blade in her fist.

He straightened, laughed and tossed away his dagger, showing her his empty hands. She straighted reluctantly, fingering her stone knife, and finally thrust it into a phondle-skin sheath tied by thongs to her loincloth.

When she smiled, the pale round oval of her face, framed by shining black hair, was inexpressibly lovely. He felt a small pulse thud hotly at the base of his throat as he watched her bare body move in the moonlight.

"I am Thongor of Valkarth, the chieftain of this band," he growled. "And I thought you were the vanguard of a troop of Shembian soldiers!"

She voiced a husky laugh. "I am Zoroma of the Pjanthan,"

she said, "and I feared you were a troop of," her voice dropped, "—*ghosts!*"

He gave a grunt of laughter. "We are flesh and blood. But, tell me, girl, what are the Pjanthan? Never have I heard of them till now."

"Jungle hunters," she answered. "There are many tribes like ours in Kovia—how can you not know this?"

He rubbed his jaw ruefully.

"Frankly, I know nothing of Kovia, save for the jungles around Shembis the Dolphin City. We are bandits who raid the Shembian caravans, but now we have been chased deep into this jungle country, unknown to us, by the Sark's soldiers. I fear we raided one caravan too many!"

"It is as I thought," she said enigmatically. "You are strangers. Few dare come into these regions of the jungle— even the legions of Shembis never enter here."

Thongor wondered why—wondered if the answer to that question might not also explain the curious retreat of the warriors of Dorgand Tul—but before he could ask, his sentinels, attracted by the sounds of their struggle, and the conversation, came over to where he and the girl stood, to see if everything was well with their chieftain. And by the time he had reassured them and, learning that the girl, Zoroma, hungered, saw to it that the remnants of their meal were put at her disposal, the girl's curious remark had slipped his mind for the moment.

She slept the remainder of the night in his bed of leaves, under his cloak, while he stood guard to make certain that none of his men, who had not seen a woman in weeks, did not abuse the hospitality he had offered her.

Many times her eyes stole to his stalwart figure as it stood before the overhanging rock, black and silvered bronze in the moonlight. But, at length, she fell into a fitful slumber, from which she did not awaken until dawn.

They broke their fast on cold water from the stream and the small scraps of meat and cheese that remained uneaten. Then they pressed forward. Thongor was still uncertain as to whether the pursuing troops had retreated completely or were circling around, so he moved his men out early with all possible speed.

Zoroma rode his kroter and he walked alongside the beast. The trail through the hills was rough and rocky, but they made better speed over clear, dry ground than they had the previous days, hacking a path through dense jungles and the muck of rotting leaves.

The sun burned high above like molten gold in a cauldron of searing brass. They were hot and dusty, but he urged them on, with brief and infrequent rest stops.

"Do your people, the Pjanthan, dwell nearby?" he asked her.

"No. Many leagues to the west."

"How is it, then, that you are roaming these hills alone, so far from your tribe?" he asked.

"I am searching for a youth who is . . . lost," she said.

"A brother?"

She shook her head. "My lover. Him who . . . was to have been my mate." There was a note of somber sorrow that haunted her low, hesitant voice.

"And your people would not assist in your search? They would permit a mere lass to stray so far, in so hostile a land, all by herself?" He grunted and spat. "Mine are a savage people, too, and no soft-gutted city-dwellers. But rather than permit a maiden to venture alone into peril we would sacrifice half the fighting strength of the clan!"

She moistened her lips hesitantly.

"They . . . they fear to penetrate the borders of this region," she said in low tones. And she explained that it was under a bad omen; she used a term which we would translate as—*taboo*.

He said nothing. His people, too, knew the terrors of the darkness and the curse of all omens. The Black Hawk people of Valkarth were not immune to the strength of the taboo . . . but never would the stalwart heroes of the North have permitted shadowy terrors to come between them and the protection of their womenfolk. Privately, he decided that these Pjanthan were either weaklings, or fools—or both!

But he did not want to offend her.

Frequently that morning as he strode along beside her kroter his lambent gaze strayed to her bare brown thighs, rounded calfs and slender, tapering ankles . . . to the proud lift of her naked young breasts, her sleek flat abdomen, the rondure of her little rump. And, whenever she thought he was not looking, the girl's huge dark eyes took in the swelling arch of the boy's deep chest, his flat belly, his long, powerful arms.

It was nearly noon when they came upon the white grinning skull mounted on a black pole, set up like a silent warning directly in their path.

IV

The Shadow of Shan Chan Thuu

Zoroma shrieked as the naked white skull loomed up in their path. The kroter shied nervously and Thongor growled an oath and sprang to catch the bridle before the beast could panic into flight.

The girl sat shuddering, her terrified eyes fixed on the grisly emblem of warning that stood grinning at them from atop the black pole.

Thongor examined it narrowly.

"We passed such a thing in a jungle clearing yestereve," he said. "I thought it a warning sign reared by the Beastmen, but the hairy folk of the jungles would not be here in these harsh hills. Do you know what this thing means, girl?"

"It bears the Sign of Omm," she said weakly. "The emblem of Shan Chan Thuu?"

"And what might Omm and Shan Chan Thuu be?" he growled.

Her face pale, her dary eyes haunted by fear, she shuddered, for all the baking heat of the dusty hills. It was as if a clammy, crawling wind blew against her naked spine.

"Have you never heard of Omm?" she asked faintly. "Indeed, you are strangers to the jungles of Kovia. . . ."

"I told you our accustomed territory lay to the north, in the wilderness of Chush," he said impatiently. "Come—out with it, girl!"

"Omm is a legend in this land . . . an age-old city that dates back to the dark days of Time's Dawn . . . when the Children of Nemedis first came into this realm out of the Ultimate East, to lay the foundations of the Nine Cities!"

Her voice fell to a whisper, and there was something in her tones, a crawling note of cold menace and elder evil, that lifted his nape hairs and roughed the skin of his forearms with the thrill of premonition.

"No man knows where the Lost City of Omm lifts its eon-crumbled towers, but legend whispers that it is the cradle of an evil deviltry . . . a lore of science-magic foul with the slime of chaos, and black with the horror of man's cruelty," she whispered. "Such is the unholy legend of Omm . . ."

"And what of Shan Chan Thuu?" he pressed. "Is it some black god of the Pit?"

She shuddered. "Perhaps that is what he is, after all . . . but he was mortal once, an ancient devil-wizard out of Omm who came into this land and raised his black citadel among these very hills, wherein to pursue unmolested by his sorcerous brethren his strange worship and his stranger arts! That was two hundred years ago, men say. . . ."

"And he lives yet?" Thongor demanded, incredulously.

The girl shrugged slim, bare shoulders, tawny, pink-tipped breasts lifting. They say he prolonged his life beyond the normal limitations of mortal flesh . . . that he bartered his soul to chaos for some vast magical price—"

"—The Emerald Flame!" a voice gasped behind them.

Thongor turned to see that his lieutenant, Chelim, had heard the girl's fable.

"Have you never heard of it, lad?" Chelim grunted, his shaven pate gleaming with perspiration, his powerfully muscled arms gray with rock dust. "A fabulous jeweled treasure—I've heard the same tale as the wench relates—the old Omnian sold his immortal part to possess it! They say 'tis a wealth of gems of a kind unknown to men—the ransom of a dozen emperors! And the old wizard long since dead!"

A speculative gleam shone in the fierce eyes of the young barbarian.

"Gems, eh? And this death's head means we are approaching his fortress, or whatever it is? It is supposed to warn men away from his treasure house?"

The girl nodded. Thongor and the burly Chelim exchanged glances.

"What do you think, Chelim?" the youth growled. "Will the men let old fables fright them from a treasure like this?"

White teeth flashed in the bald giant's tanned face.

"Not Jorn's Raiders, lad! They'd dare the horrors of the Pit itself for a handful of gold!"

The girl watched them but said nothing.

"Where is this place?" Thongor asked. She pointed.

"Directly in our path, but—"

He waited. "But—what?"

She bit her lip. "Nothing . . . ."

After a brief consultation with his warriors, Thongor led

the march forward. Some of the men had demurred: that scrawny little thief, Fulvio, whined that it was not wise to disturb the bones of dead wizards, for life clings long about the dust of those sorcerers who have sworn the awful Vow to Chaos. But Thongor laughed and mocked their fears.

"I have faced and fought gods, ghosts and devils—men, magicians and monsters, ere now," he grunted. "And never yet have I found a thing that cannot be killed!"

And so the bandits rode on, ignoring the grisly warning that grinned down at them from the black stake, the ominous crimson symbol coiled between its bony brows.

And Zoroma rode with them. But now she was silent, and her face was tense and haunted.

For all the hot noonlight, it seemed to her that they rode through gathering shades of darkness . . . as if a dread shadow lay over all this dead, dry land.

The shadow of Shan Chan Thuu!

V

Black Citadel

As the long shadows of late afternoon stretched across the rocky hills of Kovia, they came within sight of the ruined tower.

It had been built atop a round knoll and it thrust high up above the surrounding barrens.

Gaunt and stark and ominous was that dead citadel, the only sign of man in all this waste.

Thongor studied it with narrowed eyes, thoughtfully. It was odd, he thought, that the transition from lush, steaming jungles to this harsh and barren land should be so abrupt. One moment they were cutting a path through sweltering underbrush—the next their bootheels crunched in dry soil where not a single blade of grass grew. He had not even glimpsed a mold or lichen, such as one might find underneath boulders or on the shadowed base of rocky cliffs, even in the most desertlike of wildernesses.

It was more than odd—it was uncanny!

It was as if that black citadel that thrust its broken walls up into the dim gloaming were the center of some cosmic contagion that had cast its evil blight over all this land about, draining the life and the vigor from every living thing.

Not one single sign of life had they seen since leaving camp the night before. Not so much as a crawling scorpion, a carrier hawk or a venomous serpent.

All of this land was a land of death. . . .

From this distance, the citadel was a black, featureless mass—a clotted cluster of shadows, of which no details could be discerned. But it was evident that the structure was of far greater antiquity than the legends hinted, for the extent of decay was extraordinary: Thongor could see fallen columns, shattered architraves and entire sections of wall that had collapsed into moldering ruin. Surely, the passage of a mere century or two could not account for so extensive a degree of ruin. It would take millennia—perhaps even eons—for a stone structure to crumble like this, particularly in a desert wilderness, whose aridity should preserve worked stone, not hasten its decay!

The rocky eminence whereupon the black citadel stood was in the exact center of a vast bowl-like depression, a disc-shaped valley, like some enormous crater. The floor of this crater was a stretch of desiccated sand—dead as the surface of the moon.

They rode across the breadth of this huge depression, the hooves of their kroters crunching and squeaking in the crystalline sand. Thongor stooped and picked up a handful of the strange stuff. It was not sand at all, but rock—stone that had been subjected to some weird force that had sapped the hardness of the mineral until at length it crumbled into this coarse substance.

Under the pressure of his fingers, the sand crystals crushed to fine powder, like dry wood ash.

What uncanny force had leached the solid strength from living stone?

They rode on.

As they drew nearer, it became easier to make out the details of the structure. And they became aware of its true size—distance, a trick of perspective, or perhaps the absence of any nearby object large enough to measure it against, had somehow concealed the truth of its proportions.

It was the largest stone edifice Thongor or his warriors had ever seen. It may well have been the most enormous man-made structure on Earth at that time. Indeed, it would have dwarfed even the pyramids of Egypt, or the mighty Sphinx herself, had those relics of ancient Atlantis been built in the age of Thongor, the dim Pleistocene.

The colossal stone wreck was one of incredibly detailed and curiously unfamiliar architecture. The eye became lost in a maze of balconies, towers, colonnades and buttresses. The mind was baffled and confused among the mad profusion of wall and arch and wing and extension. It was not so much one building as a cluster of buildings, all built together in a rising man-made mountain of stonework. The nature—the origin—the uses—of the citadel were impossible to make out.

It was like nothing else on Earth.

The extent of the decay was incredible.

The outer walls, which were as much as twenty paces thick, and built of solid stone, had crumbled and lay fallen, scattering the slopes of the high place with enormous cubes of broken stone, each weighing several tons. Minarets were toppled and square turrets leaned crazily or strew the earth with rubble. The whole outer surface of the enigmatic ruin was worn and pitted, as if bathed for countless centuries in the glare of some intolerable radiation. From the rough, porous condition of the outer walls, Thongor got the feeling that solid *inches* of stone had melted into powder, sifting down from the face of the structure.

As they approached nearer, they became aware of yet a further element of mystery.

They felt an uncanny sensation of being close to some enormous and living—*thing*.

It was hard to say precisely what there was about the shadowy citadel that gave them the feeling that it was, somehow, alive.

Like a titanic idol, hewn from a solid mountain of dead black stone, carved by the denizens of some unthinkably remote eon, it squatted, brooding, amid all that dreary waste of death and desolation.

There exuded from the dark structure an aura of cold menace.

The black openings of windows gaped like the eye-sockets of a skull. The cold wind of fear blew from the towering colossus, like a chill and fetid breath from the mouth of the Pit itself.

The men muttered among themselves, signing their breasts with the names of half a hundred gods and totems and protective spirits. Thongor alone remained impassive. He had looked death and horror in the face ere now—and he had laughed!

When all the west was a welter of crimson vapor whereon Aedir the Sun lord lay expiring in scarlet and gold, they reached the summit, and colossal portals loomed before them like the yawning jaws of a dead behemoth.

Within they found a vast, echoing hall whose roof, supported by stone columns like marble sequoia, was lost in clotted shadow far above. Galleries and antechambers in incredible number branched away from this central hall. All was a murmuring emptiness of dim shadows and whispering echoes.

For a very long time, it was evident, the hall had lain untenanted.

Moldering rubbish littered the stone pave of this gloom-drenched hall wherein one hundred men could have marched abreast without brushing the walls to either side. Thongor poked among the rubbish of dry leaves, rotten bits of cloth and nameless scraps of ancient leather—and the toe of his boot dislodged a human skull!

Zoroma stifled a cry.

He knew she was thinking of her lover. But this could not be he. The bone of the skull was brown and scabrous with antiquity.

Thongor dispatched some of his troop to explore the nearer galleries, while assigning to a limping rogue named Randar the task of stabling the kroters in an antechamber close by the front gate. Then, while a few men under the command of a grizzled old swordsman from Thurdis marched off to take a look at the far end of the colossal hall, he drew his lieutenant, Chelim, to one side.

Zoroma stood, staring blankly about her with wide, apprehensive eyes, absently fingering a protective amulet of white crystal that hung between her breasts. She did not notice as they stepped apart for a consultation.

"Well, what do you think?" Thonger inquired.

Chelim rubbed his nose, which had been broken once or twice and clumsily reset, and sniffed.

"I don't like it, lad," he muttered. "I get the feeling this place is somehow *alive*—watching me—waiting for me to take a false step, before it pounces; or does something even worse."

Thongor grunted: he had the same feeling, and he liked it little. "This can't be the citadel of Shan Chan Thuu," he grunted. "Not if the old Omnian sorcerer only lived two hundred years ago! This place had been abandoned for thousands of years—and its true age must be measured in millions of years. Look at that area of wall: the facing stones have decayed away, littering the floor with dust. Why, it would take ages to do that."

"Aye, lad—and those columns, see how they're cracked and split and pitted? I've seen the sides of *mountains* that looked younger . . . well, the old legend must be wrong; the sorcerer must have found this place as it is, and made it his dwelling, rather than building it himself."

"I think you're right," the youth grunted. "No one man—wizard or no—could build anything this big. It is a task that would require a nation." He paused, fingering the hilt of his sword. Then—

"I have heard that in the ages before the Father of the Gods created the first of men this world was ruled by wily and malignant creatures known as the Dragon Kings of Hyperborea . . . and that they entered into the land of Lemuria when all their land was lost beneath the eternal snows of the boreal pole."

"Yes, I've heard the same tale. . . . You think this is some ungodly palace or temple or shrine left over from the fall of the Hyperboreans?"

Thongor nodded. "I do. For I have seen many of the kingdoms of man, and looked upon his cities, yet never till this hour have I seen this fashion of building . . . not in my homeland, or among the shadowy foothills of Mommur, or in Kathool or Thurdis or Zangabal, or even old Tarakus, the Pirate City or any of the cities of the Dakshina. This is, must be, a survival of some forgotten age before the coming of man."

Chelim's face was stolid. "Gorm alone knows what pre-human deviltry these ancient walls have looked upon . . . or what shadowy forces may linger within, waiting for the chance to spring to life again . . ."

Thongor uttered a rude expletive.

"Keep this in mind, friend. I've seen much that the world affords in the way of dangers—ghosts and monsters and dark gods—but never have I encountered anything that could do me physical harm and which could not itself be destroyed!"

Chelim grinned. "Aye, there is that! Sharp steel is a mighty remedy against things in the night. . . ."

The leader of the men Thongor had dispatched to explore

the farthest reaches of the hall came up to them then, and they held no further converse.

"Well, Thad Novis, what's it like at the other end?" Thongor asked.

The grizzled old Thurdan paused to catch his breath from the long hike. "Just more of the same, Thongor: galleries leading off in every direction, chambers opening into halls and corridors—this temple, or whatever it may be, is like a city, a whole city under one roof!"

They ate what few scraps were left, finished the ale, and bedded down for the night in the echoing vastness of the central hall, save for those whom Thongor designated as sentries of the first watch.

That night the first of them died.

VI

The Thing That Walks in the Night

Deafening, filled with unendurable agony and horror, the scream rang out through the gloomy castle!

Wakened suddenly from fitful, uneasy slumbers, the bandits sprang up, cursing, snatching up their weapons, staring about for the enemy that had struck suddenly and without warning—but there was nothing to be seen.

Thongor, who had taken a small antechamber off the central hall for his bedchamber, appeared naked in the doorway, Sarkozan, his broadsword, glittering in his hand.

Sentries peered about with wide eyes and white faces, but nothing untoward was to be seen. Yet *something* had happened—they could not all have dreamed that horrible shriek!

At Thongor's command, a head count was taken, and one man was found to be missing. It was a fat, red-faced rogue called Kovor. He had bedded down with the main body of the men, who lay in a ragged circle around the huge bonfire they had built against the night chills. Now his pallet was empty.

One of the bandits suggested Kovor might have stepped outside to answer a call of nature. Thongor dispatched searchers to investigate, but they found nothing.

Urging the sentries to be wary, Thongor bade his men return to their interrupted slumbers, and withdrew into his little room again. But hardly a single warrior of the band so much as closed his eyes through all the rest of that fear-haunted night.

At dawn, the men refreshed themselves with water from the small quantity they had dipped out of the running stream the night before, when they had camped in the hills. Then the young barbarian organized them into search parties and carefully directed the exploration of the central portion of the monstrous edifice.

Lest anyone become lost in the maze of suites and corridors and chambers, he commanded them to scratch the symbol of an arrow on the sill of every portal through which they passed, pointing back the way they had come, so that in any eventuality they should all be able to find their way back to the central hall. They trooped out, under search leaders designated by Chelim.

They found what was left of fat Kovor an hour later. A runner was sent back to fetch Thongor and the girl.

"We could *smell* it before there was anything to see," panted the wild-eyed bandit as he guided the chieftain through the maze of dusty chambers. "Then we found—*this!*"

Zoroma moaned, covered her eyes and turned away.

Even Thongor, toughened as he was, felt his belly writhe and heart sicken within him as he peered beyond the portals of the room of horror.

It was a huge, square room, unadorned, its floor one solid piece of unbroken stone. The only element of decoration was a square design cut in the exact center of the floor.

Floor, walls and ceiling were besplattered with gouts of blood and gobbets of raw flesh. The stone chamber stank like a slaughterhouse.

Kovor had, literally, been torn apart. No fragment could be found that was any larger than a man's thumbnail. His sword, dented and broken, lay in one corner. His reeking gore flecked and dribbled the interior of the hollow stone cube like a ghastly scarlet dew.

Chelim, who had also been summoned, came up and stood at Thongor's shoulder, a grim, sickly look on his ugly face.

"What kind of thing could have done anything like . . . this?" he muttered. "There isn't even enough of him left to bury and say a couple of words over . . ."

"Fat, puffing, complaining old Kovor . . ." Thongor said slowly.

There was not much else that a man could say.

All that day they searched the endless rooms of the vast citadel, but nowhere did they find any sign of recent habitation.

If the ancient Omnian sorcerer had, in truth, made this unearthly castle his habitation, they had yet to come upon the place wherein he had dwelt.

There would be books, bits of furniture, athanors and crucibles and aludels and the other apparatus of the magical sciences.

That night, ferociously hungry, they again settled down to sleep, but terror haunted the dreams of every man, and they started awake at the slightest sound.

Toward morning, the second man died.

Thongor staggered to his feet, kicking aside his cloak, cursing vilely, knuckling the sleep from his bleared eyes, grabbing up his naked broadsword. From her pallet across the chamber. Zoroma stared, white-faced.

"Not—another one," she whimpered.

But it was so. The echoes of the mad scream still sounded through the vastness of the gloomy structure.

The second victim was discovered to be one Orovar, a stolid, close-mouthed Pelormian who had few friends among Thongor's troop.

They did not find his bloody remnants, although they searched all the next day. But he was missing, that was certain.

Thongor questioned his sentries closely. He had put the fear of death into them the evening before, threatening to disembowel any man who slept on sentry duty. But he knew the men were so frightened they would not have dared to fall asleep, not if they had gone a week without rest. Only one of the sentries had heard or seen anything in the least suspicious. None of them had noticed Orovar creep stealthily from his pallet, but one hesitantly said he thought he had seen something—something tall and black and thin—walking silently in the night. He had thought it was a trick of the eyes, of his overstrained nerves, or just a curious shadow cast by the flickering of the flames. But now he was no longer so certain. . . .

Something that walked in the night.

Something tall and black and thin.

Something that—*killed*.

That next morning, Chelim drew Thongor aside, leaving the old Thurdan veteran, Thad Novis, to organize the search parties.

"What do you say, lad—shall we leave this place before it takes us one by one?" he asked.

Thongor's strange gold eyes were inscrutable.

"Is that what you advise, Chelim?"

The huge Zangabali shrugged, the golden hoops in his ears glinting in the morning light.

"You are the chieftain," he grunted. "But we have no food or water left, and are not likely to find any in this accursed ruin. And the men are very frightened by now, and are beginning to whisper among themselves. All the jeweled treasure in the world will not tempt them to stay much longer in this devil-haunted mausoleum. Thus far you have held them here because they admire and trust you; but before too much longer their fears will get the better of them and they will begin slipping away, by ones and twos, into the hills."

Thongor folded his arms upon his chest, and bent his head, brooding on the stone pave. At length he lifted his black mane and looked at Chelim.

"You can leave, if you like. But if I go from this place now, without finding the solution to this mystery, it will haunt me for all the rest of my days," he said.

VII

Zoroma Vanishes

Thongor came awake suddenly. He could not tell precisely what had awakened him, but something was wrong. Those ultra-keen senses of the barbarian, which are dulled and vestigial in softer, city-bred men, triggered him to alertness. He lay motionless, pulses drumming, searching the gloom with keen eyes and listening ears.

He had found it difficult enough to get to sleep, his belly growling with hunger and thirst raging in his throat like a small red demon, but eventually he had drifted off into a fitful, uneasy slumber. Now some faint signal, some vague premonition of danger, drove sleep from him.

Lifting himself on one elbow, he searched the darkness of the far corner of the room where Zoroma slept.

He had not touched her, although he wanted to, and although he sensed her own response to his manhood. Not since he had learned she mourned her lost lover. Although a barbarian, the boy was not without a certain rude chivalry in such matters. But he could not trust the more ruffianly of his bandits to leave her unmolested—hence he had offered her the protection of his presence. Now his eyes searched the corner where her pallet lay.

And saw that it was—empty!

A tingling shock drove the last vestiges of sleep from him. He sprang to his feet, buckling his warrior's harness about him, dragging on his boots loosely, not bothering to buckle them securely. His face was grim and impassive, and his eyes burned like fiery coals. If anything had happened to the girl—?

Out in the vastness and echoing silence of the central hall he found the sentries awake and alert, and he questioned them urgently. None had seen or heard anything unusual, and not one of them had noticed the girl as she had crept from the small side chamber she shared with the barbarian youth.

"Shall we rouse the men?" asked one of the guards. Thongor considered briefly, then shook his head, tousling his coarse black mane.

"Let them sleep if they can. The wench cannot have left more than a moment or two ago, and she cannot possibly have gone far. I shall search for her myself," he growled.

Snatching up a burning brand from the fire, he strode off into the darkness.

Some undefinable impulse led him in the direction of that dread room in which fat Kovor had met a terrible fate. He could not have explained his reasons for selecting this goal, but he had long since learned to trust his hunches, for the barbarian had a wilderness trained intuition, better developed than most.

The gigantic pile of masonry echoed about him, ringing with his rapid strides. He strode along, searching every shadow with alert eyes, scrutinizing the dusty pave for some trace of Zoroma's small bare feet. His cloak rustled behind him and his loose boots flopped. He bore the torch in one hand; the other held the hilt of his naked broadsword.

She had either taken another direction, or she had moved more rapidly than he had guessed likely, for it took him some ten minutes to reach the distant chamber wherein Kovor had so horribly died at the hands of the unseen opponent.

The enigmatic structure was as dark and silent as a tomb. And tomb-like was the noisome stench that hovered in the cold, dusty air. Thongor uttered a low growl, as might some prowling predator who detected the scrutiny of invisible eyes.

At length he came to the portal of the cube-shaped chamber and peered within.

There was no sign of the vanished girl.

The crusted flakes of Kovor's gore, dried now to brown scabs, still clung to walls and ceiling and floor. But although he searched every corner of the stone chamber, he found no token to suggest that Zoroma had come this way.

His brows knotted in bafflement. Every presentiment in his savage breast urged him that she had stood in this room but moments before, yet she was not here. His jungle-trained nostrils almost caught the warm, sweet odor of her tender flesh hovering on the stale fetor of the air. But his eyes found no evidence that she had come this way.

Baffled, he prowled on. But the endless rooms beyond were deep in the dust of millennia. No one had entered them in countless ages, that was obvious.

He doubled back and entered the room again. He stood motionless, searching with every sense for the slightest sign of something wrong. There was—*something*—about this room that obscurely bothered him, but he could not give a name to the vague unease that stirred his primitive soul.

It was an odd room, the walls totally devoid of any ornament, unlike most of the others, whose surfaces were sculptured with weird and alien geometrical designs in low relief.

The only attempt at any sort of design was the shallow square cut in the exact center of the floor.

On sudden impulse, he squatted down and peered closely at the crack in the stone floor, holding the crackling torch closer.

A muffled exclamation escaped his lips.

Earlier, when he had scrutinized the room following the strange doom of Kovor, the cracks that formed a perfect square in the floor of the chamber had been thickly packed with dust.

Now that dust was—*gone*.

His strange gold eyes narrowing in thoughtful surmise, the

young barbarian studied the square design cut in the solid stone of the floor.

Could it be a trapdoor, leading to unknown regions below?

They had not, in days of searching, found that portion of the black citadel wherein Shan Chan Thuu had made his magical laboratorium. Could it not lie in unexplored crypts hollowed out of the heart of the hill?

He inserted the tip of Sarkozan in the crack and probed and pried.

Was it only his imagination—or had the stone block shifted ever so slightly?

Now he wedged the blade of his small dagger in the other side of the crack, and played both steel blades against each other for leverage. The stone slab creaked—groaned!

Working with infinite care, wary of snapping either of the steel blades, he slowly wedged the sword and dagger deeper into the knife-thin crevice, and began to work the slab loose.

When he had pried the stone slab up at one end so that he could get a grip with his fingers, he released the broadsword and closed his hands over the lip of the slab—and threw all the steely strength of his mighty thews into one tremendous effort.

With a harsh rasp of stone against stone, the slab lifted slowly.

And Thongor stared down into a weird and wonderful world.

VIII

The Crypt of the Sorcerer

From the mouth of the black opening a green glare flickered. It bathed his impassive features in a lambent jade luminance.

By that elusive radiance the youth perceived a flight of worn and ancient stone steps that descended from the level of the secret door.

Sheathing his dagger but keeping the great Valkarthan broadsword bare in his hand, the young barbarian stepped through the trapdoor and lowered himself until his booted feet touched the topmost step of the ancient stone stair.

He descended cautiously, eyes roving from side to side, alert for the slightest sign of danger.

Beneath the floor of the citadel he found an immense cavity hollowed from the stone of the hill whereon the edifice was reared.

At the foot of the stair he found the stone floor bed besplattered with a ghastly crimson. His jaws tightened grimly. The splattered gore must be the remnants of Orovar of Pelorm, who had vanished on the night following the disappearance of Kovor. But what, then, of Zoroma? Did the tattered remains of her young body bedew some far corner of the crypt? Perhaps—and perhaps not.

He recalled that, as yet, the ghastly scream that had twice rung out to signal the demise of two of his band had not yet sounded the death knell of the jungle girl.

He prowled through the crypt without finding anything of further note.

Here and there portions of the stone floor were encrusted with a noisome, scaly residue that suggested the dried blood of earlier victims. He searched on, seeking the source of the curious flickering green light that dimly illuminated the recesses of the enormous vault.

In the far wall he found a dark opening and strode in warily, finding a gloomy passage of ancient stone. Cautious as a jungle cat, he padded through the dark passage, which soon widened into a vaulted chamber even more enormous than the one he had quit.

Huddled in one corner, Zoroma lifted dulled eyes and tear-wet cheeks to him.

"*Gorm!* Are you unharmed, girl?" he burst out, surprise and relief mingled in his tones. Woefully, she nodded.

He strode over to the corner where she sat huddled.

"How came you to this dismal place?" he inquired. She shook her head mutely.

"I . . . I know not. It was like a dream. I seemed to hear a voice that called my name . . . a voice that seemed to come from a great distance. And I followed it, like one entranced . . . followed it to the room where your man, Kovor, died."

"And found the trapdoor in the floor?"

She nodded listlessly.

"It stood open, and a dim green light beat up from the opening in the floor . . . still the far, faint voice called, and it seemed in my dream that I could not resist the urgency in that voice . . . it drew me on . . . down the stone stair . . . to this place, where I found . . . I found. . . ."

Her words died in a choked sob. Bare shoulders shook as thick waves of her shining black hair fell across her tear-stained face. And it was then that, peering about, he saw that this corner too was scaled with the dry crust of long-shed gore.

"Alatur!" she sobbed, holding out one hand.

"Your lover?"

She nodded mutely. Clenched in her fingers a bronze talisman flecked with dried blood could be seen. She wept, and he let her weep, knowing it the best remedy for woman's sorrow. He raised his head and peered about alertly.

"A voice that calls one, as in a dream, to the hidden place of death," he mused. "There must be more to these crypts than this—come, lass. Let us explore further."

Fear leaped suddenly into her great dark eyes.

"Should we not be gone from this place before . . . before . . . *it* . . . comes?"

He revealed white teeth in a swift, wolfish grin.

"Probably you are right," he growled. "But it goes against my ways to retreat from danger—and never yet have I faced a foe that cold steel could not kill!"

He helped her to her feet and they went forward through the green-lit gloom.

As his eyes roamed about restlessly, ears straining to catch the slightest sound, he felt the pressure of unseen eyes, but could see nothing but bare, worn stone about him. The walls of these crypts radiated an almost tangible aura of cold menace, but still he went forward, searching for something to kill.

Why had not the unknown, murderous thing torn apart Zoroma? Was it perhaps because it sensed his own presence, and the swiftness of his approach? Perhaps . . . he would find the answer to that mystery soon enough, he somehow guessed.

He would find the answer to many mysteries here, he knew.

They came at length into another chamber, larger than all the others. And on the threshold, Thongor halted abruptly, amazement written upon his features, and an oath of astonishment on his lips.

The floor was heaped and littered with treasure!

The far walls bore chests and shelves of ancient wood,

whereon moldering objects lay scattered. Huge old books of thick-leaved parchment, bound between boards of carved wood, or plates of ivory, or bound in the scaly hide of dragons.

A long bench of black marble bore instruments of the sorcerous arts—a brazen astrolabe, a huge hourglass filled with dark crimson powder, mortar and pestle, and a great deal of broken crockery—the remnants, he doubted not, of crucibles and vats and cucurbits and other devices of the alchemic art. There was even a gigantic instrument of verdigris-eaten bronze, a weird conglomeration of rings and hoops, with an engraved bronze sphere at the center. Thongor dimly recognized it as an armillary sphere, whereby a necromancer may follow the movements of the stars and planets through the celestial circle of the zodiac.

Over everything lay a thick gray blanket of dust, and the heavy webs of dead spiders festooned the walls.

The floor was heaped with a splendor of treasure and trash.

Bits of old, worm-eaten wood, dried bones, the withered remnants of ancient mummies, globes of dusty glass, the wink and flash of gems, thick gold coins, bright goblets of precious metals, crumpled scrolls and scraps of antique parchment, rust-gnawed blades of dagger, axe, sword and spear, dented helms, casks of gems, all manner of bottles and vases and phials, filled with colored powders or nameless oils—all lay jumbled together in a trash heap of decay and neglect...

With a muttered oath, Thongor strode over to examine the drifts of wreckage that bestrew the floor. Gems crunched under his boots and ancient coins spilled, clattering, down the sides of the heap as he disturbed their ancient rest.

It was from this moldering pile that the lambent green light shone.

He dislodged a clattering avalanche of broken bottles and spilled jewelry as he dug down through the heap.

Suddenly green flame bathed his bronze torso in flickering light. A muffled exclamation burst from his lips as he gazed down at the incredible thing his searching fingers had discovered.

"Thongor! What is it?" Zoroma cried.

He turned, grinning exultantly in her direction, holding up the flashing object he had found.

"The Emerald Flame—by all the gods!"

IX

Secret of the Emerald Flame

It was an incredible thing—and its value must have been fabulous. It was like a great collar and heavy pectoral, but it was fashioned entirely from strange gems whose like the barbarian youth had never before encountered.

The gems varied in size from that of a kernel of corn to great lumps as large as hawks' eggs.

They were uncut but polished smooth, and they were the pale, lucent green of clear water or the fresh bright jade of young leaves.

In the heart of the jewels an elusive wisp of flame danced and flickered. This wavering flake of fire was the fierce yellow-green we call chartreuse. Not all of the gems contained this wisp of flame at their hearts—there must have been a couple of hundred gems in the heavy collar, which, when worn about a man's throat would lap over his shoulders, chest and back, covering them with a mantle of flickering jade fire. Some of the jewels were dead and dull and lusterless, but most were alive with inner flames that danced with an ever-moving semblance of life.

Thongor stared at the treasure in his hands, for incredible it was in very truth. There was the ransom of a hundred captive kings in his heavy handful of living green fire.

With the wealth this collar represented a man could purchase an empire—nay, a dozen!

He laughed delightedly, drunk with the exultation of his discovery, and lifted the collar to set it about his throat—

And then a bony, claw-like hand clutched his ankle in a vise-like grip of steel.

He stared down, his face contorted with astonishment.

The hand was scrawny as an eagle's talons: scarce more than bare bone sheathed in scaly, desiccated, parchment-like skin, woven together with dry sinews like cords of cat gut. It was the hand of a thing long dead and withered . . . but it clung to his ankle with incredible living strength and tenacity.

He stepped back, dragging his captured foot. A thin, gaunt arm appeared, coins and parchment tatters spilling away.

Dried flesh hung in ropes and tatters to the brown old bone. But the thing, somehow, *lived*.

Now the rest of the mummy came into view, a hideous thing with a bony mahogany face that was as fleshless as a skull and to whose bald brow a few tatters of desiccated skin yet clung. The eye sockets were deep and hollow, mere black pits of shadow, but within them eyes blazed with cold, awful fires of malignant hatred. The eyeballs themselves, Thongor could see, had dried to beads of yellowing gum, but still they burned with cold, inhuman vigor and intelligence.

His skin crawled with a thrill of horror as he saw that the dust of centuries filmed those naked, burning eyes!

Behind him somewhere the girl screamed with sheer terror as the living dead thing arose into view, clutching his leg in an unbreakable grip.

And Thongor somehow knew that even after centuries of death, Shan Chan Thuu was still the Keeper of the Emerald Flame, and by whatever nameless sorcery animation lurked yet within its withered flesh, the mummy of the old Omnian magician still guarded its ancient trust.

Thongor swept his sword up and chopped an awkward blow at the scrawny arm. But it was tough as sun-dried leather and although the keen edge of Sarkozan cut through a shred of dried flesh and snapped a thread of gristle, naught else was accomplished. The vise-like grip on his boot tightened inexorably. Already his ankle was numb from the paralyzing pressure of those withered talons.

On sudden inspiration, he recalled that in his haste in dressing he had not bothered to buckle the boots securely. Thus, with a twist of his leg he tore his foot out of the boot, leaving it in the grip of the mummy's hand, together with a few square inches of his hide.

He sprang backward, clumsily, thrusting the collar of glittering green flame into his girdle so as to free his hands.

The grinning jaws of the long-dead sorcerer gaped in a soundless howl of rage. Convulsively, the bony claws closed on the empty boot like a steel trap. And then Thongor saw the ferocity and demoniac strength that had torn his men asunder into bloody gobbets—for in a mindless fury the claws of the mummy ripped and tore the tough leather of his boot into rags!

His jaw tightened grimly. If once those bony claws closed on his flesh, he would be maimed for life.

Whatever the nature of the force that animated the wizard's

mummy, it lent unbelievable strength to the withered lich of Shan Chan Thuu.

Now the thing came lurching down the mounded treasure toward him, bony arms reaching for him, eyes aflame with a reptilian ferocity.

Behind him the girl watched, her face milk-white, hands to her cold cheeks, eyes wide and filled with horror.

X

When Dead Men Walk

Thongor circled the stone chamber slowly, fending off the mummy of the ancient wizard with the gleaming steel of the broadsword.

With jerky, ungainly strides, the thin brown thing stalked after him, its burning gaze fixed on the mass of gemmy flame that flashed and scintillated at his girdle.

It closed with him suddenly, and the youth took his stand and swung the mighty broadsword in a whistling blow that caught the mummy full in the side.

The impact of that slashing steel would have slain a living man. Gaunt ribs, over which leathery hide was stretched drum-taut, crunched and splintered. The mummy staggered, but did not seem to feel the blow in the slightest.

Another stroke caught the mummy's forearm, splintering the bone and shattering the wrist joint. The blow, which would have put any mortal warrior out of action, did not in the slightest impede the skeletal lich. The young barbarian felt his skin crawl with horror.

How do you kill a thing that is already dead? he wondered.

Again he circled the chamber, followed by the staggering mummy that stalked tirelessly after him, bony arms outstretched to rend and tear his flesh.

Fumio and Orovar had, doubtless, stood still, mesmerized by the uncanny powers of the dead sorcerer—helpless to move as the grasping claws ripped their bodies asunder. But Thongor was free of the spell—which indicated that a man who was awake was immune to the magic of Shan Chan Thuu, who gained his powers over the minds of sleeping men by whispering to them in their dreams his eerie, siren song.

It occurred to Thongor to wonder for what reason the mummy had lured the two men and the girl, Zoroma, into his grasp. Merely to protect his treasure of ensorcelled gems? He frowned thoughtfully: it was not likely, for until he had penetrated to the secret crypt, they had not known of its existence, and thus posed no threat to the mummy's treasures.

Why, then, this bestial fury—this necromantic urge to kill?

Suddenly, it came to Thongor, as if by sheer intuition.

That collar of green gems, some of which were inwardly lit by eerie, writhing emerald flames, and some of which were dead and dark, unlit and lusterless.

Something the boy knew of the dark, perverted cult of chaos, for his adventures had brought him into proximity with their grisly worship and unholy rites ere now. He knew that the gifts of chaos were never bestowed freely . . . that always the seeker after wisdom and power had a grim and terrible price to pay.

What price had Shan Chan Thuu paid for his magisterium?

Thongor had a horrible suspicion that he already knew.

For each weird gem in that mighty collar the old Omnian wizard had taken a human life . . . and the flickering, restless flames that beat within those green crystals, as prisoners might beat against the bars of their cells . . . *each flame was a captive soul!*

And there were still a score or more of dark, lusterless gems at whose cold heart no captive flame danced!

"Great Gorm!" he breathed hoarsely . . . and the curse was more than half a prayer.

No reason, now, to wonder that life clung with unnatural tenacity to the dried, dead mummy of Shan Chan Thuu. . . .

For his spirit would not be free of its ancient curse until every crystal which composed the Emerald Flame was horribly in-lit!

Zoroma watched as the young warrior circled the stone-walled chamber again and again, followed by the shuffling steps of the untiring mummy. The horror of their predicament gradually dawned upon her frozen mind, which was gripped in the icy clutch of supernatural terrors.

Why had she violated the precepts of the tribal elders and sought out this haunted castle? She had known that her lover, Alatur, was lost . . . for no man who entered the realm of Shan Chan Thuu ever left it alive.

Her vain and foolish quest had accomplished utterly noth-

ing. And it would soon bring a ghastly doom down on herself
and on the stalwart barbarian boy who now battled so
heroically—but so hopelessly—against the animated mummy
of the ancient wizard.

Thongor, too, knew that it was only a matter of time before he would fail to elude the grasping claws of the mummy.
And once that bony grip closed on his arm, he would be
helpless to oppose its unnatural strength.

His strength was failing even now. Days of toil and tension, sleepless horror-haunted nights and the lack of food and
water—all these had taken their toll even of his magnificent
young physique. In a moment—or an hour—his weary legs
would falter or stumble, and the claws of the mummy would
seize him in their unbreakable grip . . . and those mad eyes
burning from black pits sunken in that gaunt, grinning skull
would be the last sight he would see in this life.

Fiercely, he redoubled the fury of his attacks against the
stalking dead man. Sarkozan whistled through the fetid air,
smashing a thigh bone here, slicing through a taut liga-
ment—terrible crippling blows that seemed to cause the walking dead thing no discomfort.

One shattering blow stove in the side of the bald bony
brow, extinguishing the mad glitter of one scummed, dusty
eye in a shower of splintering bone. Yet on it came, grinning
with a rigor of hellish mirth!

Another terrific blow cracked the bony pelvis. A web of
black lines ran jaggedly through the dry brown bone, but did
not slow its tireless advance.

The weary boy was panting with effort now, his face black
and congested, his naked breast rising and falling. The broadsword in his hands seemed to weigh like a ton of lead and
the taut sinews of his arms trembled with the effort of wield-
ing it. It was only a matter of time before—

Zoroma screamed!

His booted leg stumbled against the ruin of a broken chair
and suddenly he felt himslf falling. The broadsword spun
away from him and rang like a struck gong against the stone
flags of the pave.

Then he lay sprawled, his feet entangled in the broken
rungs of the chair, the air knocked out of him by the impact
of his fall—and before he could clamber to his feet again, the
mummy lunged like a striking serpent and he felt the dry,
bony claws clutching at his throat and stared up through rising red mists into the single glaring eye of Shan Chan Thuu!

XI

Flaming Death

The clutch of the bony claws was crushing his throat. A numbness went tingling through his body and his skin crawled with loathing at the touch of the dead sorcerer.

Dimly, through the rising haze that obscured his vision, the young barbarian stared up into the ghastly, grinning visage of the mummy as it loomed above him.

Its bony jaws worked soundlessly, and he could smell the dust-dry odor of the breath that blew from between the brown fangs, sour as sweat.

He fumbled desperately, seizing the gaunt wrists in his numb and suddenly powerless hands, and strove to tear the vise-like grip loose. But all his young strength was helpless to dislodge the clutch of the mummy.

The muffled thunder of his pulse was loud in his ears. Faintly, as if from a vast distance, he could hear Zoroma screaming his name.

Then blackness rose about him and it seemed to Thongor that he fell with weird slowness through veils of dim vapor, ever darkening around him . . . and he knew that soon his mighty spirit would be but one more captive flame flickering within an eternal prison of cold crystal.

Terror broke the cold paralysis that had seized the girl. She sprang forward, crying Thongor's name, casting about her frantically for some weapon to use against the murderous mummy.

On a long low table of acid-stained black wood she spied a heavy carboy of clouded glass, and snatched it up.

Sustaining its massive weight with numb, trembling hands, she staggered to the struggling pair—raised the heavy container above her head—and brought it down with a shattering blow upon the naked skull of Shan Chan Thuu.

Bone crunched, glass cracked, and a noisome chemical stench permeated the air suddenly.

The whole back of the mummy's skull was crushed inward by the force of her blow, and from the broken carboy rivulets of a heavy fluid seeped, crawling over the bony back and shoulders of the sorcerer.

Suddenly it staggered erect, releasing the half-conscious barbarian youth. It peered about at her with one mad blazing eye. She stood frozen, watching a strange and miraculous transformation take place.

The heavy fluid, which had soaked into the desiccated flesh of the mummy—*smoked!*

Burst into flame!

An oily metallic vapor went whirling up from the mummy's wriggling, jerking torso. Now its entire upper thorax was one seething mass of crackling flames!

Whatever virulent fluid the carboy had held—some powerful acid, no doubt—the centuries had not lessened its fierce potency!

As the mummy, wrapped in crackling flame, went staggering away, she dropped to her knees beside the half-conscious youth and cradled his head on her bare thighs. Was he dead? Had the crushing claws quenched his young vigor?

No—he lived—for now his perspiration-smeared chest rose and fell, drinking the fetid air deep into his oxygen-starved lungs. Even as she watched, the blackness drained from his congested features and his eyelids flickered. The youth voiced a hoarse, inarticulate growl and forced himself up on one elbow, staring with amazement at the wizard's mad contortions.

As if it was capable of feeling pain, the burning mummy staggered and cavorted about the stone-walled chamber, writhing and flapping its flaming arms, cavorting in a macabre dance of death.

The ghastly scene was made all the more gruesome by the utter silence of its struggles. For although the bare fanged jaws moved and mouthed horribly, as in mute agony, no sound escaped it.

Frozen with horror, they watched the dance of the flaming death!

The leathery flesh and dried bones of the mummy had absorbed all of the acid the heavy carboy had contained. Now it seethed scarlet flame from head to foot. Even as they watched it blackened—shriveled—dwindling like a moth caught in a flame!

Immune to pain, to crippling blows, the supernatural vitality that animated the mummy's form was helpless against the one enemy to which it was vulnerable—the healing purification of naked flame!

"Look—the thing has the collar!" Thongor croaked, pointing.

And it was true! As it tore loose from Thongor, feeling the bite of the virulent acid, the mummy had snatched its jeweled treasure from Thongor's girdle. Now it brandished the Emerald Flame amid the seething fury that was rapidly consuming it.

One hip joint, eaten through, collapsed, and the burning mummy fell to the stone flag, coming apart. An arm dropped, twitching, from the blackened rib cage, sooty claws still scrabbling and clutching. Within seconds the mummy crumbled in the midst of the roaring fire, which died to glowing coals, and then to a heap of white ash where a few lumps of unconsumed bone protruded.

Thongor limped over to inspect the remains of the enchanter's mummy. The skull was a blackened shell, hollow and cracked in the heat. It fell to pieces at his touch. From the pile of ashes, crumbling bits of bone, and scaly, blackened gristle, he drew forth the jeweled collar, smeared and dull with ashes. He wiped his hand across the glistening crystals.

They were dead and dull. No longer did the dancing emerald flames inwardly illuminate them. Mere lusterless bits of smooth crystal now, devoid of beauty or value.

Obviously, when the life force of the mummy was extinguished in the flames the spell was broken whereby the souls of his murdered victims were chained within the gems. Thongor dropped the dead crystals with a little grimace of disgust.

By mid-morning they had reached the ring of hills that enclosed the vast, bowl-shaped depression.

Thongor reined in his kroter, and turned for one last look at the black citadel that thrust its wilderness of turrets and cupolas skyward from the rocky knoll at the center of the valley of death and desolation. Rarely had he been so glad to shake the dust of any place from his heels.

Where she lay in his arms, seated before him astride the kroter, Zoroma trembled at the memory of the horrors they had endured in that ghastly ruin.

Grinning, Chelim reined up beside his chieftain.

"Where now, Thongor?" he inquired.

The young barbarian flexed his powerful arms as the girl lay back against his chest, her warm cheek laid trustingly upon his mighty heart.

"Anywhere at all where we can find water and game—due

north along the coast, I think; the sooner we get back into Chush the happier I will be!" he said.

The massive Zangabali grimaced and spat. He turned his gaze to where the fortress of Shan Chan Thuu loomed in the distance.

"After the nights o' fear we spent in that haunted mausoleum, I'll be glad to face Dorgand Tul and his spearsmen again," he laughed. "They, at least, are mortal! Give me a foe you can kill with a thrust of good, clean steel, and I will stand against any enemy. But this battling against shadowy sorcerers is not for the likes o' me!"

Thongor grinned. "Aye, but still, we did not come away empty handed," he growled. Chelim blinked in puzzlement— then grinned at the girl nestled demurely in the circle of the young barbarian's arms.

"Say, rather, that *you* did not come away with empty arms—but what of the rest of us?"

Tongor grinned and dug one hand into the pocket-pouch of his girdle. He held out a fistful of gold coins and glittering gems and laughed at the expression of astonishment that crossed Chelim's heavy features.

"In Gorm's name, man, you did not think I came away from that crypt of nameless horrors in such a hurry that I failed to fill my pouch, did you? There's enough loot here to buy you all women and weapons and new mounts at the next city we enter!"

The slack-jawed astonishment faded from Chelim's features and was replaced by a grudging admiration.

"Well . . . perhaps I did underestimate you," he grunted. "I doubt that *I* would have lingered in that gloomy cavern long enough to pick up loot."

"Nonsense," Thongor snorted. "Why fear? The mummy was dead at last. But, come, let us get on. Ahead lie good, comfortable jungles—complete with streams of fresh, cold water, and game. *Game!* Gorm's blood, it has been so long since I last had a good steak that my belly has almost forgotten the taste of meat! Tell the men to ride west, Chelim—I'll have a hot meal before I curl up in my pallet to sleep this night!"

He thumped booted heels in the ribs of his kroter and rode past the burly Zangabali. Noticing with a grin how the arms of his young chieftain tenderly enfolded the slim form of the jungle girl, Chelim laughed. Thongor was thinking of more things than filling his hungry middle, Chelim knew, and it would be hours before the young barbarian finally—slept!

They rode off through the dusty hills, bound for the jungles of Chush and a host of new adventures.

VALUSIA

Valusia was the invention of the Texas writer Robert E. Howard, who founded the modern school of sword and sorcery and created the famous Conan. He wrote (or started) a bookful of tales about an Atlantean savage named Kull who became king of elder Valusia when Atlantis was only a primal wilderness filled with barbarians.

All but two of these stories were rejected by *Weird Tales*, so Howard tossed them in the trunk, sat down, and invented Conan. The manuscripts of the earlier stories were unearthed after Howard committed suicide in 1936. I was asked to finish them as best I could, and they all went into a book called *King Kull* which Lancer Books published in 1967.

The book is out of print; the publishing company is defunct; and the most recent edition of the Kull stories returns to Howard's original text, omitting my contributions. So I reprint the best of my posthumous collaborations on Kull here.

RIDERS BEYOND THE SUNRISE

with Robert E. Howard

"Thus," concluded Tu the Chief Councillor, "did Lala-ah the Countess of Vanara flee with her lover, the Farsunian adventurer, Felnar. And thus she hath brought shame to her husband-to-be, and to the very throne of Valusia!"

Kull the king, who sat listening with his fist supporting his chin, grunted. He had paid scant attention as the old councillor told the tale of the young Countess of Vanara and how she had left a noble of Valusia waiting to wed her on the very steps of the Merama Temple while she fled with her lover. And he could not see why Tu attached so much importance to these somewhat sordid but, after all, common doings.

"Yes, I understand," Kull said impatiently, "but what have the amorous adventures of this runaway Countess to do with me—or with Valusia's throne? I blame her not for running away from Ka-yanna. By Valka, he's as ugly as a swamp devil and has a disposition just as amiable. Why fill my ears with this tale?"

"You do not fully grasp the implications, Kull," the old councillor said, with the patience one must accord to a barbarian warrior who happens to be a king. "You come from far Atlantis, and the ancient customs of great Valusia are still unfamiliar to you. Let me explain. Lala-ah, by deserting her betrothed at the very horns of the altar, has thus committed a gross offense against the highest tradition of Valusia. And an insult to Valusia is an insult to the king of Valusia. For this, royal law decrees she must be brought back to the City of Wonders for trial.

"Then, too, she is a countess and cannot wed a foreigner without the king's consent, for we have also a law regarding the marriage of nobles. And in this case, your royal consent

113

was neither given nor even asked. Valusia will be an object of scorn among the Seven Empires if it is seen that we allow foreign adventurers to carry off our women with impunity, and permit even Valusians of noble birth and title to flout our ancient laws without punishment."

Kull rubbed his chin, brooding sourly on the thousand and one ignoble tasks a king must undertake. He must break up this girl's marriage for no reason save that a law inscribed ages ago by some mumbling graybeard on a rotting scroll must be obeyed!

"Name of Valka," he grumbled, shifting restlessly on the mighty throne. "You Valusians make a great to-do over these things—custom and tradition! I have heard little else since first I sat in the Topaz Throne. I like it not, Tu! In my land women mate with the men whom their hearts choose . . . of course, we were only savages. . . ."

Tu nodded sagely. "Aye, Kull. But this is a civilized realm where all obey the laws. In your homeland of Atlantis men and women run wild, unhindered by precedent and tradition. But here we have a civilization. And civilizations are naught but entangling webs of custom and regulation that set strict limits on their peoples so that all may live together in safety."

"*Safety!*" Kull repeated. "I think little of 'safety' that is imposed by dusty laws—give me the safety a strong-thewed warrior insures, through the valiance of his fighting skills and the keen edge of his sword! *That* is Kull's notion of safety!"

"Aye, lord king," Tu said soothingly. "The concept, if you will permit me, of a man raised in savagery."

Kull laughed. "The more I see of what you call civilization, the more highly I think of what you call savagery! But say on, Tu, for I perceive you are not yet done with your arguments."

"Only one argument more, O king!" Tu said. "And it is but this: the countess hath a strain of royal blood in her, for her mother was a cousin to Borna, the king you overthrew to gain the throne of Valusia! She hath, thus, a certain tenuous but legal claim upon the throne—and this claim the adventurer Felnar of Farsun might press, if he be as ambitious as are most of his kind. Dare we—dare *you*—risk a rival claimant to Valusia's throne?"

A feral light flashed in Kull's tigerish eyes. This was, indeed, an argument! He had seized the Topaz Throne and meant to hold it. An inarticulate growl sounded deep in his corded throat. Tu, noting these signs, smiled gently to him-

self, and added the final touch: "Ka-yanna rode after his
runaway bride-to-be with an armed host. One of them awaits
without, bearing a message for you from this Farsunian adventurer. I think you should give it ear, O king!"

"Then have him in, and bid him speak," Kull growled.

Tu returned in a moment, followed by a young horseman
whose mail was much stained with road dust. The youth
made humble obeisance to Valusia's warrior king.

Kull eyed the young man fiercely.

"How is it that you carry word from this Felnar? Did you
not seize the fellow, if you were close enough to exchange
words with him?"

"Nay, lord king, I did not see him. I but spoke to a guard
on the borders of Zarfhaana. To him this Felnar left a
message which he bade the guard repeat to any Valusian that
came after in pursuit. The message was this: 'Tell the barbarian swine who defiles Valusia's sacred throne that I name
him scoundrel, rogue and vile usurper. Tell him that someday
I and my bride, whose title to the royal name is purer than
his, shall return with a thousand swords at our back to pull
him from his high place. I shall clothe Kull's cowardly body
in the raiment of women and set him to attend the horses of
my chariot, which is an occupation more fit to his lowly
birth!' "

There was an instant of utter silence in the throne room;
tension strained the very air, about to break.

Then Kull's powerful bulk heaved erect, his scepter of
State crashing to the marble flags. He stood for a moment
speechless, face black with fury, eyes blazing like gray
torches. Then he found his voice in a wordless roar that sent
Tu and the young horseman stumbling back from him, as
men retreat from a tiger's lair into which they have unwarily
intruded.

"*Valka! Holgar! Tath and Hotath!*" he roared, voice thick
with rage, mingling the names of gods, heathen idols and
hell-demons together in a blasphemous proximity that made
Tu shudder. The king brandished his mighty arms and his
iron fist crashed down on a tabletop with a blow of such
tremendous force that the heavy legs buckled like paper. Tu
shrank back against the farther wall, and the young rider, his
face white as milk, stumbled backwards toward the door. He
had dared much in giving Kull the Farsunian's insulting challenge, and he feared for his life. But Kull was far too much
the savage to identify the insult with its bearer; it is only the

civilized monarch who wreaks vengeance on the courier for bearing an insult from his master.

Kull ripped off his gem-encrusted robes and hurled them across the room. His coronet clanged after them against the farther wall, shedding its sparkling opals from the fury of his gesture. He snatched up his great sword and buckled the scabbard-belt across his naked torso.

"Horses! Summon the Red Slayers and bid them mount and ride! Where is Brule the Pict! *Move,* you slow-footed gape-jawed thick-witted oafs—!"

Tu fled the throne room, his robes flapping about his bony shanks, pushing the pale horseman before him.

"Blow the war trumpets! Quick! Summon Brule the Spear-Slayer to the king, before he slays us all!"

Four hundred warriors clad from head to heel in crimson trappings sat astride their stallions in the mighty square before the Palace of Kings, when Kull strode grim-faced from his hall. Sword crashed against shield and stallions reared back upon their haunches as the Slayers gave their king the crown salute. Kull's fierce eyes blazed with pride and ferocity as he returned their salute. These were the most terrible soldiery upon the earth. Kull's own picked cavalry, chosen from the warriors of Valusia's hill country, the strongest and most vigorous fighting men of a degenerate race. Here, too, were the Picts, lean, naked savages, men of Brule's heroic tribe. They sat their mounts like centaurs, and they could fight like demons from the scarlet pits of hell.

Kull strode up to his great war stallion, seized the half-tamed beast by the jaw-bit and dragged it to its knees in a surge of strength that drew a gasp of awe from even the strongest of his warriors. He sprang into the saddle fully armed and reined the snorting stallion with a powerful hand. Brule, chieftain of Valusia's most formidable allies and Kull's closest friend, cantered to his monarch's side, accompanied by Kelkor, second-in-command among the Red Slayers.

"Whither, O king, do we ride?"

"We ride hard and far, by Valka! First to Zarfhaana and thence beyond—to the lands of snow or the burning deserts or the scarlet maw of hell itself, I know not!"

Kull's first red fury had cooled and hardened to a cold, steely rage. His eyes flashed like naked sword-steel in his impassive bronze face. Brule grinned wolfishly.

"What seek we there?"

"The trail of Felnar, a skulking adventurer out of Farsun who carried off a Valusian woman, and we shall track this Farsunian fox to his lair if we must tread half the earth to dust behind us!"

Tu, quavering with fright, had followed Kull to the square.

"O king," he ventured in a shaking voice, "this is most unwise! Zarfhaana's emperor will never permit such force as this to ride through his realm! Forget the idle threats of this boastful bride-stealer—"

Kull transfixed him with a ferocious glare.

" 'Twas you yourself who urged me to this quest, so be silent! Tu—I leave Valusia in your hands until I return. And I shall return when I have crossed swords with this Farsunian, or I return not at all. As for the Zarfhaanan, if they forbid our passage then I shall ride over the rubble of their broken cities," was Kull's grim reply. "In Atlantis, men avenge insults. And, although I am no longer an Atlantean, by Valka, I am still a man!"

He gestured fiercely toward the east. Kelkor shouted a command—trumpets lifted, sparkling in the sun, and rang with brazen thunder—and the Red Slayers poured like a flood of steel and crimson through the broad avenues and out of the magnificent city.

People peered curiously from balcony and roof and window, to see the mighty cavalcade rumbling forth to wage war. They watched as caparisoned stallions tossed their rippling, silken manes, the clatter of their silver hooves ringing on the cobbles like a horde of goblin blacksmiths. From lancetip and spear, pennons streamed in the wind. Sun flashed from the bronze armor of the warriors. Cloaks fluttered in the wind like scarlet banners. The brave cavalcade dwindled down the boulevard, vanishing through the great maw of the Eastern Gate, and were gone from sight.

And the people of the city turned away, bending again to their little household tasks, as people always do, no matter to what portentous deeds kings and warriors ride.

Night found them encamped on the mountain slopes beyond Valusia. The hill people flocked with gifts of food and wine. The proud warriors, now that the City of Wonders lay behind them, set aside the restraints they felt among the cities of the world and talked freely with the hill folk, many of whom were kin to them. They sang old songs with them beside the night fires and repeated old jests.

Kull, grim and unrelenting, walked apart. Beyond the glowing fires under the star-gemmed skies he gazed out over mystic vistas of bleak crag and flowering vale. The harsh lines of the slopes were softened by foliage and green verdure; the deeper vales became pits of inky gloom in the starlight, shadowy realms of old magic and mystery. But the line of hills stood out bold and clear in the moon-silver. These hills of Zalgara held forever a certain fascination for Kull. They brought to mind the snowy heights of Atlantis he had scaled in his boyhood, ere faring forth into the great sunlight of the world to write his name across the blazing stars and to take an ancient throne for his seat.

Yet were they different, these hills. The craggy cliffs of Atlantis rose stark and gaunt; they were brutal and terrible with youth, even as Kull himself. Age had not softened the knife-edge of their strength; the naked stars impaled themselves upon their fang-like peaks.

But these Zalgaran hills were older, rounded. They rose like kindly gods. Green groves and great trees laughed upon their shoulders. Robes of tossing grass and meadows green as velvet clad their angular sides like thick garments. *Old, old,* Kull thought: many a drifting century hath worn away their sharp-edged splendor. Mellow and beautiful with age they lay, dreaming of olden days and ancient kings whose feet had trod their sward. *As Felnar's feet had trod them!*

Memory of the braggart's insult swept over him like a red wave, smothering his brooding thoughts, which burst forth now with remembered fury. Kull flung back his broad shoulders and glared up at the calm eye of the moon.

"Valka and Hotath doom my spirit to everlasting fire if I wreak not my vengeance on this Farsunian!" he roared.

The night wind whispered among the trees as if in mockery of his vow.

Ere scarlet dawn burst like a conflagration across the Zalgaran Hills, Kull was in the saddle at the head of his cavalcade. The glints of dawn awoke white flame from lancetip, helm and shield, as the Red Slayers wound like a serpent of scarlet and steel between the green vales and over the long undulating slopes heavy with pearls of dew.

"We ride into the sunrise," Kelkor remarked.

Brule shrugged. "Aye, and some of us ride beyond it."

Now it was Kelkor's turn to shrug. "That will be as it will be. It is the warrior's fate."

Kull observed all this from the bronze mask of his face, wherein only the eyes seemed alive. He watched Kelkor thoughtfully. Custom decreed that the lord commander of the host must be of Valusian blood, and Kelkor—Kelkor was a Lemurian. His skill in war, his courage in battle, his wisdom in council had lifted this warrior from among the unknown ranks of mercenaries to the second-highest place in the Host of Valusia. Only this accident of birth kept him from taking the highest rank. Straight as a spear Kelkor rode, inflexible, unbending, like a statue of steel. A man of ferocious, berserk fury when facing the foe, Kelkor was icy calm at other times. His absolute control over himself marked him as one born to command others. Again, Kull cursed this blind adherence to King Custom that ruled in Valusia with a power above even the king's will!

The next dawn found them trooping down out of the foothills into the yellow mystery of the Camoonian desert. All that day they rode through the vast, dreary, saffron-tinted waste wherein grew nor tree nor bush nor blade of grass, naught save eternal undulating yellow sands that rose and fell in dunes of dust. When the sun stood at noon, they briefly camped to break their fast. The heat was intolerable, burning down from the brass bowl of the sky. They moved on through waves of searing light. No drop of water moistened the salt waste. No bird essayed the burning vaults of heaven. No sound broke the moaning of the perpetual hot wind, save for the creak of their leather, the clank of steel, the rustle of sand moving under the horses' weary hooves. Brule, even Brule, wilted in the white heat; he stripped off his brazen corselet and hung it on a baggage horse. But Kelkor rode bolt upright, unwavering under the burden of full armor, and seemingly untouched by the furnace heat of the day. No bead of moisture touched his leather face.

"Steel clean through," Kull murmured in admiration. Given to blind rage himself, he envied the Lemurian his iron control.

Two days of scorching travel brought them out of the sands of Camoon and into the wall of low green hills that marked the verge of Zarfhaana. Here they halted before two Zarfhaanan guards. Kull spurred forward to deal with these sentinels.

"I am King Kull of Valusia," he said abruptly. "We follow the trail of Felnar, an abductor of women. Seek not to halt nor hinder me. I will be responsibile to your emperor."

The two sentinels stepped aside, nodding the host forward, and when it had vanished in the distance one turned to the other with a grin.

"I win the wager! Valusia's king rides himself on Felnar's track."

"Aye," the other made reply. "These barbarians are hot for honor and eager to avenge their own wrongs. Had he been a true-born Valusian, you had lost, by all the gods!"

The vales of Zarfhaana echoed to the drumbeats of Kull's horsemen. Here had he paused to dispatch a message to the Zarfhaanan emperor in surety of his peaceful purpose, and here he had caught up with Ka-yanna, the vengeful and betrayed bridegroom. As they halted briefly to confer, word sped to north and south, west and east that Kull of Valusia rode into the sunrise. The peaceful villagers flocked to see the mighty Valusians.

". . . So, according to your intelligence, the abductor rides ahead of us with many days' advantage," Kull mused grimly. "We must follow hotly on his trail. No point in questioning these peasants, for Felnar will have bribed them with much gold to lay false scents and lie to us."

Ka-yanna curled his thin lips in a vicious smile. "Let *me* question them, sire! I will wring truth out of them, like water from a twisted rag. . . ."

Kull did not even try to disguise his contempt. "Torture? We are friendly with the Zarfhaanans. Their lord permits our armed passage through his domains; torture of his peasantry is too much to expect him to swallow."

"What cares the emperor for a few wretched villagers?"

Kull swept him aside. "Enough! Kelkor—the map."

They bent over the parchment whereon these lands were etched in blue and green and crimson inks.

"He is not likely to venture north," Kull mused, "for beyond Zarfhaana in that direction lies the sea, swarming with rogues and pirates."

"Nor south," said Kelkor firmly. "That is the land of Thurania, hereditary foe of his nation."

Brule considered. "To my thought, he will strike on east as he has been traveling. That means he will cross Zarfhaana's eastern border somewhere near the frontier city of Talunia and go on into the wastelands of Grondar. Thence he will probably turn south, seeking an open road for his own land, Farsun, which lieth west of Valusia. He will make his way through the small principalities south of Thurania. He can go nowhere else."

"Aye," Kull nodded agreement. "But here lies a strange thing. If Farsun was his goal all the time, why strike out east—in the opposite direction?"

"Probably, sire, because all borders of Valusia save for the eastern are closed during these troubled times. He could never have gotten through the closely guarded roads without having a pass from the king. Much less could he have carried the countess through the borders!"

So they rode east, on and on through long, lazy days. The kindly countryfolk feasted them at every halt with plenteous Zarfhaanan foods, waving aside proffered payment. *A soft and lazy land*, thought Kull, *helpless as a wide-eyed lass before the coming of some ruthless conqueror!*

Their hooves beat out a steel music through the dreamy vales and verdant forests. He drove the Slayers hard, giving them a bare minimum of grudged rest. For ever before him like a mocking phantom floated the elusive face of Felnar. His heart gloried in the hot lust of revenge, the relentless hatred of the savage before which all other desires give way.

The frontier city of Talunia they reached by dawn. The host made camp at the forest's verge and Kull entered the city with Brule at his side. The gates opened at the sight of the royal signet of Valusia and the symbol of free passage sent him by the Zarfhaanan emperor, which was a gold seal in the likeness of a fierce gryphon with a lion in its hooked beak.

"Hark ye," Kull said, drawing aside the commander of the guards of Talunia's gates, "are one Felnar of Farsun and Lala-ah of Valusia within the city? They would have ridden out of the west some three days since."

The commander nodded. "Aye, king, they entered some days since at this gate, but as to whether or no they have left the city I cannot tell."

Kull put into his hand a gemmed bracelet unclipped from his own left arm. "Listen, then, and heed: I am but a wandering Valusian noble, companioned by a Pictish slave. None need know aught else than this, understand?"

The soldier eyed the costly bauble covetously and pocketed it. "Aye, lord. But what of your warriors encamped by the woods?"

"Their camp cannot be seen from the city, since an arm of

the forest curves betwixt. That bracelet also paid for your lack of knowledge as to my force, eh?"

"Valka's name, sire! I am a soldier of Zarfhaana—how can I be so false to my emperor and his viceroy who rules the city as to pretend ignorance of a foreign army! I think not you plan any treachery, but—"

Kull's eyes flashed gray flame. "The emperor's sigil binds you to obedience! Keep silent, and all will be well. I but seek a Valusian traitor, and no harm to Zarfhaana."

The gate commander reluctantly obeyed, and Kull and his Pictish comrade strode into the city. The bazaar was already astir, although dawn's bright banners were not yet unfurled across the sky. Kull's giant stature and Brule's bronze nakedness drew curious eyes, but such reaction was only natural. Kull had flung a dusty cloak over his royal armor and thus hoped to pass without undue comment.

They found a small tavern and secured a room, then sprawled in comfort in the low-ceilinged drinking room to sip ale before the morning fire and see if they could overhear any of the news they sought. Kull had been in civilization long enough to learn that more information can be found in a wineshop than in the chamber of a king's chief spy. They drank and stood others to a stoup of wine, and the long day wore by, but not a word of the fugitive couple came to their ears, despite their leading questions. If Felnar of Farsun and the Countess of Vanara were still in the city they certainly hid their presence. Kull would have thought that the presence of a dashing gallant and a beautiful heiress of blood royal would have set idle tongues wagging from one side of Talunia to the other, but such did not seem the case. Was his surmise wrong, then? Had the couple fled instead of staying to rest?

Night was falling, drowning the streets in purple, when Brule and his master left the tavern to seek information in the streets. The narrow ways of the old city were athrong with a jostling crowd of night revelers. Torches and lanterns flared, guttering in the night wind. Then Brule clamped one hard hand on Kull's arm and nodded to their left, where the black mouth of an alley yawned. Within the alley's mouth a ragged, crouching figure stood, beckoning to them with a claw-like hand. Trading swift glances and loosening their daggers in their sheaths, they stepped to the dark entrance.

A withered crone with bleared eyes stood there, hunched

with age, a ragged, filthy mantle wrapped about her lean shoulders.

"Kull—Kull—what seek ye in Talunia's winding ways?" she crooned in a shrill, croaking whisper.

Kull's fingers closed over the dagger hilt.

"How know you my name, old mother?" he demanded.

She cackled. "The market has many eyes to see with and many tongues to whisper—and, though I be old, I have keen ears!"

Brule swore softly under his breath, and grasped her arm.

"You'll have a slit throat, too, unless you tell us what we want to know, old crone!"

The old woman paid no attention to the threat. Her rheumy little eyes leered craftily from the dark shadows.

"Hark ye, Kull, I can lead ye to those ye seek. But—have ye gold?"

"Enough to buy for you a life of ease," he replied.

"Good! Aye, good! 'Tis hard enough to be old, without ye be poor as well! Then listen . . . listen well! The two ye seek know ye are about. Even now they make ready to flee as soon as it be dark enough. They hide in a certain house; soon, soon, they leave—"

"How?" asked Brule, suspiciously. "Talunia's gates are shut with sunset!"

"Aye, aye—but horses await them at a postern gate in the eastern wall! The guard's been bribed—aye, young Felnar has friends a-plenty in Talunia-town!"

"Where is this house?" Kull demanded.

The crone stretched out a dirty palm.

"A token of yer good faith, sire! Let me see th' color of yer gold. . . ." He put a fat gold disk in her gnarled hand. The old woman snuffled it, bit it and seemed satisfied. She cackled gleefully and shuffled back and forth in a grotesque parody of a curtsey.

"This way! This way. . . ." She hobbled off down the black alley. Kull and the Pict strode after her grimly, well aware that vile treachery might lurk in these dismal haunts and hovels. They followed her bent, shuffling form through one filthy lane after another, past whining, bedizened wenches who ogled their stalwart inches and sent simpering smiles after them . . . at last, coming to a halt in the most squalid quarter of all, before a huge dark house with tight-shuttered windows and grim black walls. The crone whispered to them with fetid breath that Felnar and the countess abode in a room at the head of the stairs. Kull nodded grimly, thoughts racing.

"Brule, follow this woman to the place where the horses await—I know the postern gate, saw it when we reconnoitered the walls at moonrise—I will go within."

Brule protested. "But Kull, you can't go in that black place alone! Bethink you—it might be an ambush!"

"Do as I say. Wait within sight of the horses, I will join you there. Felnar may give me the slip—you be on the watch to seize him if he appears before I do."

"And me gold? Where's me gold?" the crone whined. Kull eyed her fiercely.

"You'll get your gold when I know whether you led me to Felnar's lair or not! Go now with Brule."

As they melted into the darkness Kull entered the black house, groping before him with wolfish gray eyes seeking the faintest trace of light. Dagger at the ready, he ascended the creaking old staircase stealthily. For all his vast bulk, the king moved as swiftly and as silently as a hunting leopard—a trick learned from a savage boyhood in the forests of Atlantis.

Even if the watcher who sat at the head of the stairs had been awake, it is doubtful he could have heard Kull ascend. As it was, he awakened only when an iron hand clamped over his mouth—awakened only to fall in a deeper sleep when a massy dagger hilt crashed against his temple.

Kull crouched for a moment over the unconscious guard, keen ears searching the silence for a hint of movement. Utter silence reigned. He stole to the door of the chamber the crone had named. *Someone was within!* To his straining ears came the whisper of faint words, the creak of a floorboard— with one tigerish leap Kull crashed through the door and was within. He paused not for an instant to weigh chances. For all he knew or cared there might have been a roomful of armed assassins waiting for his arrival.

The room was black as pitch, save for the silver moon-path on the floor and the open window. Two black forms broke the white rectangle of the window—*they were escaping!* In the cold glare of the silver moon he caught a flash of dark eyes in a girl's piquant face—and a man's laughing face, darkly handsome. A roar of bestial fury broke from his lips as he crossed the empty chamber at one bound and sprang through the window, catching the rope down which the two clambered. Once in the alley behind the house, he saw the two dart into the shadows of a maze of leaning hovels. He shot after them on swift-thudding feet, but the alternate bright moonlight and inky gloom confused his sight. A silvery mocking laugh floated back to him and another laugh, a man's, full-throated with hearty amusement. He wasted no time tracking them through the weird labyrinth of tilting walls but raced through the night for the postern gate where the horses were to be.

And found the horses there, aye, and Brule and the crone as well, but no sign of the two mocking fugitives. Kull cursed like a madman. Felnar, that sneaking, treacherous scum, had outwitted him! The horses were but a blind—the couple had either gone to earth in another house or had escaped by some other route. If so, perhaps he could still catch them!

"Swift!" he bellowed, leaping astride one of Felnar's steeds. "Haste to the camp and rouse the Red Slayers—I follow Felnar's trail! After me with all the host!" And, tossing a fat purse stuffed with gold to the crone, he galloped into the night.

All night Kull rode like a demon, striving to pare away precious moments from the lead Felnar and the countess had gained. Their trail lead dead east. East to Grondar, even as Brule had predicted! He bent low over the horse's neck, its flowing mane whipping his face, and drove the spurs against its side. East to—Grondar, the Shadowy Land!

The stars were paling in the west and dawn came stealing across the eastern skies as Kull's panting steed toiled up the ramparts of the eastern hills and came to a halt at the summit, where the great pass cleft the hills with a gigantic notch like the cut of some stupendous scimitar of the gods. This way the Farsunian and the girl had come: there was no other pass through this wall of cliffs that stretched a thousand miles, forming a natural border between Zarfhaana and Grondar. He forced his weary, lathered steed to the high point of the pass and rested there, hands crossed on the saddlehorns, staring ahead.

There lay Grondar, aswim with purple gloom, awaiting the dawn which already pearled the horizon. It was the easternmost realm of the Seven Empires—the last stronghold of mankind—and naught lay beyond it but empty wilderness, stretching on unto the very utmost Edge of the World. Surely, soon, he would confront the Farsunian—sword to sword! Not very much farther into the unknown east could Felnar ride. . . .

Down the steep slope his eyes traced the road. The cliffs fell away sharply into a vast plain . . . mile after empty mile of dreary savanna, where tossing grasses nodded before the morning breeze. *And there—that fleeing dot on the road ahead—Felnar!*

He spurred forward, down through the pass and down the cliffs and down into the misty plains of Grondar. No time to wait, to permit Brule and Kelkor and the Red Slayers to catch up with him . . . the two he sought rode only a little way ahead. True, his steed was winded, but Felnar's horse must be just as weary, and more, as it bore a double load.

The pass was guarded by a lonely watchtower wherein two Zarfhaanans stood vigil. They waved and shouted at him as he thundered by, but he made no response and they did not come after him. They came sleepily out of the tower to stand staring after him down the white road that smoked behind his flying hooves. The sun stood bold on the mysterious horizon of the utmost east, like a ball of red fire. The mist that mantled the grassy land seemed to catch that fire and became a crimson haze into which Kull rode, a black figure, horse and rider merged into one, like a black basalt statue set against the Gates of Dawn.

"Another!" the first guard commented laconically.

"Aye," his companion said dully.

"He rides into the sunrise. *Fool!*"

"Aye," the other repeated with a low laugh.

"They ride into the sunrise . . . and whoever rides back from beyond the sunrise, eh? In all the years that we have watched. Eh? Who ever comes back?"

"None."

Brule and the host caught up with Kull by mid-morning. He stood, waiting for them, with a grim-set face, gray with road dust from head to toe, beside the corpse of the horse.

"I almost had him," Kull growled, as he swung astride one of the slayer's stallions. "But he turned in the saddle and shot the horse with an arrow, curse the luck! But he's still riding east, due east. . . ."

The host moved forward through the swishing grass. They spread out in a broad front, eyes peeled for a sign of the two they had pursued so long. Kull suspected Felnar and the countess would try to turn away south any time now, for no one could wish to ride very deep into legend-haunted Grondar the Shadowy Land. So they rode in open formation,

Brule's Picts ranging like lean wolves far afield to the north and south.

But still the tracks of Felnar's steed bore straight east, straight into the sunrise.

They grew uneasy at this darkling land. Men whispered strange rumors of Grondar on the edge of the world. Here travelers never came, for Grondar was a weird land, and the men herein, if they were indeed truly men and not dark things disguised in manlike form, had little or naught to do with the western lands. Nor did Kull strive to send a messenger to Grondar's king to request free passage, as he had done among the Zarfhaanans. For it was darkly rumored Grondar had no king. Sorcerers ruled it, men said; some said demons. Any land that stood so close to the Edge might well be ruled by things that dwelt—*Beyond*.

They rode without rest or pause all morning, till the horses were nigh to foundering. Their heaving sides were lathered; foam dripped from gasping jaws; their eyes rolled whitely. But they were war horses of Valusia, sprung from noble lines that had been bred and interbred for a thousand years, and they kept going.

How Felnar, mounted on a single steed, managed to retain his narrow lead for so long was a mystery to Kull. He began to suspect strange things, dark things. Perhaps this weird land of Grondar was fraying at his tight-stretched nerves and all this eerie desolation and misty endless pain were casting a spell over his mind, but he began to think . . . of sorcery.

They saw them toward noon of the second day. A dark band of men, mounted on shaggy black ponies, standing deathly silent as if waiting for the Valusians to approach. Kull rapped out terse commands to his weary men, commanding caution and courage.

They rode up to the Grondarians, Kull at the fore, with Kelkor and Brule at either hand. Then, bidding the men hold their ranks, the three detached themselves and rode forward, up to the line of Grondarians. Kull studied them with narrowed eyes; strange silent men they were, four hundred strong, warriors from the look of them, with tight, dark faces and unshorn black hair that blew on the wind. Fierce, silent men, lean and hard, roughly clad in glistening black leather, with glittering swords that sparkled so bright in the zenithal noon light that it hurt the eyes to look at them. Strange, dark, silent men with yellow eyes and shields of buffalo hide whereon were painted uncouth symbols of terrible demon's faces and monsters such as he had never heard, even in the grimmest fables or most black and whispered myths.

The master of the men of Grondar was old, old, years sat heavily on him, and the beard and flowing mane of hair that drifted on the wind was gray as weathered stone.

"Strangers, what do ye in this land?" he asked, his voice low and heavy.

"We pursue fugitives from justice who fled from our own land," Kull answered in a level voice. The cold yellow eyes of the ancient glared at him with strange mockery.

"Justice? Speak ye of justice, stranger? I have heard the word ere now, but here in Grondar on the Edge of the World we speak little of justice. We speak of the Will of the Gods, or of the Demons of the dark, whichever Will be stronger!"

"That may be," Kull replied in a voice without inflection, "but we wish to pass on. We have no dispute with Grondar or her gods. All we seek are the two that ride ahead to the east—"

The yellow eyes flashed in the worn, leather-hued face.

"*East,* ye say, stranger? Ye ride east?"

"Yes, until we have caught the two we follow," Kull said, and wondered why, at his words, ugly laughter broke among the dark, silent men of Grondar. The ancient leader laughed too—a wild, mad, pealing laughter, filled with cold cruelty and mockery, terrible to hear from human lips.

"Then ride on, stranger! Ride on . . . east, ye say? . . . ride, ride, and the Will of the Gods, or of the Devils of the Great Dark, be with ye at the end of your journey! Whichever be strongest. . . ." The ancient's cold, ringing laughter followed Kull as he rejoined his troops. They rode in silence past the host of Grondar, on into the haze of noon, and the old man sent one last mocking cry after them:

"Ride on, ye fools, ride on! *Those who ride beyond the sunrise . . . never return!*"

All that afternoon they rode in silence through the whispering grass and saw naught of the Grondarians. It was as if the mists and dim grasses and echoing silences of the Shadowy Land had swallowed them up.

Toward dawn of the next day they came to a great river that cut through the dark plain like some enormous moat around a castle of the gods. A vast, level expanse of slow, sliding, pale water it was, with the mist floating from it and the red sunrise mirrored within the rippling water until it seemed like a river of molten fire. Here they halted. They could go no farther. Yet the track of the Farsunian led directly up to the reed-grown shore.

Out of the sunrise came gliding a flat raft, poled across the sullen, dully gleaming floods by an old man. He was aged, but mightily built, huger even than Kull, and he towered in haggard strength like the rugged ruin of some kingly fortress the ages had blighted but not yet overthrown. No Grondarian he, for his face was lined but pallid, and his eyes, beneath white lowering brows, no slitted yellow fire-eyes like those of the dark men of Grondar but great luminous orbs ablaze with strange wisdom.

"Strangers, would ye cross the floods to that which lieth beyond the other shore?" he asked in a deep, quiet voice.

"Aye, that we would," said Kull.

"Then come, king, for I perceive ye to be royal and mighty, as mortals measure might and kingliness. Come— *alone*—for my boat can bear but one beyond the sunrise!"

Kull surveyed the old ferryman closely.

"What lies beyond the sunrise, old man? A city?"

"Nay, those who pass these floods of the Stagus have done with cities. Naught that man knoweth lies beyond . . . for this is the end of Grondar the westernmost of all mortal lands and the last of the Seven Empires. Beyond the river lies naught but the World's Edge, the boundary of the earth."

A murmur ran through the Red Slayers at these ominous words. Brule swore thickly, and bade Kull to stay here, to return, and leave the Farsunian and his wench to whatever dark fate waited for mortal men beyond the sunrise, but Kull was adamant.

"I have come thus far; I will complete the quest," Kull said.

"Come, then," the old ferryman bade, and his great eyes blazed with strange light. Kull boarded the raft and the old man poled forth from the shore where the Valusian warriors stood silently. They floated out on the broad breast of the crimson Stagus, and soon the dim dawn mist concealed the shore they had left behind. Kull regarded the mystic figure with suspicion.

"Who are you, old man, who ferries wanderers at the World's Edge?" The ferryman smiled at him through the veils of fog, and his voice echoed like distant thunder in the hills.

"I am of the Elder Race who ruled this continent of

Thuria ere Valusia was, or shadow-fraught Grondar, or any
of the realm ye know," he said softly, and Kull felt a thrill of
wonder and awe go through him. For Valusia was nigh as ancient as time itself: Valusia was old, old, when the peaks of
Atlantis and elder Mu were but isles of the sea! And a shudder of some emotion stronger than awe ran through Kull's
mighty form, for he knew that dark and terrible peoples had
ruled Valusia over the dim ages before the coming of mortal
men to these lands. Among them were the terrible Serpentmen who were not men at all but demon-things that
masqueraded as human; such had he driven forth from Valusia when the kingdom fell to him, but such he knew still lived
and lurked in hidden corners of the Seven Empires.

But the ancient ferryman sensed his thoughts and smiled.

"Nay, king of men, I am not a servant of the Snake. Ere
they came hither, the Elder Race ruled. Long was the Earth
ours, but now are we gone from it, returning to that legended
realm from whence we came . . . the east, beyond the sunrise. 'Twas from the east, ye know, that in Time's First Dawn
flew out over the lands of men the great Ka, Bird of
Creation. We saw Ka fly, his ebon wings enshadowing the
stars of Time's Dawn, and we shall see him return again into
the east in Time's Sunset when all things end. . . ."

Beyond the crimson floods of the Stagus the land lay flat
and drear like the plains of hell. Kull strode into the swirling
mists, leaving the motionless figure of the ferryman standing
terrible and tall, staring after him with luminous eyes.

The desertland rose slowly in bleak hills. Dawn blazed
overhead, but this weird land beyond the river was cloaked in
mists and naught could the king see of the sky above. He
plodded forward relentlessly.

And they were waiting for him there on the crest of the
hill. No longer did they flee his coming, but stood silently, the
girl and her lover. Kull felt a sense of unreality; he had
sought the two fugitives for ages, it seemed, and ever had
they fled his coming. Now they stood waiting for him, and a
sword gleamed in Felnar's right hand.

Kull came up to them, peering at them through the whirling fog. Rage and joy swelled his heart, thickening his
throat.

"At last, dog of Farsun, you run no more!"

"Aye, Kull," the slim, dark-faced man said with a laugh
that sent prickles of an eerie premonition up Kull's spine.

"Aye, the flight is over . . . the quest is done . . . *and the masquerade is finished!*"

His voice rose in a shriek of triumph and his sword, as he lifted it, flashed with a terrible glare of green flame as if enchanted. By its weird emerald light, Kull saw the girl clearly . . . as she faded, vanishing into thin air like a swirl of mist, a smile of mockery on her pale features to the last!

"Name of Valka!" he swore. "What devil's sorcery is this?"

Felnar's thunderous laughter boomed about him and the man's form became shadowy, growing huger in the dim mist, the face changed . . . changed into. . . .

"Sorcery indeed, O Kull, that has tricked you and lured you near the World's Edge where your gods can no longer shield you nor aid you against *my* wrath!"

The mist cleared, and Kull saw the man's face. *It was no face, but a mask of naked white bone!* A grinning, fleshless skull atop a warrior's gaunt and powerful body, a skull of ivory in whose empty, shadowed sockets burned twin livid tongues of dancing flame in lieu of human eyes!

"Thulsa Doom!"

The death's-head leered at him like a nightmare phantom from the scarlet pits of hell and the sword flamed with green radiance that flickered across the white bone, lending it the illusion of life and motion.

"Aye, Kull of Valusia, Thulsa Doom, the mightiest of earth's wizards! I warned you when we last met that I would return to joust with you again—and the hour hath come!" A peal of hideous laughter rang from the skull's gaping jaws, and Kull felt his blood run cold. Thulsa Doom, the greatest master of black magic in all the Seven Empires! Once, he had sought to lure Kull into the deadly waters of the Forbidden Lake through a similar trick—Kull well remembered Delcardes's cat and its ageless wisdom and whispering voice—then Kull's luck, or the hand of his watching gods had intervened to save him from the wizard's trap; but now they stood together face to face, in the dim lands that bordered the World's Edge, and here no god could intervene.

"I, who once served the Serpent, swore to bring you down, cur of an Atlantean savage, and now the time is come! You were a fool to trust in outward seemings—the countess lives still in Valusia, drowned in an enchanted sleep, and it was but a mist-demon from the World's Edge that rode with me hither, a fog-phantom that wore her likeness, even as I donned the likeness of the Farsunian! But now we are met,

Kull, and from this meeting only one of us will ride back from beyond the sunrise!"

They fought there in the mist, sword against sword, and the wizard was strong and tireless as a statue of black iron, while Kull was bone-weary from days of hard riding and nights without rest. Steel rang against steel, and at each touch of his blade against the sword of green fire Kull felt strength drain from his body. His arms weighed like lead; his brain dulled with weariness; his mighty chest gasped for clean air, as if he fought beneath cold dead water that crushed against him, numbing his flesh.

He knew then that the skull-faced wizard fought with a magic weapon. But he fought on, drawing on wells of strength that he had never tapped before. And as he fought the wizard's cold voice stung mockingly in his ears.

"Aye, Kull, fight—fight! Fight, till the last drop of strength drains from you and you fall like an image of stone at my feet! For with each stroke you meet, Atlantean, my charmed sword draws strength from your arm and pours strength into mine . . . and know, Kull, that fight as you will, I cannot be slain! *For I died, as men know death, long ages ago . . . naught that lives can die . . . twice!"*

Exhaustion hung on Kull like a thick armor of solid lead. Although the swirling mists were cold and damp, sweat poured down his face, stinging his eyes. His lungs were filled with fire, his throat dry as mummy dust. He would have traded his chance of Paradise for a draught of cold red wine.

And then from somewhere beyond the whirling mists a voice rang urgently, calling his name. . . .

"The sword, Kull! Change swords with the devil—strike it from his hand!"

He knew not from whence those words came, but in his weariness his numb hands obeyed the voice without thought. He struck hard, feeling his strength drain to numbness as the green sword lay flat against his own—then twisted up and out, with that trick all swordsmen know, to lock blades and disarm an enemy—and lo!—the green sword went flying and Thulsa Doom was unarmed.

Through the mist strode the unexpected figure of Kelkor the Lemurian, wet from crown to toe, for he had swum the broad Stagus, unable to let his king face battle alone in an unknown land. And in one hand he clutched the fallen sword of green fire, proffering it to the weary Kull.

Kull grasped it by the hilt, feeling a thrill of eerie force travel up his arm from the tingling blade, and he laughed harshly and flung his own good steel at Thulsa Doom.

"Now, fall to, wizard! Let us see how your trickery works now!" he croaked from a dry tongue.

Again they fought there in the timeless mists, but now the tide had turned. Each time Kull's flaming blade met the wizard's steel a bolt of thrilling strength flooded into his weary body. Tiredness drained from his aching muscles. His vision cleared and his numb brain became alert. The dull, leaden armor of exhaustion fell from him, piece by piece, and he fought superbly, beating back the silent wizard, driving him to his knees!

Now it was the turn of Thulsa Doom to feel the cold breath of fate blowing upon his nakedness! His limbs glistened with perspiration, trembled with exhaustion, while his breast heaved, and he panted for air. Dead thing though he was, and powered with vital magic force, the ageless wizard felt his artificial life drain from his body drop by drop before the Atlantean's relentless advance . . . he called upon the Serpent, his voice rose in a shrill cry of mad terror, invoking the demons who once had served him . . . but he learned with a terrible and merciless finality that a trick can be turned to strike back against the trickster . . . for here in the shadowy realm near the World's Edge, where neither god nor demon hath power, his devils could aid him no more than Kull's gods could come to the assistance of the Atlantean. . . .

It did not end soon. But it did end. Kull thrust the green blade deep into Thulsa Doom's chest. It cut through his laboring heart, and Kull left it there as the blade drank in the wizard's strength, green radiance blazing brighter and brighter as the life faded from the wizard's body, which shriveled slowly into a mound of gray dust.

Kull left the sword where it lay and turned to clasp Kelkor firmly by the hand.

"Lemurian or no, claim from me the high commandership of the Red Slayers," he panted. "I have defeated a devil's magic here—I doubt not I can defeat an empty law in Valusia!"

Brule met him at the water's edge when he came back across the silent rippling flood of the Stagus with Kelkor.

"Did you come to the World's Edge, Kull?" he asked, when greetings were done. The king laughed hollowly.

"Valka's name, Pict, I saw it not! 'Twas nigh to the edge of life I came, instead!"

"What now, Kull? Whither now?"

The king drained a skin of wine and wiped his lips with a great sigh of relief.

"Back whence we came. 'Tis a long road, but the land lies free before us! They say that no men ever rode back from beyond the sunset, aye, perhaps—but we have shattered other myths ere now, O Brule!"

Kelkor's voice rang like iron: "Forward—the Red Slayers!" And the trumpets blew.

The way back into the west was long and hard and weary, but it ended at last. And at the end lay Valusia, and home.

ANTILLIA

Antillia was a myth which arose during the Dark Age out of misinformed geographical speculations concerning islands in the Atlantic. Many such islands were rumored to exist, and when you don't know anything for certain about a place, it's all too easy to make up stories of its fabulous marvels. In the fifteenth century a yarn got started about how seven bishops and their flocks, who fled Spain to avoid the Saracen invasion, sailed west and settled on Antillia.

Maps drawn before Columbus show Antillia (or Antilha, Antigla, and so on) as being so similar to Cuba in shape, size and location that once people had gotten to Cuba considerable credence was given to the idea that pre-Columbian seamen had reached it. That's why to this day Cuba and its neighboring islands are called "the Antilles." Some versions of the story make it seven isles instead of one big one; and Lewis Spence thought it more or less contemporaneous with Atlantis, and slightly to the west, so the Atlanteans could migrate there after their own island-continent sank. (Spence was no fluff-headed author of flapdoodle like Churchward and some of the Theosophists. He was an erudite man and his books are closely reasoned; still and all, he's probably mistaken.) When L. Sprague de Camp and I came to write our novel *Conan of the Isles* we decided to set the story on Lewis Spence's Antillia, then inhabited by a degenerate remnant of Madame Blavatsky's Atlanteans: what the hell!

Recently I have returned to Antillia as the scene of a new series of fantasies written (I hope) with humor and elegance, somewhere between Clark Ashton Smith and James Branch Cabell, with a little Jack Vance thrown in for seasoning. I have taken up Spence's idea that Antillia flourished sometime between the foundering of elder Mu

135

and the rise of savage Atlantis to civilization, and I've moved it a bit farther south in the Atlantic so as to get it away from the Atlantis.

Here is the first of this new cycle of tales.

THE TWELVE WIZARDS OF ONG

I

"The air elemental, Fremmoun, has recently returned to the earth after a journey to the third planet of the star Srendix, where he discovered the long-lost Compendium of the sorcerer Paroul," the demon reported sullenly.

Intrigued at this intelligence, the young karcist, Chan, questioned the captive diabolus further on this point without, however, learning more. Satisfied at length that the infernal spirit possessed no further details on this matter, Chan uttered the Greater Dismissal, broke the circle of luminous powder which had confined the demon, suffused the invocatorial chamber with camphor and strode from his house for a turn or two through his gardens.

Deep in thought, the youghtful karcist strolled the gem-strewn path which meandered through his pleasaunce, absently driving an archeopteryx from his mandragora beds by hurling a well-placed opal. With a gutteral squawk, the ungainly feathered reptile flapped away through the tall stand of nodding cycads that bordered the garden.

The implications of the demon's message were most alarming. On a sudden impulse the young karcist returned to his house, belted on his Live Blade, took up his Waystaff and a purse stuffed with potent amulets and strode off to visit his nearest neighbor.

Chan's house of red stone stood on the southern slopes of Mount Ong; the mountain was a nexus of occult forces and many fellow practitioners of the Secret Sciences made it their home. The domed dwelling of his nearest neighbor, Hormatz, a theomancer, rose on the same slope a bit higher than Chan's house; toward it the impulsive youth headed without further cogitation.

The dome, a handsome edifice of bronze and smoky crystal, stood amid a grove of feathery tree fern. Chan found the decrepit theomancer, his senior by a dozen centuries, busied making oblations to a squat, yellow jade idol of Muvian craftsmanship. The elder nodded perfunctory greeting at his approach. Without ado the karcist informed his senior colleague of his information regarding the sylph Fremmoun. The old theomancer was not impressed.

"I fail to see the reason for your concern," he said absently. "However, I will consult my idols if you require further data on the matter."

"I would indeed appreciate it," the youth admitted. "But can you not see the horrendous implications? Paroul was the preeminent sorcerer of the last epoch. It is a matter of common knowledge that Fremmoun is subject to Nelibar Zux. Zux, once he has mastered the Compendium's contents, will thus become the most advanced sorcerer of our day."

"I still fail to perceive the cause of your perturbations," the theomancer reiterated.

"Has not Sarthath Oob, the leader of a rival enclave, sought for some time to enlist the sorcerer in his coven? What a coup it would be for him—and what a loss to us!"

The aged theomancer paled as the full import dawned upon him at last. The wizards who dwelt about Mount Ong had long since formed a local enclave. They were twelve in number, lacking only a final member to total thirteen, at which number they could become a full coven. A rival enclave, that headed by the nefarious Sarthath Oob, was in an identical predicament. Both enclaves had made overtures to the sorcerer Nelibar Zux but without success. Were the nefarious Oob to succeed in persuading Zux to join his group, it would be a coup of considerable value: at once he would achieve full covenhood for his group, thus outranking the enclave of Mount Ong, to say nothing of the prestige he would gain for his group, since Zux, his occult authority newly enhanced by mastery of the long-lost Compendium, would be the supreme sorcerer of the age, his presence lending enormous luster to the coven of Sarthath Oob. The prospect was horrible to contemplate, and Hormatz hurried to consult his collection of gods.

These divinities ranged in size from an amulet of blue paste the length of your middle finger to a rough-hewn monolith of porous lava the height of a full-grown stegosaurus. Some were squat and fat, with features jovial, complacent or sleepy. Others glared beneath crowns of woven vipers, leered with fangs of sparkling black obsidian or howled in graven wrath, brandishing skulls and scorpions in the grasp of multiplex limbs.

In oracular response to the theomancer's queries, a brass godlet from the Southern Polar Continent informed them that Fremmoun had indeed borne with him from the star Srendix a ponderous volume bound in diplodocus hide, whose contents were, however, unknown to him.

A triple-headed eidolon from age-lost Hyperborea, fashioned from a pillar of flint, reported that the sorcerer Nelibar Zux had recently canceled a scheduled tour of the astral plane and remained in the seclusion of his subterranean palace, presumably deep in study of the famous Compendium of advanced sorcery.

The remainder of Hormatz's collection of carven gods professed ignorance in the matter.

"Perhaps the brothers, Themnon and Thoy, can inform you as to the current activities of our rival, Sarthath Oob," suggested the decrepit theomancer. The young karcist offered hasty thanks and departed at once for their abode.

The necromancer Themnon and his twin, the warlock Thoy, dwelt together in a mansion of gray stone on the east face of Mount Ong. Chan selected the shortest path, but it was late afternoon before he reached their mansion, a somber and ominous structure, built on a glassy scarp of glittering quartz which overhung a deep chasm. The mansion bore up a crest of turrets; scarlet lights flickered in its tall, pointed windows; potent runes, cut in pillars of harsh corundum, protected the dwellers therein from unwanted visitors. Before the portal of scaly and verdigris-eaten bronze, a heavy slug-horn hung. Chan set it to his lips and sounded an echoing call. In a few moments the magical fence flickered and went dead; he strode between the pillars and up to the door, which creaked open on rusty hinges. To the worm-eaten lich who served the necromancer and the warlock as butler Chan crisply stated his business and was ushered into a gloomy hall hung with moldy tapestries thick with cobwebs, while the magically animated cadaver stalked into the farther recesses of the mansion to fetch his masters.

II

Themnon was a tall, gaunt necromancer with dull eyes like

unpolished smaragds set in a dour, wrinkled visage. His brother, the warlock Thoy, was short, bald and sleepy. They served the young karcist a black, heady wine of mediocre Atlantean vintage in cups of luminous orichalc and listened without comment to his urgent tale. Chan well knew that naught could excite the necromancer unless it were a newly excavated mummy or an interesting corpse; but the squat warlock was less phlegmatic and more given to social conviviality.

Upon the conclusion of his account, the twins conducted him into the depths of their gloomy mansion. By crumbling stone stairs, made slippery with slimy lichen, they descended to a deep crypt whose stone walls held flaring torches which shed a guttering orange light over a clutter of sarcophagi. Cadavers lay strewn about on the stone floor in various stages of advanced decay. Several closed wooden coffins were drawn up beneath the flickering torches; their lids obviously served the brethren in lieu of desks, for portfolios and tomes lay helter-skelter upon them and scrolls of parchment fashioned from the membrane of pterodactyl wings were tumbled about in a litter of periapts and tomb figurines. The stench of the place was frightful.

With the casual ease born of long practice, gaunt Themnon animated a favorite decomposing lich and queried it as to the current affairs of Sarthath Oob. Chan listened intently but could make nothing from the slurred, liquescent syllables of the animated corpse's mumbled reply. Themnon was accustomed to a certain lack of articulation on the part of his decaying corpses, and easily interpreted the slobbering speech: the leader of the rival enclave had departed that noon from his residence amid the Desolation of Skarm, which lay on the other side of the island, for an unknown destination. Chan could guess all too well that his destination was the famous subterranean palace of the sorcerer Nelibar Zux. He thanked the brothers and hastily departed from that ominous crypt.

Achieving again the open air, he spied the hut of the fair young witch, Azra, far below him at the base of the mountain and upon a sudden whim descended the glassy scarp by means of a narrow ledge which zigzagged down the cliffy face to the brink of the chasm.

On his way he passed the hovel of the shaggy and unkempt old alchemist, Phlomel: a miserable lean-to, a mere shack, filled with stench and bubbling messes, belching forth at that moment a nauseating yellow smoke. He could picture the wild-eyed old souffleur within, acid-stained smock flapping about his skinny shanks, his flying beard smelling of sulphur, as he hopped busily about from alembic to athanor, from crucible to cucurbite, amid roaring fires, seething smokes and amazing fluids. Although the alchemist was a fellow member of the enclave, Chan saw no means by which Phlomel could help him, and thus he passed his hovel without a visit.

The pleasant hut of the witch Azra, who was the only feminine member of the Mount Ong wizards, was situated at the base of the eastern slope at the head of a grassy glade hemmed in by tall bamboo. Like Chan, the witch girl was yet in first youth. Indeed the green-haired girl, with her ripe lips and eyes of sparkling quicksilver, had often prompted him to erotic fancies. Her supple, tawny, high-breasted body and ling lissom legs were entrancing, as was the languor of her smile and the honeyed warmth of her slow, soft, husky voice. Her charms had inspired him to certain overtures which, however, she laughingly rebuffed in a casual way which deprived her refusals of the sting they might otherwise have inflicted on his masculine vanity.

By now the sun had declined in the sky and the west was one splendid vault of tangerine flame. A cheerful light shone from the windows of Azra's hut and it guided him across the darkening meadow to her door where the witch girl greeted him with a friendly smile and an invitation to enter. His pulses thrummed at the beauty of her lithe form, which her carefree costume—consisting of a silken scarf tied loosely about her hips and a small idol of green porcelain suspended between her bare, pointed breasts by a thong—did little to conceal.

Azra's hut was cozy and comfortable. A magical fire of sizzling blue flames danced on the stone hearth without need of arboreal fuel. A cage of woven rattan housed a tame archeopteryx which squawked and snapped its fanged beak at his entry. A decoction of herb tea simmered in a kettle hung above the flames and fresh mangoes and pawpaws were arrayed temptingly in a wooden bowl on the table. The fragrance of the tea and the glossy rondure of the ripe fruit recalled to Chan the fact that he had not eaten since long before his invocation of the diabolus, mid-morn at least; thus without hesitancy he accepted Azra's invitation to dine.

While at table with the nearly nude witch girl, Chan conveyed a brief narrative of the day's adventures and the disappointing failure of their colleagues, Hormatz, Themnon and

Thoy, to suggest a remedy. The green-haired girl responded with sympathy to his woeful tale.

"Tomorrow evening a full meeting of the enclave is scheduled," Azra reminded him. "Surely our brethren in full council should be informed of these dire events and may perchance arrive at a mode of redressing them."

He agreed that the best course to follow was to lay the matter in the collective laps of the enclave, and to postpone any further efforts of his own until the following eve. Then, warmed by the tea and excited by her casual state of undress, he again made amorous overtures. And again she smilingly denied him her body and gracefully eluded his embrace in such a manner as to cause no affront. His protests—that night was upon them and his own house far above, while her bed was capacious enough to shelter both of them—went unheard. And so he was forced to trudge wearily up the mountain again to his own house of red stone and to his empty, lonely bed.

III

Eldest and most powerful of the twelve wizards of Ong was the Archimage, Doctor Pellsipher, who resided in a villa of rose marble and mellow ivory atop the utmost peak and pinnacle of the magic mountain. The Archimage served the local wizards as magister, or presiding officer, of their enclave, and Chan had no doubt but that Doctor Pellsipher would turn a most sympathetic ear to his urgent news. For nothing was more dear to Pellsipher's heart than his ambition to preside over a full, authentic coven, and the fact that their enclave lacked a thirteenth member, which was the chief prerequisite for covenhood, was a matter of considerable complaint by the membership in general and Doctor Pellsipher in particular. They had often discussed means of enticing or persuading or coercing one more practitioner of the Secret Sciences to join them on the slopes of Mount Ong, and it was the Archimage himself who most frequently voiced the opinion that their thirteenth member should be a sorcerer. As the enclave already consisted of an Archimage, a karcist, a theomancer, a witch, an haruspex, an alchemist, a warlock, a necromancer, a conjurer, a magician, an astrologer and a theurgist, there were few occult disciplines not represented among them. Thus they could pick and choose as to adding to their enclave a diabolist, a sorcerer, a thaumaturge or an

enchanter. And it was the emphatic opinion of Doctor Pellsipher that a full-fledged sorcerer was what they most needed.

Pellsipher's villa was complex and baroque, all balconies
and cupolas and ornamental balustrades, minarets, pavilions
and belvederes. While it clung to the very pinnacle of the
mountain's crest, the remainder of the peak had, by afreets
subject to the doctor's art, been leveled into artificial terraces,
which now bloomed with lush gardens and exotic pleas-
aunces. Archaic sculpture rose amid the nodding cycads; gaze-
bos stood in lotus pools; arched bridges spanned wandering
artificial streamlets; paper lanterns swayed from the palmy
boughs of club-mosses and tree-ferns, glowing like luminous
and cycloptic eyes through the purpureal dusk. The villa was
a faerie structure of carven ornamentation; jeweled mosaics
twinkled through rows of fluted pilasters, fountains splashed
in miniature courts, screens of fretted ivory shielded nooks
and niches where lamps of pierced silver shed a warm
luminance.

Despite his concern and the importance of the occasion,
for one reason or another Chan was the last of the wizards to
arrive for the meeting of the enclave. He was admitted by a
voiceless figure of sparkling brass, one of the marvelous au-
tomata for which the Archimage had been famed for several
millennia; it looked like a man in jointed, fantastical armor,
the visor of his helm closed. But Chan knew it was an ingenious clockwork mechanism and neither alive nor mortal.

He was ushered into the great domed hall, which was
roofed by a vast cupola of milky glass supported atop twenty
slender pillars of spiral-fluted rose quartz. His eleven colleagues were already in attendance: Spay, Phlomel, Velb the
Irithribian, Themnon, Thoy, Master Quinibus, Azra, Hormatz, Kedj the Conjuror, Zoramus of Pankoy and Doctor
Pellsipher. He bowed slightly to their host and magister and
made his apologies for his unseemly lateness.

"Tut, my boy, not another word! These monthly assem-
blages are, as ever, mere informal social gatherings, and strict
attendance is neither desired nor enforced," the Archimage
rejoined in a hearty manner. This Pellsipher was a large,
jovial, not-unhandsome man, whose good humor and elephantine courtliness made him generally popular with all,
despite his pompous and pontifical tone. He customarily
dressed in the height of Antillian fashion, and this evening he
was, as usual, resplendent in a nine-tiered hat of scarlet
crepe, a many-pleated cloak of striped pink and vermilion

taffeta, high-laced buskins of orange plush and a beautifully
draped undertoga of peach silk with a tasseled violet fringe.
He wore a jeweled talismanic ring on each finger and in his
left hand he bore an ivory baton carved to the likeness of a
winged caduceus. This last was a mere ornament; his Blasting
Rod, the badge of his science, was too uncouth an instrument
to be borne into polite society.

Patting the young karcist on the shoulder affably, Pellsipher guided him to a long table where a cold buffet supper
had been laid out by mechanical servants. Chan had not
eaten before arrival so he did not scruple, but heaped a porcelain plate with stuffed figs, smoked oysters, cheese paté,
miniature sandwiches, a dab or two of mint jelly and small
cubes of spiced meat speared through with silver toothpicks.
A brass servitor was at his elbow with a crystal goblet of
chilled, sparkling yellow wine.

"Ah, my dear friends, how delightful to see you all here, in
splendid health, I trust, and making excellent progress in your
art? Azra, my dear, ravishing as always! My good Phlomel, I
declare we have civilized you at last: a clean smock, on my
aura!" Pellsipher boomed expansively.

Munching away, Chan covertly eyed the witch girl. She
was somewhat more formally dressed for this occasion than
she had been on their last meeting, although her raiment still
left her deliciously rounded and coral-peaked right breast
bare. The rest of her was gowned in platinum lamé: a gorget
of iridium was clasped about her throat, set, he observed,
with uncut but polished emeralds and moony pearls from the
isle of Zatoum, which set off, respectively, her sea-green hair
and lovely quicksilver eyes.

Still chatting with Phlomel the wild-eyed old alchemist,
who did indeed look somewhat less disreputable this evening
than on previous occasions, the jovial Pellsipher was interrupted by Spay, the tall and bony haruspex, who dourly observed
that, clean smock or no, Phlomel's dingy beard still was redo-
lent of sulphur and chemical messes. Pellsipher nodded,
beamed and overrode this comment by inquiring after the alchemist's progress. In his croaking voice, rusty from disuse,
Phlomel reported happily that he had achieved the Green
Lion transformation and was well on the way to synthesizing
the Azoth, as the ultimate goal of all the sages of his profession was called. Spay grumpily commented that by the time
the disheveled old *pouffleur* achieved his Azoth young Atlantis
should have joined elder Mu beneath the waves, but no one

was listening as Pellsipher was by then loudly interrogating his colleague, the eminent magician Zoramus, on the progress of his breeding vats—Zoramus being involved in a century-long experiment in the creation of artificial homunculi.

The suave, courtly magician, a tall and distinguished gentleman in a narrow robe of lavender satin sprinkled with minute golden amulets, silver slippers and a heavy pectoral of massy gold which was, Chan knew, a genuine magical relic of antique Hyperborean work, quietly rejoined that his latest mutations were only partially satisfactory. He was then attempting to breed a flower-headed human, but the hybrid proved cretinous and had to be dissolved in the acid tanks.

"Regrettable, most regrettable," tut-tutted Pellsipher. "Your vat creatures will yet earn you the well-deserved applause of your fellow magicians; persevere, my dear chap, persevere!"

"Such is my intention, Magister," Zoramus assured him, smoothing his neat silver beard with a carefully manicured left hand. "The error doubtless lies in the blending of nutrients, for I embued the creature with an excellent brain and his idiocy must be traceable to a faulty blend of protein froth. I know the brain was of the finest for I procured it myself from a strapping young male slave from the island of Thang, and before attempting the surgical transference I myself tended to the slave's tutoring."

"Splendid, my dear fellow! Persevere; success will yet crown your endeavors, I am certain of it!" beamed the Archimage.

As the magician stepped to the buffet, their genial host turned to query the dreamy-eyed astrologer who stood at his elbow.

"Master Quinibus, I will have your opinion on a most interesting artifact I recently procured on the isle of Ompharos; it was uncovered in the Valley of Silver Tombs by a ghoul of my acquaintance; a fellow of disgusting habits, of course, but no mean antiquarian, I assure you!" Drawing the languid astrologer aside, he indicated a ceramic cylinder of brick-red, incised with time-worn cuneiform, which stood on a jasper pedestal.

His plate empty, Chan left it on the table and followed Themnon and Velb and Zoramus who were drifting into an antechamber where low curule chairs of mastodon ivory were drawn in a half-circle about a modest podium. Once these mandatory social amenities were concluded, the business session would commence and he could present his information to general discussion.

IV

As Chan expected, his presentation of the matter to the assembled wizards threw the throng into a fury of consternation, and repeated remonstrances by their magister failed to restore the enclave to quietude.

When at last order was established, Pellsipher asked for suggestions from the floor.

"As you all know," he said in a state of quivering agitation, "this matter lies close to my heart, and I cannot but hold it a problem of the gravest import. We all owe a debt of gratitude to our young karcist for pursuing the event and thus bringing it to our attention. I will now hear queries or motions from the floor. Ah, my dear Velb, your hand is raised: may we have silence for our esteemed theurgical colleague."

Velb the Irithribian, a dwarfish little theurgist noted for his waspish temper, spoke up first.

"Sorcery is a discipline alien to my own studies," he observed. "What is this Compendium and who is this Paroul?" In his pontifical, expansive manner, the Archimage explained that the sorcerer Paroul had been an ornament to the reign of Gledrion, Grand Prince of Ib, an island to the east, in a remote epoch. "The practice of sorcery," he went on, "employs spoken spells, mantra and cantrips. A master sorcerer, such as the distinguished Paroul, bends his efforts to composing new, more complex and powerful cantrips. Of such is the famous Compendium composed; possession of the volume gives one access to the most advanced mantra ever created."

Velb the Irithribian tugged at his perfumed indigo beard. "Very well! But what is all this about the star Srendix, a luminary, I believe, found in the constellation of the Gargoyle? How did this book find its way thither?"

"Since a sorcerer's power lies in written spells, anyone who captures such a volume from its rightful owner gains possession of his full art," Pellsipher explained. "Unlike, for example, a witch—such as our charming Mistress Azra here—whose supernatural powers derive from a learned knowledge of herbal lore and natural philosophy; or, for that matter, a theurgist such as yourself, who commands the diabolic and celestial intelligences through usage of the Names of Power, which reside in your memory and not on the parchment page."

"Yes, yes," Velb snapped pettishly. "But what of Srendix?"

"To insure his privacy and safety from envious and malign fellow practitioners of the Art Sorcerous, the distinguished Paroul caused a winged elemental to transport himself and the contents of his librarium to this distant orb whereon certain afreets bound to his service constructed a palatial abode to his own design. Millennia passed and eventually Paroul succumbed to his innate mortality—which can be postponed for an era or two, as every wizard knows, but which cannot be put off forever."

"Whereafter this Nelibar Zux dispatched his sylph to the ultra-telluric abode and thus gained possession of the precious Compendium, I see, I see." Having the matter thus detailed to his satisfaction, the theurgist Velb lapsed into thoughtful silence.

Some further discussion eventuated; at length the obvious course was agreed upon: the Ong enclave would send a delegation to the subterranean palace of the augmented Zux and reiterate their offer of membership. As night was wearing on and argumentation over the precise composition of the delegation might well consume the remainder of the time, Pellsipher took the matter into his own hands.

"Naturally, I, as magister of the enclave, shall head the delegation and tender our invitation in person as a mark of respect. As to the further members of the party, I select our young karcist, Chan, who, as the individual most responsible for bringing these events to our attention, has a vested personal interest in their successful conclusion. Yet a third representative is needed: I suggest our esteemed colleague, Zoramus."

"Alas, my latest crop of vat creatures are approaching their maturity and I cannot, at present, spare the time," responded that individual.

"Very well: Master Quinibus, then."

The astromancer declined as well, pleading a rare conjugation of the planets demanded his attentions. Pellsipher became disconcerted. The remainder of the enclave were disappointing choices: Phlomel made a poor appearance; Spay the haruspex was distinguished enough in his person, but his Art, like that of Kedj, was hardly high enough in the hierarchy of the Secret Sciences to form a good impression on the mind of Nelibar Zux. He was debating between the remainder when the witch girl stood, her lithe figure sheathed in sparkling lamé, her sea-green hair pouring down her slender tawny shoulders.

"If the magister will permit, my work does not demand my presence for some days and I will be happy to join the expedition," she said in her warm, throaty voice.

And thus it was decided. They would depart at dawn.

V

Chan rose before dawn, nibbled absently at a hearty meal laid out for him by captive spirits, while selecting his wardrobe and magical appurtenances for the voyage to Zatoum, where dwelt the sorcerer. He chose high scarlet boots, a brief kilt of rust and umber wool, patterned after his tribal tartan, and a loose while silk blouse to be worn under a tough jerkin of canary leather. Around his shoulders he slung his famous Live Blade in its dragonhide scabbard and baldric; to his shoulder tabs he affixed a cunningly designed Weather Cloak with cairngorm brooches; and he took up his waystaff, although it did not seem likely he should need it. Still, you never know.

Thus accoutered, he summoned his attendant spirits, demons, afreets and intelligences, sternly bade them keep to the premises, tend to his various long-term magical experiments, ward against intruders, rogues, thieves and interlopers; he then sealed the windows and portals with potent wards which could be released only by the proximity of his own aura and strode up the mountain to Pellshiper's villa.

In a columned arcade of the eastern wing he found the jubilant Archimage and the witch girl preparing Pellsipher's rare aerial gondola for the sky voyage. The Archimage affected an elaborate undertoga of mauve gauze, pleated and gathered in many folds, over which he wore an expensive Armor Cloak that was a product of troglodytic enchanters. A quiver strapped to the magister's back contained slim homotropic javelins of frail glass suffused with the venom of the horned Cerastes serpent, a loathly ophidian found in the Gorgon Isles. The old magister bore with him his mighty Blasting Rod which hummed and thrummed with power. His far-seeing helm of magical crystalloid he wore upon his brows: it gave him an unwontedly martial and even heroic appearance.

The witch girl was clad in an abbreviated tunic of tough

woven silver fibers, magically rendered supple; high-laced sandals and sparkling greaves of perdurable orichalc guarded her lovely shins; her breasts were protected in cups of silver filigree, and a small oval buckler, composed of seven thicknesses of brontosaurus hide, tanned in the bile of basilisks and riveted together with diamond screws, was strapped to her forearm. She wore a coronet of silver set with fire opals and her seaweed-green hair flowed unbound over her shoulders. Chan found her ravishing, her usual nymphette beauty enhanced by the Amazonian war dress. She bore no visible weapons, but pouches and flasks of potent liqueurs and powders hung from her metallic girdle.

As he approached through the slim alabaster columns of the arcade, Chan observed the famous gondola which lay on the tesselated pave of alternate squares of iridescent black jade and lapis lazuli. The slim-hulled boat was constructed of light, polished wood: perhaps twenty feet from stem to stern; it was equipped with three comfortable chairs bound firmly to the inner structure with leather thongs. A silken canopy shielded the occupants from the sun and the elements, raised on twisting, gilded poles. Gondola-like, poop and prow rose in graceful spiraling foliations. Chan had heard much of the famous vessel but had never chanced to see it before, and much less to venture upon the unstable winds therein.

"Ah, my boy, a perfectly timed arrival," the genial Archimage beamed at his approach. "My aerial contrivance is prepared and ready; naught restrains us from an immediate departure. After you, my dear!"

Helping the witch girl clamber aboard, Doctor Pellsipher guided her to the rearmost of the three chairs, indicated that Chan should make himself comfortable in the midmost, while clambering with agility surprising for one of his not-inconsiderable millennia into the foremost.

Ingenious belts strapped them securely in place, so that a chance wind might not dislodge them from their seats. When his colleagues were securely harnessed, the magister activated the magical adjuncts of the vessel. These consisted of a bulbous flask of thick crystal wherein a mixture of pulverized cinnabar, powdered emeralds, crushed orichalcum nuggets and desiccated moontree seeds seethed in a slime of hissing acids. Pellsipher had timed the transformation to a nicety: as the last belt was buckled, a sudden flash of nine-colored radiance illuminated the glassy globe. Chan perceived a roiling vapor exuded by the potent mixture. The hue of mingled azure and chartreuse was the tincture of the uncanny mist, which thickened visibly, filling the sphere until it became opaque.

At the same instant, the aerial gondola became buoyant. It trembled, shivered, wobbled—and floated up from the tessel-ated pave. Pellsipher uttered a Word; the prow veered to portside and the contrivance glided between two pillars and drfited out over the gardens. Now a strong up-draft caught and cupped the knife-slim hull. The vessel inclined steeply and shot skyward with alacrity. After it achieved a height of five thousand feet, Pellsipher halted the upward motion with a second Word; next he directed the floating skyboat due west with a third powerful vocable. And the voyage was be-gun!

Mount Ong is situated toward the thickly jungled interior of Thosk, which is the larger of the two westernmost of the Isles of Antillia. Thosk, indeed, is the second largest of the isles and its extent is considerable. Zatoum, their goal, is far smaller, and is itself the very westernmost of the archipelago.

Soon the mountain of the twelve wizards dwindled behind them. They passed over the Ymbrian Hills. They traversed the Green Plains of Nool, observing with amusement a graz-ing herd of burly aurochs reduced to the stature of Minikins from the perspective of their height. They flew across the rivers of Ska and Osk. They approached the outer suburbs of Palmyrium, the capital of the isle and the residence of the current Emperor, Mumivor, twenty-third regnant monarch of that name.

Azra's eyes sparkled with interest as she gazed down on this splendid metropolis. She had yet to visit it; this was, in fact, the first time she had even seen it, and to observe it from this unique aerial vantage point lent an extra fillip of excitement to the experience.

In truth, it was a most fair city, splendid with domes of green copper, superb with thronged minarets of alabaster, pink coral and yellow sandstone. Broad boulevards and awn-ing-shaded arcades stretched beneath them. Quaint houses roofed with indigo tile cupped secluded gardens where palmy cycads were mirrored in still ponds. Bazaars seethed with market-day throngs, crowded booths, strolling jugglers.

The imperial city passed slowly beneath them. Now the blue harbor lay below. High-prowed galleys from young At-lantis swayed at anchor along stone quays. As well, stately triremes with sails of purple and orange lay at anchor, come from the last few surviving isles of foundering Mu. Fat-bellied merchant ships from remote Antichthon, as the mysterious south polar continent was named, lay berthed beside rakish corsair galleys with slim black hulls and ominous scarlet sails.

Now they flew beyond the harbor and out over the Deep Green Sea. Thosk receded behind them; Zatoum, the last isle of Antillia, lay dead ahead.

VI

Suddenly a hoarse, raucous cry broke the whispering silence of their windy height. Chan jerked about from his dreamy contemplation of dwindling Thosk to observe a horrendous peril flapping swiftly toward them.

It was a monstrous flying reptile with clawed, bat-like wings, fanged jaws agape, red eyes burning like coals. Even an aerial voyage, the karcist discovered, is not without its hazards.

The predator of the upper air, a gigantic pteranodon, swept down upon them with such velocity that it had struck their craft before any of them could utter a protective Name or direct a single blast of deathly force. In an instant its terrible bird claws squeaked and crunched and clung to the edge of the hull. They stared into blind, mad eyes of depthless rapacity. Its stinking breath blew over them like the reek of an open grave. Even Pellsipher sat frozen, immobile, voiceless.

But Chan's Live Blade was indoctrinated for such a moment and it flashed from its scabbard and slapped its hilt into his lax palm. Almost before his fingers could curl about the pommel the curved blade of the ensorcelled scimitar had hissed in a sparkling stroke, slashing deep in the lean, scaly throat of the pteranodon. Vile, oily reptilian gore leaked from the great wound, gliding down the length of the extended neck in nauseating rivulets.

The Live Blade swung back for another stroke, dragging Chan's arm with it unresistingly. The sentient yellow crystal set in the pommel of the scimitar glittered like a living eye.

But the aerial reptile had suffered a terrible wound, and had lost its appetite. Voicing an ear-splitting screech it abandoned its prey and swerved fluttering away, the skyboat wobbling at an unstable pitch as it loosed its clutches on the gunwales.

So swiftly had the attack occurred and so swiftly had

Chan's sword beaten off the attacker that the occupants of
the gondola still sat frozen in shock. But Chan fancied he
caught a certain unwonted warmth in the gaze Azra turned
upon him; a certain admiration shone in her sparkling eyes.

Had there been sufficient leisure to indulge in self-congrat-
ulation, Chan doubtless would have basked in a feeling of
heroic manliness. But, alas, new perils were upon the travelers in the next instant.

The Archimage paled, gave voice to an inarticulate cry of
alarm and called their attention to the globe which contained
the levitational vapor. In its precipitous retreat from the
skyboat, the pteranodon must have struck either its gaunt
claws or the hard bony fore-edge of a wing against the
sphere, for it had cracked badly and the magical vapor of
buoyancy was escaping with rapidity.

Consternation seized the voyagers. As yet they had not
achieved even the beaches of Zatoum. Still the briny waves of
the Deep Green Sea dashed below the keel of their aerial
craft. True, the small jungle isle was visible on the expanse of
ocean ahead . . . but already the ensorcelled gondola was
losing altitude, sinking with alarming velocity toward the
waves.

Pellsipher pressed the talismanic alexandrite he wore on his
left thumb to the broken sphere and activated a potent
Sealing Spell, thus halting the escape of any further vapors.
The black zigzag cracks melted from view as the glassy substance healed its fractures. A portion of the buoyant vapor
still remained within the crystal orb, but not, however,
enough to alleviate markedly their unfortunate decline.

But wizards are seldom at a complete loss to arrest an un-
happy turn of events.

Doctor Pellsipher activated his Flying Ring, a fiery carnel-
ian set in a hoop of black silver on his left index finger.

Azra plucked from her knap a packet of iridescent powder
and sprinkled it about the gondola: this, we may assume, en-
gendered weightlessness and was used by sorceresses of her
rank to fly to the sabbat.

As for Chan the karcist, he uttered a summoning Word
which commanded a minor sylph, and bade the airy spirit to
sustain the sinking gondola with all its strength.

Between the three varieties of magic and what little remained of the buoyant vapor in the flask, the gondola managed to reach the shores of Zatoum safely, permitting the
exhausted voyagers to disembark on dry land. But having

done so, the craft, its sustaining powers vitiated, lay lifeless on the coral sand and would fly no more.

Drained by the tension, anxiety and precipitous employment of their wizardly powers, the three adventurers sprawled gasping on the shores of the jungle island. A league of dense vegetation, crawling with venomous reptiles and a-prowl with hungry predators, lay between them and the subterranean palace of Nelibar Zux. Formerly they had intended to loll at their ease in the flying gondola while it traversed these steaming fens and thick jungles; now they must struggle afoot.

These were the thoughts which raced through their minds as they sprawled on the powdery sands. Nor were they pleasant considerations.

At length Pellsipher, recovering, rose and examined his precious craft anxiously.

"I do hope, Magister," said Chan, "that the injuries to your boat are not permanent, else we shall be marooned here without hope of returning to Thosk."

Pellsipher reluctantly shook his head. Sighing, he said, "The craft itself is not injured in the slightest, but without recourse to the lifting powers of the vapor it is as useless to us as if 'twere shivered to splinters."

"Are the vapors dispersed beyond hope?" the witch girl queried.

The magister shrugged gloomily. "The admixture of ingredients whose interaction produces the buoyant vapor yet remain within the sphere. In time, I trust the chemical action will generate sufficient gas to render my gondola skyworthy again. However, I estimate that it will be no less than twenty hours before we can expect to be airborne."

"Twenty hours!" Chan cried. "And Sarthath Oob departed in his flying chariot yesterday morn! Surely he has arrived long since and is even now seeking to enlist the sorcerer in his abominable coven. All is lost, then."

Pellsipher had, by now, regained much of his lost ebullience. "Not so," he countered. "If we cannot fly, we can at least walk. This isle is minuscule compared to Thosk, and surely 'twill take but a few hours to gain the portals of the underground abode of Zux."

Chan glanced dubiously at the jungle which hemmed in the small beach like a solid wall of greenery, but said nothing.

"Come," puffed Pellsipher with determined cheerfulness. "There is no time like the present; well begun is half done; and the journey of a thousand leagues is conquered in the first step. These and other homely apothegms suggest we had best be up and walking!"

They advanced to the borders of the jungle. Chan drew his scimitar and began to cut a passage through the tangled growth.

VII

After an hour or two, the young karcist was content to pass the sword into Pellsipher's hands and lag behind.

"My Live Blade is tireless," he admitted. "But I am not!"

Pellsipher chopped vigorously at the vines and branches which intertwined to obstruct their path. "Tut, my dear boy! No apologies are necessary. This scimitar of yours is marvelously keen, I must say." He paused, admiring the glittering edge. "After being put to this yeoman labor, 'tis still as sharp as a fine razor."

Chan explained that it had been forged, in Tartarean fires, from the burnt-out core of a fallen star and tempered seven times by plunging the smoking steel into the bile of a crucible of seething venom. 'Twas the work, he noted, of cunning Troglodytes.

The dense undergrowth gradually diminished as they penetrated deeper into the interior. Now the lofty boles of tall Jurassic conifers soared to either side like the columns of some awesome cathedral. As Chan hacked a clear path through a bush of bristling spiny leaves some intuition bade him hesitate.

He uttered an exclamation of surprise and halted, seizing the magister, who was blundering along at his heels, and restraining his progress forcibly.

"What in the name of thirty devils is it, my boy?" the Archimage demanded testily as Chan jostled him aside.

"Look!" Chan cried, pointing downward at the base of the spiny-leaved bush. His companions halted, and Azra sank to her knees with a gasp of marvel and amazement.

A village of Minikins lay at their feet. A cluster of tiny huts, cleverly woven of dried grasses and roofed with thick rubbery leaves. The village warriors had noted the approach of the full-sized humans and had given the alarm. As the travelers bent in fascination over the scene, diminutive mothers, scarce a finger-length in height, scurried for shelters dug under the roots of the bush, bearing to safety babes no bigger than small fat grubs, while the males, armed with slender, sharp black thorns, formed a protective ring about the outskirts of the tiny town. They brandished boldly their minuscule weapons, shrilling faint war cries.

"A rarity! A genuine curiosity!" Pellsipher exclaimed. "Seldom are Minikins observed in their natural habitat these
days; pray note, my friends, the cunning of the tiny creatures,
whom the chance step of a careless beast could crush to a
damp smear: to protect themselves from this ever-present
peril they construct their miniature metropolis under this
spiny and unpleasant bush whose jagged edged leafage would
doubtless be avoided by most tender-skinned animals. Note
further the admirable use the small beings have made of the
castaway artifacts of nature!" He drew their attention to the
war helms of the Minikin civic guard, which were hard hollow acorns; to their shields, the horny carapace of dead
beetles; to their swords, tubular thorns, charged with a poisonous or stinging nettle-venom which oozed in oily droplets
from the keen points thereof; and to their armor, consisting
of chest-coverings, gauntlets, greaves and loin-guards cut
from the dead, discarded skins of serpents.

Chan marveled that a folk so small could be so brave; he
reflected that boldness is an attitude of mind not relative to
matters of mere size.

In a low, clear whisper—softened so as not to burst minute
eardrums—he said, "Do not fear us, little men; we will not
harm you. Observe that I halted my companion lest he unwittingly trample you underfoot."

The leader of the Minikin war band, a handsomely formed
young princeling, brandished his thorn and bowed. "Our
thanks for your kindness, sir traveler!" he shrilled in a piping
voice. "Seldom do we receive aught but brutal and careless
treatment from Big Folk, hence forgive our natural alarm
and threatening motions, if you please!"

Chan repressed a smile at the thought of being "threatened" by warriors no taller than his forefinger was long,
but replied in courteous words to this polite speech. Their
alarm ended, the lady Minikins were timidly emerging from
their protective burrows under the roots; they clustered in
whispering groups, shyly holding up their babes to Azra's
admiration and piping faint comments to each other on her
mode of dress. They also eyed the broad shoulders and muscular thighs of the handsome young karcist who stood by her
protectively and giggled to one another.

As for the Minikin juveniles, who were no larger than

plump aphids, they rapidly lost their shyness of the Big Folk and scampered and played between their sequoia-vast legs. Chan dared not shift his feet lest he inadvertently harm one of them.

The Minikin princeling, whose name was Zixt, engaged Dr. Pellsipher in converse. In a shrill, piping voice, whose tones were made more audible as he employed a hollow snail shell for his speaking trumpet, he inquired as to their origins, explaining that few Big Folk dwelt on the isle and the presence of a stranger was a rare event. Listening to the exchange, Chan reflected with amusement that to such as the Minikins the isle of Zatoum was doubtless on the scale of a fair-sized continent. Prince Zixt was also intrigued at their mode of transport hither, when he learned they were visitors from the next isle come to tender their respects to Zatoum's resident sorcerer. To such as the Minikins, of course, the modest interval of sea between the two islands was a gulf of impassable vastness.

These and other queries Pellsipher answered good-humoredly. The conversation terminated in a gracious exchange of compliments and well-wishes, and Pellsipher expressed their desire to continue their journey before nightfall and requested that the Minikin juveniles be withdrawn from their proximity to his boots for their own safety, which plea was granted with all alacrity. The travelers then resumed their expedition without further ado; but the encounter was a rare marvel and one they would long remember.

VIII

During the several hours consequent to this adventure, the three envoys traversed the jungles of Zatoum without further incident. They emerged toward sunset in the vicinity of the residence of the sorcerer, and regarded with some dismay the havoc their journey had wreaked upon their persons: exquisite raiment was bedraggled, torn by thorny vines, soiled with leaf mulch, stained with perspiration exuded from their fatiguing exertions. They would present a sorry sight to the discriminating eyes of Nelibar Zux. But at least they had achieved their goal unscathed by the numerous predators whose hunting cries made the jungle gloom hideous.

The entrance to the subterranean palace of the celebrated Zux was the mouth of the cavern which gaped in the flank of a sheer cliff of glittering quartz. And "mouth" proved a term singularly apt, for the black portal was hung with dangling stalactites which almost met the upthrust of squat, tusk-like stalagmites, and the overall resembled the fanged maw of a yawning monster.

This portal fronted upon a grassy glade, and the plenipotentiaries from Mount Ong were relieved to observe no visible signs of their adversary, the nefarious Oob, thereabouts. Was it possible that his flying chariot had not yet arrived? Had he perchance encountered ill luck in his voyage, comparable to their own? Or had he come and gone, and was his purpose already achieved? Had Nelibar Zux been enlisted in the rival enclave with all due solemnities, hours since, while they were busily cutting their path through the umbrageous foliage?

Unable to resolve these doubts, the travelers made as neat as possible their disarranged garments and approached the black mouth of the cavern, whereupon they lingered for a time, uncertain of what means to call their presence to the attention of the resident sorcerer. At length they entered the gloomy portal, finding themselves at one end of an unilluminated tunnel hewn—whether by the patient workings of nature or the deliberate act of art they could not say—from the solid mineral of the cliff.

The resourceful Pellsipher evoked the powers latent in one of his several talismanic rings, molding a sphere of pallid radiance out of thin air. This luminous orb floated before them as they cautiously traversed the length of the cavern; it shed a vague but sufficient light whereby they could proceed without fear of treading upon an unseen viper in the dark.

At the nether end of the cavern they observed a portal of red marble, unwholesomely veined with blue and wetly lustrous; with a fastidious moue of repugnance, the girl Azra noted the resemblance of this curious mineral to raw human flesh.

Passing through, the envoys discovered a sequence of untenanted apartments decorated with voluptuous luxury but lapsed most oddly into a neglect which bordered on decay. Floor, walls and groined and vaulted roofs were faced with marbles similar to those of the portal without, marbles repellently suggestive of raw meat and flayed flesh. The nakedness of this stonework, however, was relieved by tapestries of superb antique workmanship, whose design and weave were subtly disturbing. Each arras bore curious curvilinear motifs, and it was difficult to perceive whether it was meant to suggest entangled human intestines, a nest of squirming serpents or a congeries of loathsome worms.

The floors of the sumptuous suites were cluttered with a litter of priceless treasure and grisly human remnants. Platinum bowls overflowed with baroque pearls and lucent amethysts; sacks burst with coins of silver, gold and precious orichalc; chests of sandalwood gaped brokenly, leaking moony opals and winy sapphires. Figurines of jade and malachite lay tossed about helter-skelter amid tangled carpets of woven and lustrous silks. It would seem they had stumbled upon the treasury of an emperor or the trove of corsairs who had amassed the plunder of a dozen cities.

But strewn amid this glittering wealth were white bones and the withered segments of mummies: a dried and severed hand lay half-submerged in uncut zircons looted from the isles that border Atlantis; human knucklebones were intermingled in a heap of silver coins cut with the cartouches of extinct Lemurian dynasties; a gaunt skull grinned toothily atop a pile of alabaster statuettes of rare Hyperborean craft.

These and other gruesome mementos of mortality, dispersed as they were amid artifacts of noble metals and precious jewelry, seemed present for no other purpose than to point a moral. Perhaps, Chan reflected, they were strewn about in such proximity to the treasures to remind the beholder that wealth is but rubbish, and death the inexorable terminus of life. If so, these mementos succeeded, for they cast a ghoulish pall over the splendid plunder.

The apartments wherethrough they wandered in bewilderment were lit with ten thousand waxen candles, and so Pellsipher dispersed his Witchlight. The forest of tapers rose at every hand, weeping thick tears of glutinous wax on gemmed icons, eidola exquisitely carved from mammoth ivory and superb textiles. But the sheer prodigality of such illumination puzzled the young karcist: why lighten the gloom of empty and untenanted chambers with such a largesse of fine tapers? 'Twas but another of the myriad mysteries of this subterranean realm.

They strolled on through vestibules choked with the dowries of empresses, through antechambers heaped with wealth sufficient to ransom a score of satraps, but nowhere in all this gruesomely littered redundancy of wealth did they espy a living thing. From the corner of their eyes a flicker of movement froze them with alarm: but, when they turned, ever and again it was to observe nothing corporeal. It was a

subtle business, the furtive twitching aside of the corner of an
arras, a stealthy slither of motion half-glimpsed in a far, dim
corner, a fleeting flicker of something caught in a momentary
reflection. But it unnerved them all; Pellsipher, pale and
sweating, wiped his heavy moon-face on a soiled and thorn-
rent sleeve, eyes showing their whites as he cast a fearful
glance at a distant ghost of movement; Azra, clutching at
Chan's arm, stifled a half-voiced cry of alarm at a mocking
swarthy face glimpsed in a silver mirror. But if they were observed, it was by furtive, slinking things that dared not challenge them.

Down a vast, uncoiling stairway of porphyry they went,
the ivory balustrade a single curving horn of some unthinkable abnormality whose true size made them shudder to guess
at; and the lower levels they found identical to those above:
everywhere a careless profusion of incredible wealth, be-
strewn with bony or mummified relics as if in grimly philosophical emphasis on the evanescence of human affairs; ever
the stealthy and secretive flicker of movement on the very
border of vision, yet never a firm confrontation with whatever being or essence made of this dreadful treasurehouse its
home.

Suddenly, amid the vastness of a hall of shadowy immen-
sity whose walls were hung with peculiar tapestries of inter-
woven swordblades and whose portals were veiled by
glistening wet human eyeballs threaded like ghastly beads on
cords of scarlet silk, they espied a ponderous volume bound
in dinosaur skin. The tome stood atop a pedestal of lead,
sealed beneath a crystal dome. It was curious that, of all the
numerous compendia of magical and occult science doubtless
included in the librarium of Nelibar Zux, one book alone
should deserve such protection. They advanced across the
glossy floor of black emerald to peruse this rarity.

As the three travelers approached, there impinged upon
their auras the vibrations of immense magical force. It was
Doctor Pellsipher who first guessed the nature of the rever-
ently enshrined book. He paled and his eyes gleamed with
half-fearful triumph.

"Ah, my dear colleagues," he whispered, "now I will hazard that this volume is none other than the prestigious and
long-sought Compendium of the august Paroul!"

As they came up before the pedestal, Chan perceived this
to have been a fortuitous guess. For even his unskillful eyes
could read the superscription of glyphs painted upon diplod-

ocus leather, whereof was fashioned the covers of the book, although he was but poorly schooled in the antique charactry current in the remote epoch of Gledrion of Ib.

"You are right!" he exclaimed. "It is the Compendium of Paroul!" His cry rang out in a thousand booming echoes which were followed upon the instant by a terrific detonation, like the knell of Doom itself. For in that fateful instant, as they stood awestruck before the Compendium, the unseen Watcher who had dogged their steps all this while, struck to immobilize them. With a terrific clangor, as of hollow metallic moons colliding, impenetrable blocks of adamant fell to seal every egress, save for a slitted window too narrow for human passage, and barred, in any event, with a razory grille. The three wizards hurled against these barriers every thaumaturgy in their repertoire, but, alas, in vain. The potent sorceries of Nelibar Zux were proof against the most persuasive cantrip, spell, potion or invocation they possessed.

They were trapped and helpless in the subterranean lair of Nelibar Zux!

IX

"My dear young friend," quavered the disheartened Pellsipher, "have you not some powerful diabolus, vowed to your service, who can shift the weight of these adamantine blocks?"

"I fear not, sir," sighed Chan. "Various of the several afreets and elementals sworn to obey my will have strength sufficient to dismember mountains at my word: but adamant, you know, is proof to the lesser sciences. Azra, perchance you came prepared with some terrific acid or all-dissolving alkahest whereby we might yet free ourselves?"

The witch-girl shook her head sadly, tousling her sea-green tresses. "I came prepared for no such exigency as imprisonment," she confessed.

"And my Blasting Rod is charged with energies sufficient to discarnate half an army," groaned Pellsipher, "but the destructive forces would merely rebound from sheer adamant and, in this confined space, sunder us all to our primal constituents! I fear we are helpless and must, therefore, wait upon the innate kindness and hospitality of our as-yet-unseen jailer, who shall doubtless shower us with apologies and gifts once he discovers us to be accredited envoys of the Mount

Ong enclave and not mere thieves, assassins or trespassers. . . ."

Through the window-slit that alone gave forth on the outer air they perceived darkness had long-since fallen and a wan and gibbous moon gleamed like a cold and ironic eye through the slit upon them.

The dinner hour had fallen, and to the gloom of their prison was added the discomfort of intense hunger; none of them had partaken of nutriment since breakfast many hours ago, and Pellsipher for one, a gourmet of the first order, felt the lack of sustenance most acutely. Thus none was more delighted than he when there melted suddenly from empty air three tables hung with snowy damask and set with platters of smoking fowl in aspic, dewy goblets of excellent vintage in bowls of snow, mounds of ripely lustrous fruit and heaps of crusted pastry sprinkled with the rarest of spices. Their senses were assaulted with the succulent odors and their vision caressed by the glitter of silver and crystal; Pellsipher was in rapture.

"Ah! Superb! our invisible but gracious host, it seems, hath no intent to add starvation to the other injuries he inflicts upon us. Currant jelly, upon my soul! Pickled beobab root! Consommé of oyster in cream sauce. Exquisite!"

They fell upon the repast and rapidly consumed the banquet to its final drop of sauce. Replete, they drowsily sought each his place of rest, and though the floor of this hall was devoid of the splendor that littered the other chambers, so fatiguing had been this long day of peril, toil and adventure that the hard floor was to them as the softest of couches.

When they awoke a sanguinary beam struck through the narrow aperture, from which they deduced dawn. That day passed in the utter boredom of their seclusion, broken only by their meals, which appeared like supernatural apparitions: tables draped in snowy napery, aglitter with gold and crystal, laden with fragrant and aromatic foods flickered into existence, only to melt back into emptiness the moment their appetites were appeased.

Toward evening of the second day of their internment, a singular event broke the monotony. A brass clouded mirror cleared suddenly to reveal the similitude of a lean man, cleanly shaven, sallow of skin, with cold, hooded, indifferent eyes, his high-shouldered form draped in somber robes of funereal purple whereupon were sewn many small garnets which twinkled and glittered among the folds of his gown like the eyes of venomous serpents. This mirror-apparition looked them over with opaque, supercilious and insolent gaze.

"Ah!" boomed Pellsipher heartily. "Our esteemed host and worthy colleague, the illustrious Master Zux, I assume?"

"The same," a sepulchral voice murmured. "And no doubt you purport to be a deputation from Mount Ong."

It was not a question; nevertheless, Dr. Pellsipher chose to treat it as such.

"To be sure, we are the plenipotentiaries of that excellent fraternity," he beamed. "I am myself the not-unreknowned Iollubus Pellsipherius Senex, Archimagos Maximus et. . . ."

"A dear colleague, but recently departed, assured me a party of thieves was en route to my habitation, drawn hither by a despicable greed to seize possession of the Paroul Compendium," the coldly suave tones of Nelibar Zux serenely droned on over the hearty voice of Pellsipher; "and, wary of such, my familiars have been scrutinizing your actions since your temerity in entering my abode uninvited and unwelcome."

"My dear sir! Upon my word as an Archimagos Maximus et . . . !"

"Hence your significant excitement upon discovery of the Paroulian codex can lead me but to one conclusion: you are no gentleman-envoys of the Ong enclave, but scofflaws, booknappers, vile and despicable burglars! It is even as my colleague predicted. . . ."

Dr. Pellsipher purpled at this suave affront and spluttered apoplectically in search of appropriate words to answer this astonishing accusation. But Chan interposed a swift query—

"Tell me, Master Zux, this colleague whereof you speak—might his name be Sarthath Oob?"

Puzzlement gleamed briefly in the chilly gaze of the mirrored sorcerer.

"Indeed, such is his cognomen, young knave. But how you could have guessed it escapes my comprehension."

"It is of no importance, sir," Chan smiled grimly. "May I ask toward what eventual punishment we are confined?"

Things were moving a bit too fast even for the wits of Nelibar Zux; and it seemed that thieves, caught in the very act, who keenly inquired as to their doom were a breed novel to his experience. Somewhat flustered, he said he was not yet decided as to whether they should undergo metamorphosis to the form of spiders and beetles or exposure to the rays of a petrifying lamp which would transform them to marble images: then again there was much to be said for transporting them to the eleventh planet which engirds Aldebaran and which is best described as a wintry hell swept by congealing ammoniac hurricanes . . . but Chan curtly bade him have the simple courtesy to leave them to their several religious devotions until such time as an apt terminus to their earthly careers had occurred to the sorcerer's sense of justice.

His aplomb considerably shaken by the unorthodox behavior of the young karcist, whom he considered a venturesome burglar, the simulacrum of Nelibar Zux obligingly faded from the brass mirror, leaving the adventurers to their solitary meditations.

X

Toward early morn Chan awoke from a miserable slumber whose serenity was interrupted by troublous dreams. Something was buzzing about his face and he batted irritably at the annoying insect which was, he perceived, a dragonfly of considerable size. Driving away the winged pest, he settled again for such repose as one doomed to be petrified into marble, metamorphosed into a beetle or transported to a remote orb of superarctic rigor might expect.

But a small piping voice sounded shrilly in his ear and brought him upright with astonishment. He stared about wildly until a minute figure stepped into view and stood in a moonbeam that filtered through the narrow razor-barred orifice.

"Prince Zixt!" he exclaimed in surprise. "Whatever has brought you all the way into this dismal charnel house?"

"A debt of gratitude owed to one whose kindness forbore to tread carelessly upon even the smallest of earth's creatures," shrilly proclaimed the princeling of the Minikins. Lowering his voice so as not to awaken his comrades, the karcist expressed his pleasure at again meeting the tiny potentate, and Prince Zixt explained that it was the common rumor of the night-flying bats that Nelibar Zux had imprisoned the Big Folk under a misapprehension and intended some deplorable doom for them upon the morrow. The word had passed from creature to creature throughout the breadth of the jungle isle, and upon hearing that his courteous friend was thus endangered, Prince Zixt had roused the warriors of the Minikin colony to his aid: mounted on swift dragonflies, whose aid a treasured store of honey drops had purchased, the minuscule soldiery had traversed the jungle, gaining entry to their prison by the narrow window which was but a slit in the wall to the Big Folk, but was wide as an open gate to the Minikins.

Chan's heart was warmed at the friendliness and courage of the tiny prince, but he could see no method by which the Minikins could assist in extricating them from the present peril. After all, if he and his comrades were impotent to raise the immense cubes of adamant which blocked their egress from the hall, the tiny strength of the Minikins were likewise of no avail.

"Not so, friend Chan," the princeling piped. "Small feet can sometimes go where Big Folk cannot tread: *behold!*"

And with a flourish, the princeling removed from beneath his spidersilk cloak a topaz scarab-ring, which to his scale had all the girth of a small hogshead.

"And what is this, pray tell?"

"None other than the talisman which controls the adamantine doors which seal you in this prison," announced Prince Zixt pridefully. "I know it to be such for the sorcerer Nelibar Zux had it tucked beneath his pillow as he retired!"

Chan was incredulous. "Is it possible that you dared observe the sorcerer in his own bedchamber?"

The princeling's laughter was like tiny tinkling bells. "Hidden in a tassel on his bed-curtains! Small size hath certain advantages, you see!"

"And small hearts can possess the bravery of many lions!" Chan swore. Awakening his colleagues, he apprised them of the situation; displaying the talismanic ring, he inquired of Pellsipher if his science were sufficient to employ it toward their release.

"Nothing simpler, lad!" the fat old archimage boomed heartily, his spirits much restored by finding an ally even in the very stronghold of the foe. "But even with the adamantine blocks removed and our mode of exeunt clear, how can we hope to elude the vigilance of the many small furtive familiars of the treacherous Zux? Surely, observing our escape, they will arouse their master from his slumbers, and we shall be in trouble all over again."

Again the tiny princeling shrilled with laughter. "The bellowing of thirty Titans in concert," said he, "could not rouse Nelibar Zux this hour—nay, nor for many an hour hence!" He then related that he observed it to be the nightly habit of the subterranean sorcerer to prepare himself a decoction before slumber, and that this potion had as its base a hot spiced wine whereto the sorcerer added two drops of the juice of crushed black poppies as an aid to slumber. (This intelligence he had learned from a gossipy bachelor spider who made his residence behind a loose wall tile and with whom Prince Zixt had struck up a brief but amiable acquaintance while awaiting completion of the nightly ablutions of Nelibar Zux.)

"I took the simple precaution of quadrupling the dosage while Master Zux was still engaged with his toilette," the princeling chuckled. Doctor Pellsipher exclaimed with a glad cry and performed a brief gavotte.

"Ten drops of poppy juice will thrust the wily old rogue into the profoundest of slumbers, wherefrom he will emerge sometime next week with a most prodigious headache," he chortled, "which provides us with sufficient time to swim back to the isle of Thosk, if such should prove necessary! My dear Prince Zixt, you are one in a million, and should ever you choose to remove your colony to the flanks of Mount Ong, you may rest assured of our benevolent protection and eternal friendship! And now, dear colleagues, gather up your gear and let us be gone from these loathsome dungeons upon the moment!"

Addressing himself to the topaz ring, Dr. Pellsipher in his most orotund basso solemnly pronounced the prodigious Name of Oommuorondus Smednivlioth—that genie under whose sovereignty the adamantine metal has been ruled since the Creation—and with an earth-shaking rumble of subterranean thunder, the colossal cubes of indestructible metal evaporated into thin air, leaving their free passage unobstructed.

They wasted little time in gaining the open air, with Chan bringing up the rear; a shrill chorus of cheers arose from the waiting host of Minikin warriors bedight in beetle-shell breastplates and acorn helmets, who brandished the stings of wasps for javelins. To this victorious huzzah, Pellsipher bowed magnificently.

Mounted anew on a fleet of fireflies, the Minikins guided them through the jungles and as dawn brightened overhead they achieved the place whereat they had earlier moored Dr. Pellsipher's aerial gondola; their good fortune continued unimpaired, for in the ensuing interval the sky vessel had renewed its store of buoyant gases; thus, as dawn gilded the waves of the Deep Green Sea, they flew safely home to Thosk none the worse for all their perils.

At the next meeting of the enclave it was, of course, the sad duty of Dr. Pellsipher to announce the utter and complete failure of his mission. His despondency was considerably mitigated, however, at the surprising news volunteered by Velb the Irithribian. It seemed the astral plane was agog: a recent meeting of the Skarm Desert coven had erupted in violent recriminations; Nelibar Zux had resigned amid a storm of allegations, and Sarthath Oob himself, the coven's erstwhile chief executive, had been driven from his high office when he failed lamentably to carry a vote of confidence. Crushed, the crestfallen Oob had departed on an extended sabbatical to the last isles of foundering Mu. And the Mount Ong enclave, full coven or no, was now supreme in all the Isle of Thosk!

"Whatever could have happened?" Pellsipher marveled at this astonishing report.

"I can independently verify brother Velb's intelligence," solemnly intoned Zoramus of Pankoy. "My own sources on the astral plane suggest that in some amazing lapse or negligence, far from his wonted and scrupulous security, the unfortunate Nelibar Zux somehow—lost—the Paroulian codex whose aquisition was his paramount claim to supremacy! This misfortune he blamed, for some reason, on none other than the triply unfortunate Sarthath Oob, whose fall from office followed thereafter most precipitously."

Pellsipher seemed dazed: "But how could old Zux have lost his prime treasure . . . yes, my boy? You have something to add to this discussion?"

Chan had arrayed his person with more than his usual meticulous taste; thus, as he rose slowly to address the enclave he cut a striking figure among his fellows (and from the corner of his eye he observed the glimmer of an appreciative flash in the quicksilver eyes of the bewitching Azra).

"Yes, indeed," he said modestly. "I believe I can offer some account of what transpired. My colleagues will recall the clever stratagem of our minuscule but lion-hearted savior, Prince Zixt of the Minikins. I refer, of course, to his theft of the topaz scarab; in imminent peril of discovery, the Minikin princeling yet retained sufficient coolness of head and fixity of purpose to purloin the talisman that would afford our release. I have learned much from the example of Prince Zixt, whose friendship I yet hope to renew on more favorable occasions; but in this particular, I have followed his precept and even in our precipitous haste to be gone from the dungeons, I yet lingered for a moment to smash a certain crystal case with a bit of floor tile. . . ."

And with a flourish the bold young karcist removed from beneath his cloak a certain cumbersome volume, bound in tanned diplodocus hide.

"The Compendium of Paroul!" Doctor Pellsipher gasped, clutching the top of the podium as he staggered back with amazement.

Amid the uproarious acclaim of his wizardly brethren, Chan had eyes only for the warm and open admiration in the languorous eyes of the girl Azra. One did not have to be a wizard to read the melting adoration in those eyes, or the invitation in those moist and parted lips. When next he had occasion to visit that cozy hut in the bamboo grove he knew to what extent he would be welcome.

And if the expedition to Zatoum had failed to enlist a thirteenth member of the enclave, what did it matter? It had at least won him the heart of the fair Azra, of the lissom form, the green hair, and the eyes of sparkling quicksilver.

ATLANTIS

Atlantis is, of course, the most celebrated of all the lost worlds of prehistoric earth. Since Plato first wrote about it in 355 B.C., more than two thousand books, articles, stories and movies have exploited this most famous of all the imaginary countries. No more glittering and fabulous realm exists in all of Terra Incognita than the island-continent of the Atlanteans.

And it has been a boon to fantasy writers like unto no other! Burroughs set *Tarzan and the Jewels of Opar* in a lost colony of Atlantis; Doyle sent explorers there in a bathysphere; Verne had Captain Nemo brood over the submerged ruins of it in a memorable scene. And Henry Kuttner, Clark Ashton Smith, L. Sprague de Camp and more writers than I have space to list, have explored its marvels. The legend remains inexhaustible, even today, when archaeologists believe they have found its original site on the island of Thera near Crete.

I had to get around to Atlantis sooner or later, and so I did in a novel called *The Black Star*, published in 1973. It was supposed to be the first of a trilogy but the publisher felt disinclined to take the other books, so I contented myself with writing the little tale which follows.

THE SEAL OF ZAON SATHLA

With dawn Tirion the Glad Magician departed from his citadel of blue marble which rose in the hills beyond Adalon the White City. His wyvern chariot was swifter than the wind and he traversed the several leagues of fields and farms and forest-mantled hills which lay between him and the Valley of the Covenant well before the flaming disk of Rhakotis, sun god of ancient Atlantis, had yet attained to the zenith.

As the keel of his aerial car brushed lightly against the greensward, Tirion dismounted, set the wards in place against the possible thief or interloper, and, tossing back his velvet mantle so that his colleagues of the Thaumaturgae could best observe the splendor of his garments, stood at the crest of a hill, surveying the valley below.

Painted wooden booths, shaded by striped awnings, formed a double lane the length of the Valley of the Covenant, and already those of his colleagues who had preceded him to the annual Fair of the Magicians were busily unpacking their wares for display, barter or sale. Above each booth a banner unfolded on the breeze the heraldic device of its owner. With lively interest, the Glad Magician perceived that several of the more celebrated sorcerers of the land were already come, and among them he spied the somber jetty pennant of Amphoth Mumivor, the mighty Necromancer from distant Trysadon, westernmost of the cities of Atlantis.

Already, earlycomers were bustling about, examining the books and pentacles, scrolls, crumbling stone tablets, periapts and amulets and talismanic rings set forth for sale. Abandoning his pose, Tirion descended the slope. He had come to purchase, not to sell, and he desired a first chance at the various bargains of his anticipation.

169

Although the sorcerous brethren of Atlantis were all members of a mighty fraternity, the Thaumaturgical Brotherhood, yet, like members of their profession anywhere else, they were generally at odds and enmity. Few magicians could call a colleague "friend," and to most masters of the Secret Sciences, a fellow practitioner was almost automatically to be considered a foe or, at best, a rival. But once a year a truce was declared here in the Valley of the Covenant, and during the space of seven days the various wizards and enchanters of the realms around could mingle safely. To this annual fair Tirion had come, for he suspected certain rare magical instruments which he desired to purchase might be offered.

The grassy lane between the rows of booths was not yet crowded, so the youthful magician had a fine opportunity to peruse the goods on display. There were a variety of implements, such as arthames and bollines and other magic tools, and many books, some of them, he observed, monstrous volumes inscribed in the uncouth hieroglyphics of elder Lemuria and age-lost Hyperborea. He paused to scrutinize one huge book whose vellum leaves were bound in mastodon leather, and as he glanced at it his eye was caught by a twinkle of light from the next booth adjoining, and the magician whose booth it was came bustling over.

"Ah, young sir, do I not address the famous Glad Magician of Adalon?" the seller cried, and Tirion smiled and nodded. His frank visage, merry eyes and pranksome nature had made him notorious. The other, a plump and balding wizard from Illurdis, thickly bearded and jovial, rubbed his hands together, shrewdly noting the size of Tirion's purse and the volume he was glancing through.

"A rare find, young sir, a rare find! Genuine Hyperborean, my word upon it! Indeed, I have the unsolicited opinion of no less an authority than the mighty Amphoth Mumivor himself that the work may be considered an authentic Ommum-Vog!"

Tirion smiled blandly and carelessly let the volume close. The works of Ommum-Vog, the prehuman archimage of elder Hyperborea, had all doubtless perished beneath the Ice Mountains which had destroyed the whole of that legended kingdom ages ago; the book, doubtless, was a forgery.

Noting his action, the Illurdan snatched up a tablet of black jade inscribed with cryptic cuneiform.

"If the volume be not suited to your needs, sir, consider the fabulous antiquity of this! A Lemurian artifact of enormous age: the hands of Sharajsha himself are said to have in-dited here the thirty-seven Secret Formulae of his art."

"Indeed?" Tirion elevated an arched brow inquiringly. "But the cuneiform is unknown to me, and certainly not High Lemurian?"

The fat wizard winked in a sly, conspiratorial manner, and hissed: "A secret writing; an artificial language; a code of the Master Magician's own devisal. Had you but the key to the cryptogram. . . ."

"But alas, I have it not," smiled Tirion, and turned on his heel to examine the wares in the next booth.

These, however, were pentacles of Sfanomoë—by which name the ancient Atlanteans knew the planet Venus—and, as Tirion possessed no particular interest in the starry sciences, they did not engage his curiosity for long.

The fair was bustling now, and the lane quite crowded. Gray-robed enchanters, black-hooded diabolists, astromancers in violet robes with silvery mitres on their brows, smiling and half-naked young witches with sea-green hair and amber eyes, gaunt sorcerers in scarlet from Ulphar and Darinth, enigmatic seers and diviners from the north and even a few swarthy magisters from dark Gorgonia across the ocean on the shores of great Thuria, all were here for the great fair.

Many there were who knew Tirion, and some of these turned sourly away from the Glad Magician, some indeed muttering curses beneath their breath. Tirion laughed and his eyes danced with mischief. He had tricked many of these sour-faced ones, one time or another; he had few friends, many enemies, but he carelessly laughed and strolled on.

At length the black-draped booth of Amphoth Mumivor appeared, and young Tirion paused to study the display of wares. Among the many trinkets and baubles were several astonishing rarities—a talismanic opal with the cartouche of King Nemmaridus; a set of broken red clay tablets from the ancient ruins of Pythontus; a scroll of pterodactyl-skin parchment which bore the Eleven Glyphs of Arammonzon; and even a small yellow enamel tomb figurine from the accursed and long-deserted necropolis of the City of the Golden Gates—but there was one artifact alone that seized and held his amazed attention.

This object, a small seal of blue sapphire, was encased in a globe of unbroken crystal and it was set far back from the

clutter of talismans. At the very sight of it, Tirion stiffened
and a gasp of astonishment escaped him.

"By Evenor the Earthborn! It cannot be—"

A sepulchral voice addressed him. He glanced up to see a
tall man of indeterminate age, robed in ebon satin, his sallow
skin and oblique, depthless eyes of somber black flame denot-
ing his descent from purebred Lemurian ancestry. It was
none other than the mighty magician of Trysadon, Amphoth
Mumivor himself.

"I perceive, young Tirion, that you have discovered my
chiefest treasure," intoned the black-robed necromancer.
"Your taste is impeccable."

Tirion strove to master his excitement, and to dissemble.

"An intriguing bauble," he said in an unsteady voice which
strove for a semblance of casual interest. "An amulet of the
First Empire, I believe?"

"It is a sigil and not an amulet, my young friend, and as
you have already discovered for yourself, it was fashioned in
the age of royal Caiphul many millennia ago," said the necromancer in a somber voice. The Glad Magician bent nearer
to make out the enigmatic hieroglyphs wherewith the sigil
was inscribed. Excitement bubbled up within him, and it took
all of his power of will to compose his features into something resembling serene and idle curiosity.

"Oddly enough, I am interested in sigils of that era," he
laughed. "This looks to be an example of rather fine workmanship dating from a most interesting dynasty. Shall we
say—twenty pieces of gold?"

As he held his breath in suspense, the solemn eyes of the
black-robed necromancer fixed upon him. After an interval
that seemed at least a century long, Amphoth Mumivor
shook his head sadly.

"You dissemble, young sir, and that is not an act of wisdom. We both know this is no ordinary Caiphul sigil, but
came from the hands of the great Zaon Sathla himself, the
mightiest wizard Atlantis knew in all the measureless ages before the rise of the Demon King. And a genuine Seal of
Power from the laboratorium of Zaon Sathla is worth far
more than the pitiful sum you offer."

Grimacing with chagrin that his ploy had met with failure,
Tirion raised the price, was refused, raised it again and finally, in despair, offered one hundred gold coins.

"You need not pretend, young Tirion, that you do not appreciate the true value and rarity of the Seal. It is mentioned

in the literature of our sciences as The Grand Negator, and he who bears the Seal upon his person is thus invulnerable to any malign enchantment, spell, rune, cantrip, curse or sending, of whatever potency, nature or degree. As for its rarity, the Grand Negator is all but unique. Tradition records that only two such sigils were completed before the famous career of Zaon Sathla came to its close. And this is the only Negator ever offered for open sale within the history of magic. A thousand pieces of gold would not equal a fraction of its worth."

Tirion began to perspire. What the solemn necromancer had said was, of course, completely true. The Grand Negator—and Tirion was utterly certain that this was indeed one of the only two known to exist—was worth the ransom of an emperor. And, alas, he had less than two thousand coins on his person!

He strove to bargain the price down; he offered the more unique volumes in his library—a folio of demonic portraits from the hand of Phaovonce the master demonologist—a matched collection of seventy-three periapts—a rare Gygian cloak which he happened to have with him—a contract of servitude which bound three potent elementals to a decade of slavery—even his flying chariot itself, without which he would be forced either to walk home or invoke a particularly tricksome and dangerous Air Demon. At each offer the black-robed necromancer somberly made refusal. At last, almost in tears, inwardly despairing, the Glad Magician turned rudely away and stalked off in a trembling rage, "glad" no more.

Toward midafternoon a hospitable alchemist offered sweetmeats and perfumed wine to all comers. Tirion nibbled despondently on flower cakes and drank heavily of the honey-sweet wine, but he remained sunk in gloom.

He observed that, while numerous other enchanters and witches had evinced great interest in the Seal of Zaon Sathla, none of them had been able to afford the price the Trysadonian mage had set for it.

Finally, Tirion returned to his wyvern chariot and drew forth a small packet, which he tossed to the grass, uttering a certain name. A silken pavilion sprang into being, bearing his heraldic emblem and colors. He entered, threw himself full length on a cot covered with the tawny hides of seven sabertooth tigers, and began cudgeling his wits for a means to accomplish his desires.

The Seal of Zaon Sathla *must* be his, of that he was firmly convinced. Tirion's mischievous humors, his illicit amours, his daring intervals of thievery, to say nothing of his careless tongue—all of these had made him an ever-growing number of enemies among his brethren of the Thaumaturgae of Atlantis. If he could but obtain possession of the Grand Negator, he would at one stroke render himself totally invulnerable to any form or degree of magical attack whatsoever. The potent forces locked within that small, worn, innocuous sapphire seal could ward off the most terrific blasts of magic ever devised. He *must* have it! He must! But how?

Night fell over the valley. One by one, the stars emerged to jewel the sky. As they did, Tirion, too, emerged, bearing a peculiar garment—his Gygian cloak.

He slung it about his shoulders, arranging the hooded cowl so that it masked his features and distributing the heavy folds of the garment so that even his hands were hidden. Thus rendered as invisible as a puff of idle breeze, he crept silently down the dewy slope to the black tent wherein the necromancer slumbered.

So great was his lust for the Seal of Zaon Sathla that Tirion was resolved to steal it. It would not be the first time he had stolen something he desired from a fellow sorcerer. It would, however, be the first time he had dared a crime so great as this: for to break the Covenant in this manner was a sin beyond precedent. But why should that matter? Once he had the Negator in his possession, the entire brotherhood of the Thaumaturgae could direct against him their most potent curses and spells, without so much as singeing a single hair of his silken head.

In a moment the black tent of the Trysadonian loomed before him. He paused, aware that the Gygian cloak shielded him from every eye; then he hurled against the tent and its occupant the Ninth Morphean Charm of Yammoth.

This was the most powerful sleep-compellant ever devised, and he knew that no necromancer could possibly have a defense against it, since only a true magician was learned in the charms of Yammoth.

The charm took effect instantly; hence he wasted no time in brushing aside the tent flap and gliding within. All was very dark, save for a small red ball of flame that burned before an altar of black marble. The dim radiance of this astral illuminant glittered in the crystal globe which lay atop a tabouret of inlaid mastodon ivory. By the ruby light Tirion perceived the Seal was still in place. He stretched out his hand to break the crystal and snatch up the sigil—but froze motionless, the gesture half completed.

The interior of the tent flushed with brilliance.

Awake—and steadily regarding him, despite the Gygian cloak of invisibility he wore—sat Amphoth Mumivor in a tall chair of gray crystal across the tent. One yellow hand clasped a Blasting Wand which pointed directly at Tirion's pale, perspiring brow.

About the throat of the grave, silent necromancer a blue sigil dangled. Spying it, Tirion voiced a croak of shock and dismay.

"You lied! Lied!"

Amphoth Mumivor shook his head gravely.

"I did not lie. I told you that only two Grand Negators had ever existed. One is for sale . . . *but I wear the other,*" he said. And lifting the Wand he demolished Tirion the Glad Magician with a blast of magic flame.

The Afterword:

LOST WORLDS TO COME

Do not make the mistake of thinking that I have, in the stories collected into this book, exhausted all of the lost lands of old legend. They are many and various, from the empire of Prester John to the island of Ultima Thule; from the fabulous Xibalba of Mayan myths to the dim Shamballah of the prehistoric Gobi; from the shadowy Cimmeria mentioned in Homer to the country of the Amazons described by his continuators; from the primal Gondwanaland of the geologists' speculations to the Poseidonis of Smith and de Camp—"the last isles of foundering Atlantis."

Understand: I make no promises! It may well be, with the pressure of my various commitments, that I will never get around to chronicling the strange and wonderful histories of these other half-forgotten realms of wizardry and wonder. But don't bet on it. Authors have a way of living long, and wear out their more familiar settings.

And I would like to know what Ultima Thule is really, *really* like. . . .

Happy Magic!

LIN CARTER